ABOUT THE AUTHOR

Brian Falkner was born and raised in Auckland, New Zealand. He is the author of several novels for children and teenagers, including *The Flea Thing, The Real Thing, The Super Freak* and *The Tomorrow Code*.

Prior to becoming a children's author, Brian trained as a journalist and then worked as a reporter and an advertising copywriter, a radio announcer and an internet developer. His hobbies include scuba diving, travel, amateur theatre, photography and rugby.

For more information visit www.brianfalkner.com

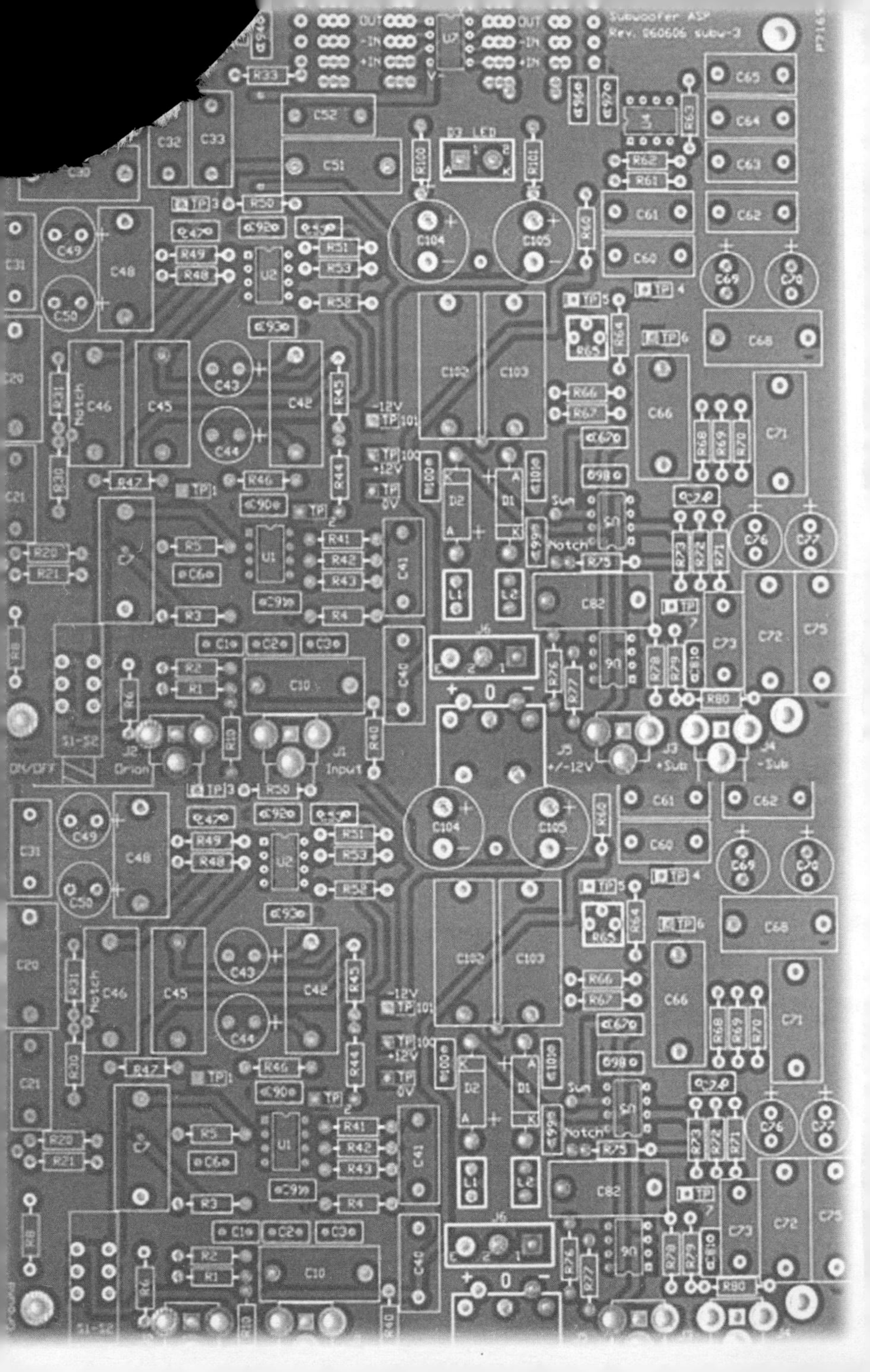

Subwoofer ASP
Rev. 060606 subw-3

brainjack

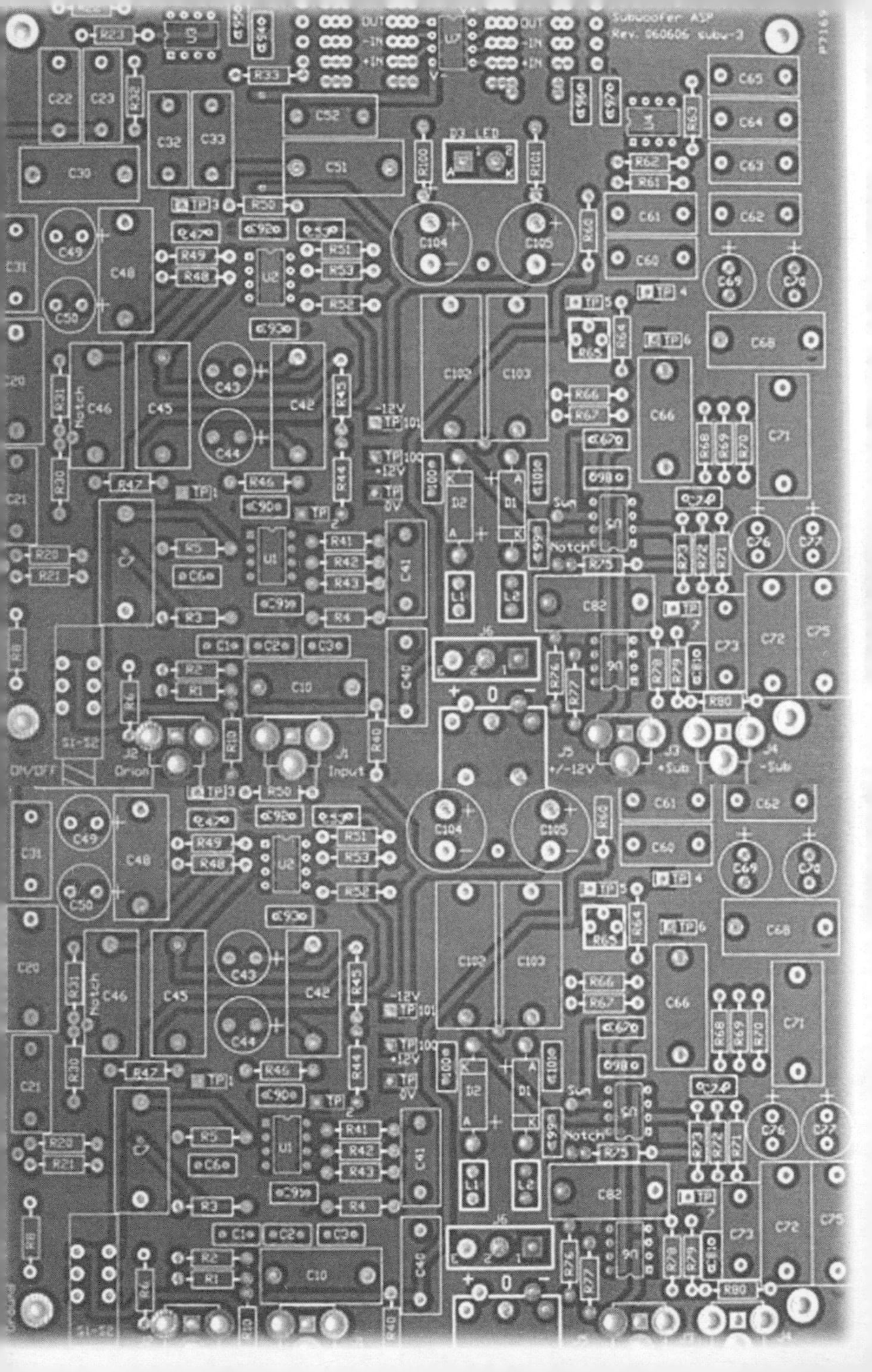

brainjack

BRIAN FALKNER

This is a work of fiction. Names, characters, places and incidents are either the product of the author's imagination or, if real, are used fictitiously. All statements, activities, stunts, descriptions, information and material of any other kind contained herein are included for entertainment purposes only and should not be relied on for accuracy or replicated as they may result in injury.

First published in Great Britain 2011 by Walker Books Ltd
87 Vauxhall Walk, London SE11 5HJ

4 6 8 10 9 7 5 3

This book has been typeset in Univers

Printed and bound in Great Britain by Clays Ltd, St Ives plc

British Library Cataloguing in Publication Data:
a catalogue record for this book is available from the British Library

ISBN 978-1-4063-2906-3

www.walker.co.uk

For my mum

BOOK TWO REVELATIONS

BOOK THREE WISDOM

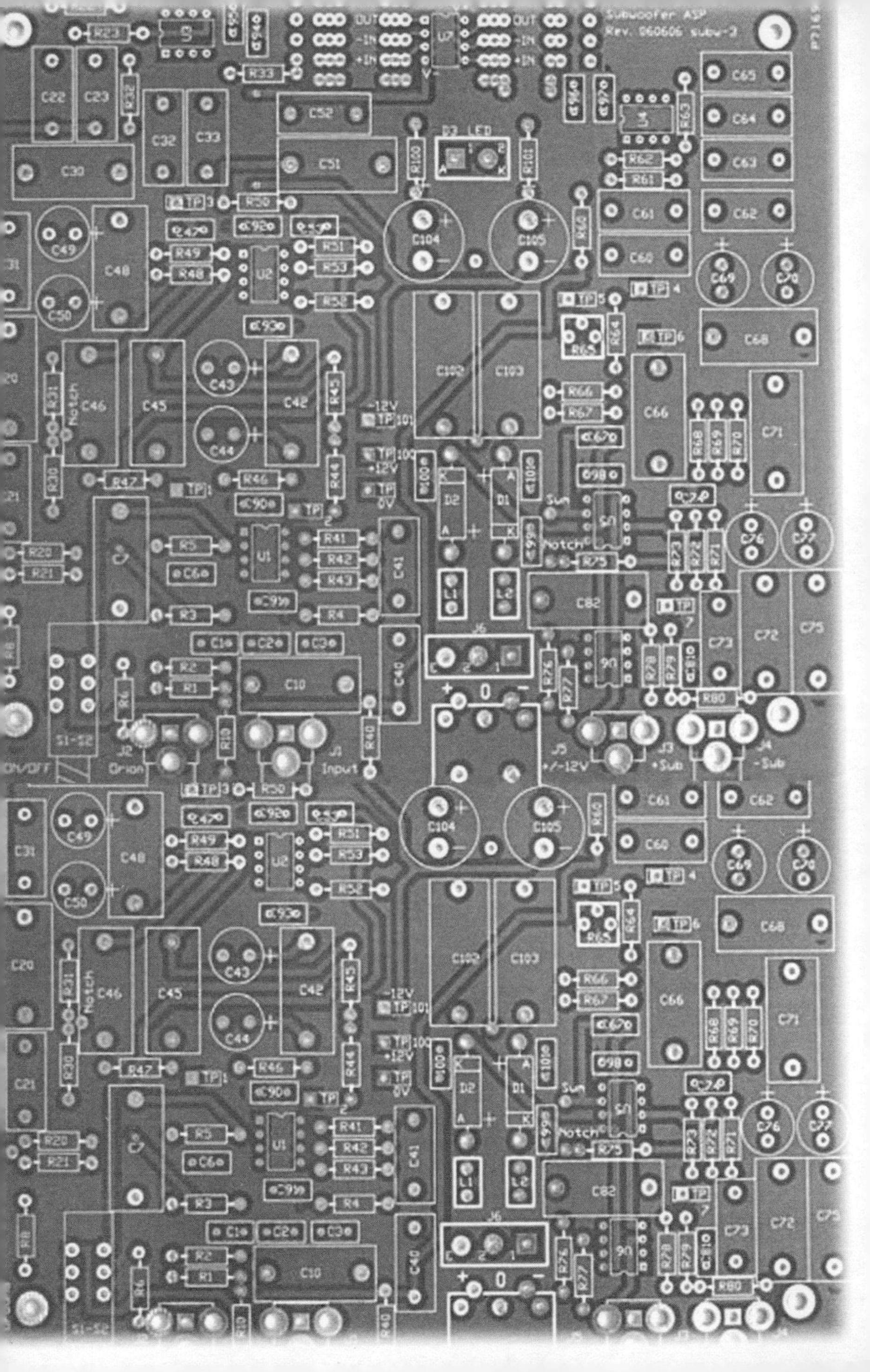

Subwoofer ASP
Rev. 060606 subu-3
OUT
-IN
+IN
D3 LED
C104
C105
C102
C103
Notch
Sum
-12V
+12V
0V
J1
Input
J2
Orion
ON/OFF
S1-S2
J3
+Sub
J4
-Sub
J5
+/-12V
J6

PROLOGUE

Right now, as you read this prologue, I am sifting through the contents of your computer. Yes, your computer. You. The one holding the book.

I am reading your emails, looking at your digital photos and images you have downloaded off the Net, opening your most private documents and having a good read, or a good laugh, depending on the content.

To be honest, most of it is utterly boring. Except for a few files. You know the ones I mean.

I know you don't believe me, and I prefer it that way, but think about this.

When you bought this book, you (or the person who bought it for you) used a credit card or a debit card. That created a record in the massive computer systems that the banks use. The systems they claim are impregnable.

But they are on the Net. And nothing is impregnable on the Net.

So I monitor those systems for transactions with the ISBN of this book. That's the International Standard Book Number. You'll find it on the publisher's imprint page on page 6. Have a look now. It's 978-1-4063-2906-3.

When your transaction went through I got an alert from one of my monitoring programs and, as I had nothing better to do, I dug a little deeper.

I got the credit card number from the transaction log and that, with just a quick poke around in the (highly secure) databases of the bank, gave me your home address and telephone number.

I crossmatched that with the internet service providers in your area to find your broadband connection. Then I checked to see if you have a static IP (that's the electronic address of your home computer). You don't, so I raided your ISP's DHCP server to get your current IP. It didn't take me long to find out where your computer lives on the internet.

Your router's firewall was a joke, and not even a very funny one. The built-in firewall on your PC was another story though. That held me up for a couple of heartbeats. I had to use your peer-to-peer file-sharing client to slip a trojan past your security and gain remote administrator access, shape-shifting a little as I did it so as not to attract attention from your antivirus software. No matter. It took me less than ten minutes from seeing the transaction to obtaining complete access to your hard drive.

So now, while you're reading this, I'm looking through your computer and having a great old time. You could race over and turn your computer off, but you'd already be too late.

I could delete a few files, but I probably won't. I could change your passwords, and lock you out of your own system, but I can't be bothered.

And I won't crash your system, or delete the contents of your hard drive, or anything like that. I am not malicious or evil, or even particularly bad.

I'll just quietly leave, and erase all trace that I was ever there.

But I know you now. I know who you are. I know where you live. I know what you've got. And if the time comes that I need something from you, something that you might or might not want to give up, I'll be back.

That time is coming. Sooner than you think.

But in the meantime, don't worry about me.

I'm not worrying about you.

Right now, I've got much bigger problems to think about.

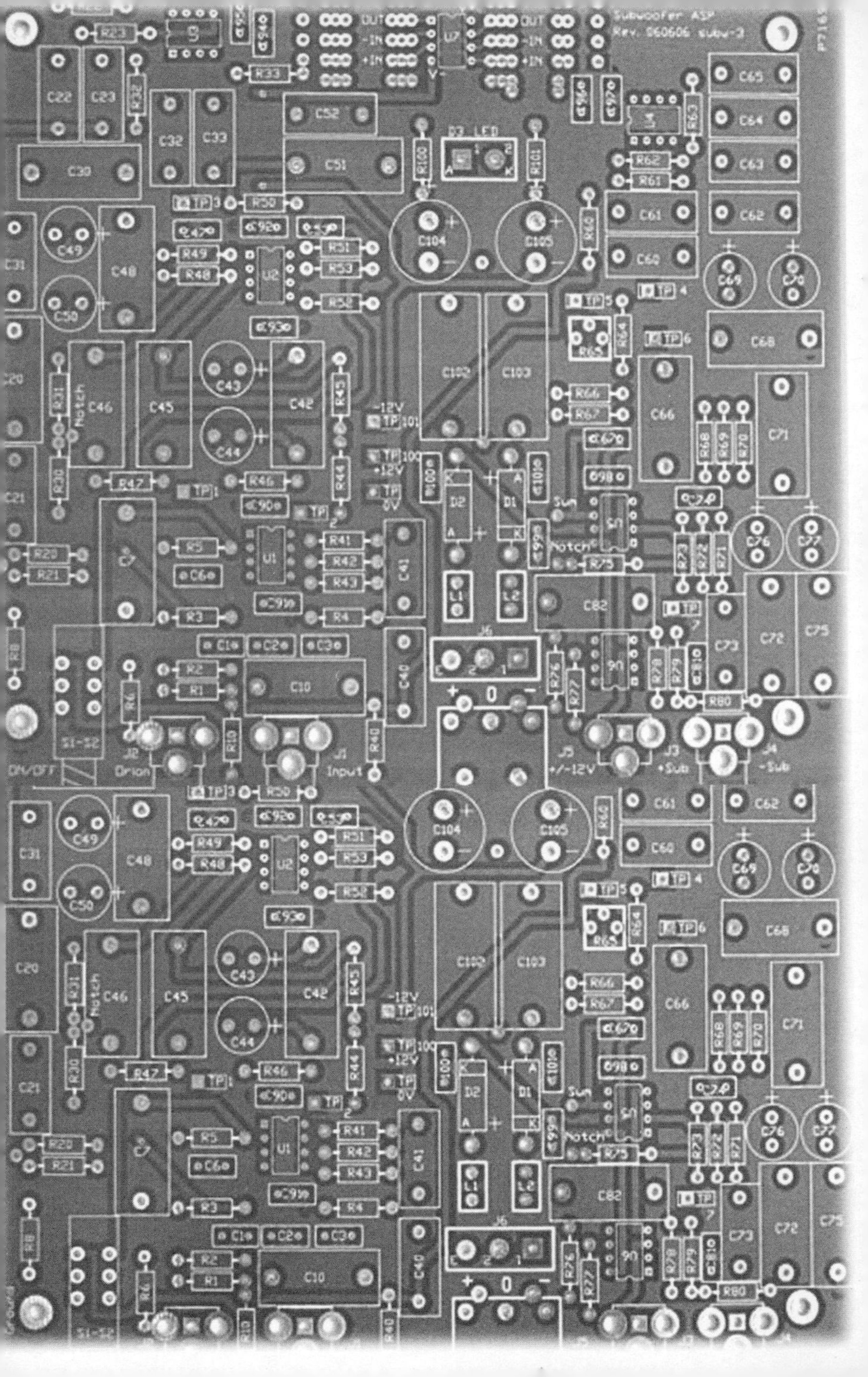
Subwoofer ASP
Rev. 060606 subw-3
ON/OFF
Orion
Input
+/-12V
+Sub
-Sub
Notch
Sum
D3 LED

BOOK ONE
BEGINNINGS

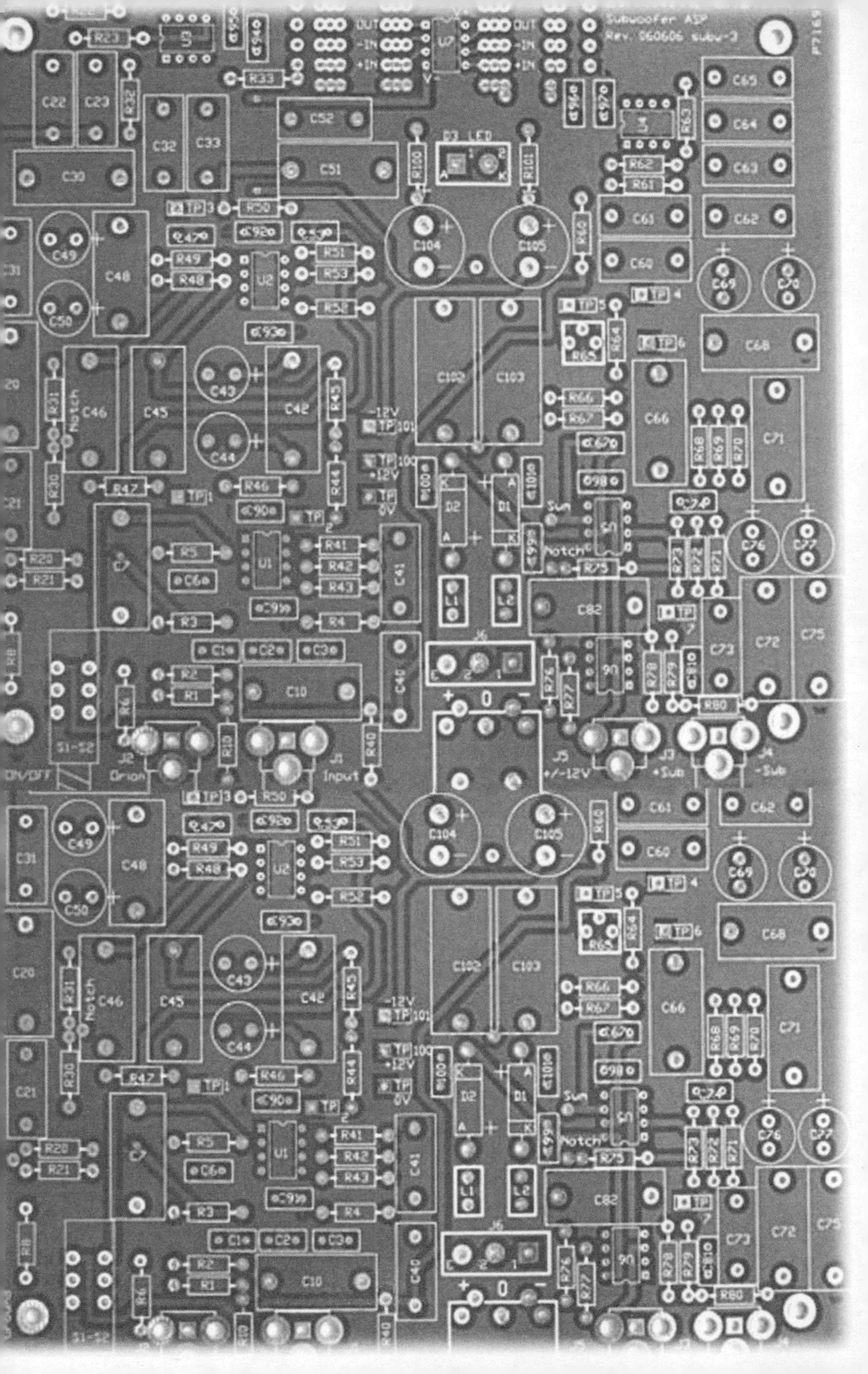

Subwoofer ASP
Rev. 060606 subw-2
Input
Orion
+/-12V
+Sub
-Sub
ON/OFF
Notch
Sum

1. DIRTY TRICKS

On Friday, on his way to school, Sam Wilson brought the United States of America to its knees.

He didn't mean to. He was actually just trying to score a new computer and some other cool stuff, and in any case the words "to its knees" were the *New York Times*' not his. (And way over the top in Sam's view.) Not as bad though as the *Washington Post*. Their headline writers must have been on a coffee binge because they screamed

National Disaster

in size-40 type when their presses finally came back online.

Anyway it was only for a few days, and it really wasn't a disaster at all. At least not compared to what was still to come.

A juddering roar reverberated off high-rise buildings

and Sam glanced up as the dark shadow of a police Black Hawk slid across the street. His breath caught in his chest for a moment as if all the oxygen in the street had suddenly disappeared, but the chopper didn't slow; it was just a routine patrol. It weaved smoothly between the monoliths of uptown Manhattan, a cop with a long rifle spotlighted in the open doorway by a brilliant orange burst of early morning sun.

He tried to remember a time when armed police in helicopters hadn't patrolled the city, but couldn't. It seemed that it had always been that way. At least since *Vegas*.

Grey clouds were seeping a dreary, misty drizzle from high over the city, but low on the horizon there was a long thin gap into which the sun had risen, teasing New York with a short-lived promise of a sunny day.

Sam cut down 44th Street and turned right at 7th Avenue to avoid beggars' row along Broadway. He took 42nd to Times Square where the tall video screens flickered intermittently or were silent and dark. The M&M's screen still worked although there were several blank spots that were said to be bullet holes.

Forty-second Street Station was crowded – jostling, bustling, shortness-of-breath crowded – at this time of the morning, but he was used to that and the subway was still the fastest and safest way to get around Manhattan.

He got out at Franklin Street Station and took Varick Street down to West Broadway. He quickened his step as he passed Gamer Alley. His nose wrinkled involuntarily at some of the odours that hung around the entrance.

Two dogs were fighting on the corner of Thomas and West Broadway but stopped as he approached. He slowed, not comfortable with the narrowing of their eyes or the jelly-strings of drool dripping from their fangs.

One took a step towards him, a low growl in its throat. The other followed, lips drawing back from its teeth.

Sam took a step backwards. The dogs moved closer, haunches high, stalking him. He stumbled backwards a few more steps. A police humvee cruised past and he half-turned towards it, hoping that the cops would stop and intervene, but they either didn't see, or didn't care.

The entrance to Gamer Alley appeared to his right. As the dogs spread out to cut off his escape, he turned and strode into the smoky unease of the alleyway.

He glanced behind but the dogs had not followed.

The walls of the alley were high and the street was narrow, a deep saw-cut across a city block. None of the dawn glow penetrated, just a tired dullness that washed through the clouds and was swallowed up by the steam and smoke from the food stalls. Gaudy fluorescent signs appeared indistinctly through the haze, promising the latest in video-gaming technology. The games they promoted were innocuous but everyone, especially the cops, knew that once inside, the full range of games, including all the illegal ones, were freely available.

People drifted past. Both men and women with the vacant stares and twitching hands of long-term game addicts.

Sam thrust his hands into his jacket pockets, hunched his shoulders and moved deeper into Gamer Alley.

A woman in her twenties, fashion-model-beautiful, sat on a blue office chair next to an overflowing dumpster. Her hair was plastered to her scalp by the rain, and droplets of water formed on the end of her nose before breaking away in a rhythmical pattern. She did nothing. She said nothing. She just sat, watching Sam as he made his way down the alley towards her. A game addict, for sure.

As he neared, the chair swivelled slightly and although her head and neck did not move, her eyes remained fixed on him.

He passed her, the chair swivelling more, her whole body turning with it to stay focused on him, her face expressionless.

His shoulders crawled as he left her behind, as if the strange inactivity might suddenly explode into mindless violence.

Ten yards past, he glanced back. She stared at him, unmoving.

"Want to buy a dog?"

The man in a shabby grey overcoat was right in front of him and he had to stop abruptly to avoid a collision.

"I, er..."

"Want to buy a dog?"

The dog in question was in the man's arms. A mangy cross about the size of a small poodle, but of no detectable breed.

"He's a good boy," the man said, thrusting the dog forwards. The dog snarled and snapped at Sam, missing his arm by a fraction of an inch.

"No, I..."

"Hardly ever bites," the man said.

"No."

Sam took a wide step around the man as the dog's teeth snapped together again in midair.

The end of the alley neared.

To his right, a door opened on a second-storey fire-escape. A man in his fifties burst out of the building dressed only in Mickey Mouse boxer shorts with a Hawaiian lei around his neck. He was carrying a coffee machine. He leaped down the metal steps three at a time, and disappeared across the street and around the corner of a building just as two policemen, in black tactical gear, burst out of the same door, hard on his heels.

Sam escaped onto Church Street with a slight sigh of relief and a relaxing of his nostrils. His cell rang, right on cue, as he turned into Thomas Street and he tapped his bluetooth earpiece into his ear.

"Hi, Mom," he said.

"What kept you?" Fargas asked on the other end of the line, his mouth full of something.

Sam looked up at the building opposite. He caught a glimpse of Fargas behind a window on the second floor, the two black circles of a pair of powerful binoculars jutting out from his long mop of unruly hair.

Sam made a discreet waving motion with his left hand.

There was a flash of white from the window that he took as a sign Fargas had waved back.

"Cut through Gamer Alley," Sam said.

There was a short pause while Fargas digested that. "Quick hit on the way?"

"Just sightseeing," Sam said. "What are you eating?"

It would be caramel corn. Fargas was the only person he knew who could eat caramel-coated popcorn for breakfast.

"Caramel corn," Fargas said. "Want some? I'll toss a couple of pieces out the window."

"Suddenly not hungry," Sam said. "Can't think why."

He walked casually past the Telecomerica building as if he had no interest in it whatsoever. He didn't even glance at it.

"You sure this is possible?" Fargas sounded a little nervous.

"I'm sure it's not," Sam said. "Be no fun otherwise. They've got industrial-strength firewalls with a DMZ and a secondary defensive ring with ASA and IPSec. Impenetrable."

"Then give it away, dude," Fargas said. "I'm not going to jail for the sake of a hack."

"Fargas," Sam said, "you're my brother and I love you but you gotta get your head out of your butt before you fart and suffocate yourself."

"I'm not your brother and you don't love me," Fargas pointed out.

"You know you're the one I'd turn gay for." Sam grinned up at the window.

"I thought you liked Keisha," Fargas said.

"I'd definitely turn gay for her," Sam said. "If I was a chick. How is she?"

"Still not interested."

"Her words or yours?"

"She's a sophomore. You're a senior. That's just wrong. Should be illegal."

"Have you asked her for me?" Sam asked.

"You can't ask her yourself?"

"She's a sophomore. She's got to ask me."

"Loser," Fargas said.

Sam said, "Okay, here we go."

The cafe was long, low and thin: a brick-lined tunnel reaching into the depths of the city block. The table Sam wanted was in use, but the smartly dressed businessman was just draining the last of his coffee so Sam loitered by the door for a moment, pretending to read the chalkboard breakfast menu until the man left.

He ordered a chai latte from the surly, mono-browed waitress and waited for it to arrive before opening his schoolbag. His bag of tricks. Dirty tricks.

His table was at the back of the cafe, deep in the heart of the building beside a large leafy pot plant with an interlaced trunk. The position had been carefully chosen.

Opening his schoolbag was both exciting and terrifying at once. It was crossing a line. It was the start of something, like strapping yourself into a roller-coaster. No, more like a Special Forces soldier going behind enemy lines, or a spy setting out on a dangerous mission that depended on skill, wits and fast reactions to stay alive.

He pulled out his laptop and from the front pocket of his bag he took a parabolic aerial, unfolding the wings and embedding it at the base of the pot plant.

"You in place?" Fargas asked in his ear.

"Yes, Mom," Sam said, glancing around the cafe.

It was about three-quarters full: mostly dark-suited businessmen and women. The occasional arty, Greenwich Village type, slumming it with the suits.

A man in his twenties with a completely shaven head and a spider's web tattoo crawling up the back of his neck was seated with a stern-looking matronly woman, possibly his mother, in a severe grey woollen dress. A small group of tourists at a table by the door were busy taking photos of each other with their cell phones and laughing.

He switched his gaze to his laptop and opened his wireless connection manager. A red light on the front panel flickered orange, then changed to green as it picked up signals from wireless networks nearby. Green like a traffic light. Green for go.

The panel on his laptop showed seventeen networks in all; the cafe's own free network for patrons had the strongest signal. The others came from all around and above him, gigabytes of data flying through the air of the cafe. Personal, confidential, private data, broadcast by people with utter faith in the security of their wireless networks.

Nor was that faith totally unjustified. With intrusion detection and high-level encryption, it would take a very special person to hack into that data. An expert. A genius. A devil. All of the above, some would say.

Someone like Sam.

Sam ignored sixteen of the signals. There was only one that interested him: an indistinct signal from a wireless access point on the other side of the old brick wall next to him, probably quite close by, but the wall degraded the signal until it was as thin as a ghost.

The parabolic aerial he was aiming in that direction had a built-in signal booster. He turned it back and forth, gauging the angle where the signal was the strongest.

"How you going?" Fargas asked.

"No problems so far," Sam murmured. "Wireless security is a contradiction in terms. Like 'military intelligence' or 'jumbo shrimp'."

"I like jumbo shrimp," Fargas said.

Sam transmitted a generic disconnect signal, dropping the other station off the network. Lost and alone, it immediately began bleating, like some kitten mewling for its mother.

He intercepted the reconnect signal and broadcast the same signal from his laptop. Less than a second later he was part of the network.

"Anything happening?" Sam asked quietly.

"A few security guards in the foyer."

"What are they doing?"

"Linedancing," Fargas said.

Sam smiled. "Okay, let's do it," he said.

With another quick glance around at the other patrons, he reached out cool cyber hands into the network, into the digital world on the other side of the wall.

2. TELECOMERICA

The New York corporate headquarters of Telecomerica are located on the Avenue of the Americas, but the nerve system is downtown in their offices on Thomas Street. It occupies forty-two floors of prime Manhattan real estate.

From the roof of the building, a forest of aerials and satellite dishes poke holes in the clouds above the city. On the ground floor, security is at its tightest, with armed guards and metal detectors on every entrance. Crash bars protect the front of the building from vehicular attack and bombproof shutters can be lowered from the ceiling in seconds, if called for. The building was designed, from the outset, to be self-sufficient and protected from nuclear fallout for up to two weeks after a nuclear blast. Back when it was built, during the so-called "Cold War" with the USSR, that had probably seemed like a good idea. Since Vegas it was a Federal requirement.

The physical security is one thing, but the electronic security is just as advanced.

A skilled hacker might make it through the outer defences but not without setting off alarms and the system administrators would shut them down before they had a chance to break through the secondary defences.

None of which mattered to Sam.

Next door to the highly secure Thomas Street facility is a small cafe, popular with the Telecomerica staff.

Just a heavy concrete wall – lined with brick on the cafe side and wooden panelling on the Telecomerica side – separates the cafe from the facility.

Sam sat at a small table on the cafe side and slowly inched his way into the computer network on the other side of the wall.

The rings of firewall security were not a problem. He had already bypassed them simply by connecting to an access point on the inside. *Behind* all the layers of expensive security.

The trick now was to analyse the network traffic: the tiny packets of data that flowed continuously like high-pressure water through the pipes of the network.

Sam's custom-built network analyser was based on a couple of the more advanced black ops programs used by other hackers but with special mods of his own. It didn't look like software at all. More like a random collection of code fragments in no particular shape or order. *Ghillie*, he called it, after the shaggy camouflage "ghillie suits" worn by Special Forces snipers.

Ghillie slithered into a small space in the network, just a shapeless pile of old code, computer droppings, lying in the memory on one of the big network routers. It lay there undetected, skimming the TCP-IP packets as they flew past, studying them, reporting on them.

The first thing Sam noticed was the silence. The TCP-IP traffic to and from the access point was minimal. There were no computers connecting to the wireless access point that he had hacked into. That indicated that the room was empty. An unused office maybe, or a conference room.

He scanned the room for peripherals: a printer, a digital projector and an interactive whiteboard. A conference room for sure.

He kept low, watching for intrusion detection programs – the network's guard dogs, smoke alarms or trip-wires.

"One of the guards is talking on his cell," Fargas said in his ear. "You sure they can't detect this program of yours?"

"Positive. What's the guard doing?"

"He's smiling. Probably ordering Krispy Kremes."

"Got a big router running hot on the fifth floor," Sam said. "Think I'll just go hide in the packet flood and hunt for a network controller."

"One strawberry, two cinnamon twists and a chocolate iced. And don't hold the sprinkles," Fargas said.

Softly, softly, Sam thought, insinuating himself into the new router, and making no further movements, just keeping his head down, watching the flow of data, looking for the software that would be looking for him.

There was nothing.

And yet...

He couldn't shake off a feeling that somewhere in the depths of the network an eye, like the eye of Mordor, was turned in his direction.

"Ever get that feeling you're being watched?" he asked.

"You *are* being watched," Fargas said from the other side of the street. "I'm watching you. Or your feet at least."

"You're supposed to be watching the guards," Sam said, as he ran a triple check for all known detection programs. Nothing.

"We can back out of this," Fargas said.

Sam ignored him and began to look around, sending tiny cyber filaments out through the network, scanning for servers.

There were hundreds of servers scattered throughout the building. Some big number-crunchers, others smaller, dedicated to a single task. The one he wanted was a network controller, one of the DHCP servers that ran the network.

It wasn't hard to find. He simply had to trace the security requests, which all had to be routed through the network controller. This was the machine with the key to the entire system, the SAM database where the network passwords were stored. Unlock that file and the network was his.

"Got the SAM file," he said. "I'm going to run a rainbow crack and—"

He froze. Something just passed right over the top of him, reading his code. Anti-intrusion! This was new though. Not so much a watchdog, chained to a post, barking at intruders, but something infinitely more dangerous. Something unseen that crawled in the dark places of the network, probing here and there with electronic feelers. A network spider. He had heard of them, had even got a copy of one and taken it apart to see how it worked, but had never encountered one in the wild before.

He shuddered as the digital legs of the dark creature probed his code, sifting through it, analysing it.

Then it was gone. Fooled by the electronic ghillie suit.

"What?" Fargas asked.

"Security spider. Just went right over the top of Ghillie."

"Pick you up?"

"Cruised straight past."

Sam traced the shape of the spider and fed it into his early-warning system. The next time the spider, or one of its kind, came crawling in his direction he would have fair warning.

Cracking the network controller was going to be tricky. He briefly considered an ARP poisoning attack against one of the network switches, turning it into a hub and making it accessible to anyone. But that would leave evidence of the hack, which would defeat the whole purpose.

He decided on a MAC spoofing attack.

Every machine on a network has a Media Access Control address, a unique ID number programmed into the network card. Sam's next trick was to find a suitable machine and "borrow" its MAC address, fooling the network controller into accepting him as an authorised part of the network.

It didn't take long. A few minutes of watching, waiting and a new computer came online. A laptop, almost certainly, attaching itself to one of the many wireless access points on the network.

Sam smiled as the laptop revealed its MAC address in the probe request, and was confirmed a nanosecond later by the probe response from the network controller. Before it even had time to authenticate the request, Sam was in, jamming the network card of the laptop for a moment while he reprogrammed his own MAC address, "spoofing" that of the genuine machines.

The network controller looked him up and down, decided that he was the new laptop and happily authenticated him.

He was in.

Someone would be calling tech support about now, Sam thought, complaining about a laptop that was not connecting to the network. But if the help desk here was like most, it would take twenty minutes to answer, and then the first advice would be to restart the laptop.

Plenty of time.

Ethan Rix put on his telephone headset and answered the call with a click of his mouse.

Business was light this time of the morning and this was his first call since coming on shift.

Most of the problems were simple technical questions that he could clear up quickly, the same problems over and over, in fact. Some people seemed to have the same problem each week, and never learned from the week before what the solution was.

The voice on the other end of the phone was complaining about a laptop that wouldn't connect to the network. As usual, he advised restarting the machine.

"First pinhead of the morning?"

He looked up. Erica Fogarty, one of the on-duty system administrators, was hovering over his desk.

"John Holden from fourth. Can't connect. System says he's already on. Couldn't be a MAC spoof?"

"Inside the firewall? Not possible." Erica shook her head.

"I'll run a check of current logins, just to be sure," Ethan said.

The spider came back as Sam was delicately probing the hard drives of the network controller. He paused and the spider passed by, although he couldn't shake off that disquieting feeling ... was it the spider? Or was there something else? That burning eye of Mordor.

There were trip-wires on the network controller.

Sections of the hard disk that, if accessed, would immediately sound the alarm. He manoeuvred cautiously around them and probed deeper into the bowels of the big server.

The SAM database is the record of all the usernames and passwords on the network, all encrypted into secure hashes with over eighty billion possible combinations.

Supposedly unbreakable security.

In fact, it took 7.7 seconds, using a rainbow crack, to retrieve the first password, and within five minutes he had the one he wanted. The SysAdmin password: the system administrator. The key to every door in the network.

Suddenly, the entire network lay open before him. Barefaced, unprotected, vulnerable.

No time though to stop and congratulate himself. He was already moving, racing through the wide-open corridors of the network.

Next stop, the primary transaction database. Millions, *billions*, of database records. A library of information, all laid out in neat rows in front of him with his new godlike SysAdmin powers.

"I'm in," he said.

"You serious?" Fargas asked.

"I am God and Harold be my name," Sam replied.

"Harold?"

"Let's go shopping. What'll you have?" Sam asked.

"One strawberry, two cinnamon twists and a chocolate iced."

"Let's start with a couple of the latest paper-thin Toshiba notebooks." Sam scanned the database as he spoke, writing and executing SQL statements, looking up product codes and making matching entries in a sales order table.

"One of those new neuro-headsets," Fargas contributed.

"Two headsets coming right up. Can I upsize you to a super combo?"

Records updated, the results window informed him a few minutes later. Just a miniscule drop in the massive Telecomerica data ocean. A transaction that never was, but which, to the computers that ran Telecomerica, was now a matter of record. An undisputed fact.

Job done. Time to leave.

He closed the SQL manager and waited – just for a few minutes to make sure that his covert operation had not attracted anyone's attention.

If Telecomerica suspected the break-in, they would run checks on the data, and that would show up the change he had made. Which would lead them straight to him.

But so far, so good.

"Excuse me, Erica," Ethan called across the room.

"Yeah?"

"You using SysAdmin?"

"Nobody uses SysAdmin. It's just a backup in case of password corruption."

"Someone is."

She came and stood over his shoulder again. "What are they accessing?"

Reflected in his screen, Ethan saw a horrified expression fall over Erica's face. "The central database server," he said.

Sam was just completing the clean-up, erasing every trace of his presence, when all hell broke loose.

The network lit up like a fireworks display as intrusion alarms went off on all the main servers simultaneously. Powerful anti-intrusion code checkers roared through the network pipes, searching, scanning for anything out of the ordinary. Spiders, not one, but a hundred of them, appeared on his radar, crawling everywhere. There were thundering crashes all around him as electronic doors slammed shut.

"Crap!"

"What is it?" Fargas asked.

"They're on to me. It's like the Fourth of July in here."

"Then kill Ghillie and get out of there!"

Frantically, Sam keyed in a self-destruct command, but hesitated before pressing the button.

"Can't do that yet," he said.

"Sam, you know if they find it, they'll pull it to pieces, figure it out and add its profile to the antiviral databases. You've got to delete it and get out of there."

It was true. If they caught and analysed Ghillie, it would be rendered useless, not just now, but always.

Still he hesitated. Without Ghillie he was deaf, dumb and blind.

"I need it," he said. "If they know the database has been compromised, then they'll look for the most recent changes and that'll lead them straight to us!"

He logged back onto the database, a desperate plan forming in his mind. As system administrator, he had full power over the database. Power to create. Power to destroy.

Gritting his teeth, he fired a data bomb right into the heart of the transaction database server. It exploded with a huge *whumph*, scrambling the database into a billion fragments.

Scanners swept over him, oblivious, fooled by the camouflage. That gave him a ray of hope. Maybe there was still a way...

"Whatever you're doing, do it fast," Fargas said.

If they are looking for something, better give them something to find, Sam thought, reaching into his bag of dirty tricks and releasing a couple of vicious viruses into the arteries of the network. The Russian Black Flu and the Japanese Kamikaze. Self-replicating, shape-shifting viruses. Nasty little critters, highly destructive and difficult to stamp out. The network security should cope with them, but it would occupy them for a few minutes: a distraction, a diversion.

What he needed, and needed urgently, was the location of the database backup files. They wouldn't be on site, but where would they be?

The SQL database management engine gave him the answer: London.

There were alternative backups in Washington DC and Melbourne, but London was the first go-to place if the system crashed (which it just had).

He digitally rocketed across the Atlantic and burst through the security in the London facility. Not bypassing the defences so much as kicking the front door down, using his SysAdmin powers as a battering ram.

Even as he did so, he realised that Ghillie was under attack. Something, *someone* – a human being not a program – was reading its code, line by line. Nothing he could do about that now. He still needed his eyes and ears if he was going to finish this.

Erica was making Ethan uncomfortable, hovering just behind him. She was on the phone now, her voice loud enough to vibrate the earphones in his headset.

"No, we don't know how they got in!" she said.

He twisted around. "Logs show a wireless router

disconnect and reconnect in Conference Three."

"Might have pirated a wireless router," Erica said, not too calmly. "I've warned and warned about wireless inside the DMZ."

"I've got viral alerts on three floors," Ethan yelled. "Variant of the Black Flu, maybe something else too."

"If it's wireless, then they're close. Get security onto it." Erica hung up and sat down at the spare terminal next to him.

"I'll take the viruses, you stay on the hacker," she said.

The backup files were stored in a SAN, Sam realised. A Storage Area Network. This SAN was well secured, padlocked as it were.

He could break it but that would leave traces of his visit. He had to pick the lock. He struggled to concentrate, knowing that they were already on his tail. He prodded the locking software gently, studying the mechanism.

"What have you done now?" Fargas yelled in his ear. "I've got security running around like their butts are on fire. Running out into the street."

"What are they doing?"

"Checking cars, stopping traffic, scanning the buildings. It's only going to take them a few seconds to figure out where you are, Sam. Get outta there! Crap, coming your way right now!"

Sam slid the laptop off the table and onto his knees as an armed guard burst in through the doors at the front of the cafe.

His heart was hammering in his chest, but casually, ever so casually, he began to sip his chai latte. It was barely lukewarm.

The guard ran his gaze around the cafe and ran back out again, shouting into his radio.

Underneath the table Sam's fingers flew across the keyboard. He was hyperventilating now and tried to force his breathing to steady, but it would not.

The locking software sprang open and he rifled through the backup files. They were encrypted and compressed, although no trouble if you had the right tools.

He carefully edited the most recent backup of the transaction database, closed it, then reset the time and date on the file back to what it had been *before* he had made the changes.

When they restored the backup files to replace the ruined database they would be unwittingly putting his data right where he wanted it.

The last thing he did, before sending a self-destruct signal, was to leave traces of a digital signature that he had stolen from a Turkish hacker. Ghillie disappeared as if it had never existed.

He grabbed the parabolic antenna, flattened its wings and threw it into his backpack. He hit the shutdown on his laptop.

"Someone just ran outside with a radio direction finder!" Fargas yelled. "Now they're all heading right your way."

Sam was already moving. He was at the rear of the cafe by the washrooms when the guards burst through the front door. He ducked across the hallway into the cafe's small kitchen, throwing on a baseball cap and pair of sunglasses as he did so, running past the hotplates and startled chefs to the service entrance at the rear.

He emerged onto Trimble Place, looking back again and again, but seeing no sign of pursuit. A police humvee went past him at speed, siren wailing.

He was so engrossed in what was, or wasn't, behind him that he completely failed to notice the security camera, mounted high on a telegraph pole, that turned to follow him as he scurried along Trimble Place. He walked a little more steadily down Duane Street, eventually losing himself in the crowds thronging their way to work along Hudson Street.

Slowly, Sam's breathing began to calm. He checked his watch and increased his pace, partly to put in more distance from the scene of the crime, and partly because he was late.

It was 8.52 am.

Time for school.

3. CHAOS

At exactly 8.59 am, as Sam Wilson was walking through the main entrance to his school, nodding to the security guards – who ignored him – and smiling at their aggressive-looking guard dogs – which snarled at him, a series of catastrophes was striking the largest telecommunications company in America: Telecomerica.

The scrambled database server was bad enough, but two nasty little viruses, the Black Flu and Kamikaze, chewed their way through node after node on the network as the system administrators and the antiviral software struggled to contain them.

Servers had to be shut down and rebuilt from scratch to eliminate the intruders and repair the damage.

The Thomas Street facility infected the Washington DC office, which spread the disease right up and down the East Coast, as far south as Miami, from where it raced across, via Albuquerque to San Diego, and quickly spread up and down the West Coast as well.

It wasn't simply the internet that went down, although that collapsed in a screaming heap right across the country and in many other places around the world as all the main US circuits imploded. The same circuits were used by the internal networks of banks and major corporations. Most had to close their doors.

TV stations went off the air. Radio stations broadcast static. ATMs all went offline. The stock exchange ground to a halt. The loss of the internet meant the loss of email and instant messaging. Cell phones just roamed aimlessly, looking for networks that no longer existed. Text messages sat uselessly in outboxes. Entire regions lost basic telephone services as the sickness found its way into other networks. Some parts of the US even lost power.

Still, nobody died. There was the occasional injury when the lights went out and some rioting in Los Angeles – what was now referred to as PVPS, or Post-Vegas Panic Syndrome – but there were no fatalities.

It took three days to sort out the chaos and get America back online.

4. URSULA

The delivery guy piled all the boxes in a stack by the door of the apartment and handed over a PDA.

Sam felt sweat break out behind his ears as he signed on the electronic screen, accepting delivery of the goods.

If they had gotten away with it, or not, this was the time they would find out.

But the delivery guy just turned and headed back to the elevators.

"Cool!" Fargas said behind him.

"Let's get it inside," Sam said, grabbing two of the boxes off the top. "We've only got a couple of hours before the convention starts."

The elevator doors opened as he did so, and Louis, the bratty twelve year old from 602, got out with a couple of his long-haired Guitar Hero friends as the delivery guy got in.

If there was ever any doubt about whether humankind had descended from the apes, Sam thought, Louis was living proof. He and his mates clearly hadn't descended as far as most other people.

"Geek alert," Louis said immediately. "Nerds in the open."

His buddies laughed. Sam ignored him and handed the boxes to Fargas.

"Whatcha got in the boxes?" Louis said. "Geek stuff? Are you building a robot in there?"

"Why don't you thump him?" Fargas asked.

"Why don't you thump him?" one of Louis's friends mimicked.

"Ignore him," Sam said. "His brain's not developed enough to argue with."

He picked up the remaining boxes and shut the apartment door with his foot as Louis struggled with a reply.

"Are you building a robot girlfriend?" Louis asked loudly in the corridor as the door closed in his face. "Can't get a real one."

Sam carefully negotiated the narrow and crowded hallway of the apartment with the two cartons.

"What's your mom gonna say about all this stuff?" Fargas asked a few moments later.

All this stuff was the cardboard boxes, polystyrene and other assorted packaging for two new laptops, two Neurotech neuro-headsets and a variety of software.

Sam folded the last of the large brown boxes flat and stacked it with the others against the wall by the window, next to the computer desk with his much older, much slower, laptop.

The desk itself was tidy, as was the rest of the small bedroom, with shoes arranged in a row inside the closet, a perfectly made bed, and rows of books, sorted by size and shape on a three-shelf bookcase against one wall.

A foot-long model of Thunderbird 2 sat on top of the bookcase, lined up with the USS *Enterprise,* the original shape from the original TV series.

Fargas was sitting on the floor, one of the new laptops on his knees and a neuro-headset next to him beside an open bag of caramel corn.

"Mom never comes in here," Sam said. "It's like my own apartment."

"And my mother hunts moose on Mars with a popgun," Fargas said, reaching out a hand to the caramel corn. Sam tried not to wince as Fargas put his sticky caramel fingers back on the computer keyboard.

"No, really—"

"Hey, dude, this chick is awesome!" Fargas said.

On Fargas's laptop screen was a picture of a stunningly beautiful girl wearing a neuro-headset.

Sam looked at his own new equipment, in shrink-wrapped cartons, now laid out neatly on his bed.

He quickly opened and powered up his new laptop, then turned his attention to the other carton.

Neurotech Neuro-Connection Pack was emblazoned across the top and *Say goodbye to your keyboard and mouse* in a flashy graphic at the lower right.

The shrink wrap disappeared with a couple of strokes

of his penknife and he opened the carton. On the top, in a flat section of the inner packing, were the manual and a Blu-ray of the software.

He put them to one side.

Below were some cables and other paraphernalia that he couldn't identify just yet and underneath another layer of cardboard was the prize itself.

He lifted it out and examined it. It was the first time he had seen a neuro-headset up close. They were still quite expensive, certainly out of the budget of a high school student, although admittedly, they were getting cheaper all the time.

It looked like a swimmer's cap, except for the slight protuberances that were the receptors. From each receptor a thin wire emerged, running backwards across the cap to the base of the neck, merging into a thick black wire which ended in four separate, multi-pinned plugs, each a different colour.

Under the next layer of cardboard in the carton he found the receptor box. A gunmetal grey box, the size of a box of chocolates. It was the biggest, heaviest thing in the carton. On the rear of the receptor device, there were four sockets, colour-coded to match the plugs.

He studied the instruction manual before connecting the cables and plugging the connector into the USB3 slot on his new laptop. He inserted the Blu-ray into the drive and installed the software then, with a growing sense of excitement, slid on the headset.

And nothing happened.

There was no strange sensation within his skull. No sudden flash of oneness with his computer. Nothing.

He looked over at Fargas, who was wearing his headset and playing some kind of simple game involving airplanes.

He loaded the training software and followed the initial set-up wizard, agreeing to the terms and conditions (without reading them) and selecting all the default options.

The Blu-ray drive whirred for a moment and his screen went entirely black, changing resolution, before a face appeared on his screen. The young woman from Fargas's computer. She was gorgeous but with a slight plasticity of skin and an unnatural smoothness of movement that showed she was computer generated, rather than a real person.

"Hello," she said in a honey-sweet voice that was entirely too natural to be simmed. A real person must have recorded the dialogue. "My name is Ursula," she said.

"Hi, Ursula, I'm Sam," Sam responded, knowing that she could not hear him.

"I'll be your tutor and guide as you discover a whole new way to operate your computer, connect with friends and family, and access the internet. Your brand-new neuro-connection," Ursula said.

"You're right. She's awesome," Sam said.

Fargas looked over. "Reckon she gives private lessons?"

"She's not real, dude. Just a bunch of pixels," Sam said.

"Works for me," Fargas said.

Sam laughed. "If she was real, I'd love to meet her."

"Get in line," Fargas said.

Ursula continued, "Your neuro-connection will allow you to put away your keyboard and mouse, and eventually even your computer screen, and interact with your computer simply by using your brain. If you haven't already plugged in and attached your headset, do that now. I'll wait," she said with a beguiling smile, then added, "If you need help with any of the equipment, press F1 now. When you are ready, press enter."

Sam did exactly that.

Ursula's face shrunk to the top right of the screen and a graphic appeared, a three-dimensional image of the headset, rotating slowly.

"You are now wearing the latest technology Neurotech 1.2 headset. Embedded sensors detect signals produced by your brain that you know as brainwaves."

Sam ran a hand over his head, feeling the slightly raised bumps on the headset.

"There are four main types of brainwaves: alpha, beta, delta and theta," she said. "The ones we are interested in are the higher frequency, but low amplitude waves, known as beta waves."

The graphic changed to show a colourful chart, a little like a topographical map.

Ursula said, "Beta waves are unique to each individual; however, certain patterns are common to all people. By detecting those common patterns, and training our patented Neuro-Sensor software to recognise your own individual patterns, it is a simple and easy process to control your computer, just with the power of your own mind. If you have ever used speech recognition software, this is a quite similar process."

Her face disappeared altogether and a screen appeared which looked like a scene out of a video game. The graphics showed a dog standing on a long winding pathway through a park. Each side of the path was lined with a row of small shrubs.

Ursula spoke. "Steer left and right to stay on the path. Concentrate on making the dog move. Focus on the dog and mentally turn it the way you want. When the dog turns to the left, press the 'L' key on your keyboard. When it turns to the right, press 'R'. This will help train the Neuro-Sensor software to recognise your brainwave patterns for left and right."

The dog started walking. The path began to curve to the left.

Sam focused on the dog and willed it to turn. It didn't. He tried to move the dog with his eyes, as if he could pick up the dog with his gaze.

The dog walked into the shrubs and stopped.

"Let's try that again." Ursula came back on screen with an encouraging smile.

"Imagine you are the dog," Fargas said, "and it is you that is turning to the left or right."

"Woof," Sam said.

The dog reappeared at the start of the path. Sam tried to imagine he was the dog, but still the dog walked into the shrubbery and stopped.

"Don't give up; you're doing well," Ursula lied cheerfully. "Press enter to try again."

Ten minutes later, he was starting to get sick of Ursula and her happy, happy attitude. A couple of times the dog had flickered a bit, as if it was trying to turn one way or the other, but that was the best he had achieved.

"Try again," she kept saying.

"I hate dogs," Sam growled.

"I know what your problem is," Fargas said.

"What?"

"No detectable brainwaves."

"I'm starting to wonder," Sam said.

"Try turning your whole body," Fargas said. "That's what worked for me at the start."

Sam stood up and this time turned his whole body to the left.

To his utter amazement, and no small relief, the dog turned hard left and crashed into the shrubs on the other side of the path.

Sam stabbed at the "L" key.

Ursula's face appeared for a moment on the screen with a huge smile. "Great work!" she said and winked.

"I think she fancies you," Fargas said.

"I have that effect on women," Sam said.

Fargas laughed and filled his mouth with caramel corn.

Sam tried again, turning to the left or the right, and found that he was able to keep the dog on the winding path for quite long periods. More importantly though, after he had pressed the "L" and "R" keys a few times, he realised that he no longer had to turn his body physically to make the dog turn. If he just thought about turning, the dog moved in that direction.

After a few minutes of doing this, still half amazed that it was actually working, Ursula reappeared with a few thoughts of her own.

"Looks like you've got the hang of left and right," she said. "Let's try up and down."

The graphic this time was a small airplane flying through a cloudy sky.

Sam pressed enter and the plane flew straight into the nearest cloud and exploded.

"Nice," Fargas said.

Sam ignored him and started over.

This time it took him just a few tries to get the hang of it, manoeuvring the biplane up and down to keep it in the blue sky part of the screen between the clouds.

As he flew on, the clouds grew thicker and larger until there was just a narrow path between them.

It took him a couple more tries before he really

mastered it, dodging up and down to keep in the blue. As he flew further and further, he noticed the plane was speeding up. The clouds came faster and faster until they were little more than a blur across the screen. Still he dodged them, flicking the little plane around the sky until at last it emerged into a bright, cloudless sky, which gradually dissolved into Ursula's cheerful face.

"Well done!" Ursula said. "Now let's put it all together."

The third game was a fish swimming through hoops in the ocean. He moved left and right, up and down, to aim the fish through the hoops. Again the game got harder as it progressed, the hoops getting smaller, the fish getting quicker. He completed the test on the first try.

"We'd better get going," he said, looking at his watch. "Or we'll miss the convention."

"Just a few more minutes," Fargas said. "You gotta try this Neuro-Doom – it's awesome!"

Sam looked at his friend's screen. Fargas was operating the computer with his eyes shut, moving around inside a virtual reality game, armed with a shotgun.

"Don't get addicted." Sam laughed.

"No chance," Fargas said. "Die, monster, die!"

"Come on," Sam insisted.

Fargas reluctantly removed his headset and closed his laptop.

Sam glanced back into the room before closing the door behind them.

The webcam sitting on top of his old laptop, on the

desk by the window, was aimed at the door, as if following them out of the room. The last time he had looked at it, it had been pointing straight ahead.

Hadn't it?

5. FREAKS AND GEEKS

The graffiti-covered door of the old warehouse opened and shut again quickly as another Darth Vader entered. Across the road, Sam checked his watch.

"Shame Ursula couldn't come," Fargas said.

Sam smiled.

"You been to one of these conventions before?" Fargas asked.

"Nah," Sam said, "I always wanted to go to Defcon in Las Vegas, but they stopped holding it after..."

He didn't need to continue. Defcon was the huge international hackers' convention. It had been held every year in Las Vegas, but the last one had disappeared from the face of the earth, along with most of the rest of Las Vegas, in a terrible nuclear cloud.

"The world is going to hell on a high-speed train, if you ask me," Fargas said, shaking his head. "And there ain't nothing nobody can do about it."

Sam checked his watch. "Time to go in. It's about to start."

"I'm really not sure, dude. I'm going to feel like an idiot," Fargas said.

"The trick is to make them feel more stupid than you," Sam said.

"And how is that going to happen?" Fargas asked.

"Don't speak to anyone. If they corner you, just act all superior and say something like 'Talk to me when you lose the training wheels'."

"Talk to me when you lose the training wheels, duckweed," Fargas tried it out in a Clint Eastwood accent.

Sam laughed, then said, "And no matter what happens, don't tell anyone about the hack we pulled off at Telecomerica."

"What's the point in visiting a hackers' convention a couple of days after pulling off the hack of the year if you can't tell anyone?" Fargas asked.

"You think the FBI can't slip an undercover agent in among the freaks and geeks?" Sam asked, pulling a C-3PO mask out of his backpack. He slid it down over his face.

"I'm leaving," Fargas said.

"Stay. It's cool. Just don't tell anyone it was us," Sam said.

Fargas stretched the elastic of a Tonto mask over his head, and said, "What do you mean 'us', white man?"

Sam took the back off his cell phone and removed the battery and SIM card and made sure Fargas did the same before they made their way across the road to the warehouse.

Defcon had been a big glamorous three-day affair with huge competing sound systems, overseas speakers, competitions, giveaways and even a formal dinner.

Neoh@ck Con was another story altogether. A convention that Sam had heard whispers about, but had never been close to. Until now. A convention for the elite, the discreet. The dark figures who moved through the shadows of the internet.

Hidden, encrypted three times over, in the code of an email about Defcon had been the address of a website. A highly secure website. Hack into that website and you found the date, time and location of Neoh@ck Con.

If you weren't smart enough to break the codes and hack the website, then you weren't invited to the convention. It was that simple.

There were two guards just inside the door. Clean-cut, broad-shouldered men with Marine-style haircuts. Hired security. They looked serious and they looked mean.

The guards stopped them with raised hands.

"Are you a law enforcement official or in the employ of any government department?" the first man asked. He said it as if reading by rote. A muscle on the side of his jaw twitched as he spoke.

Sam shook his head.

Would you admit it, if you were?

"I didn't hear that," the man growled.

"No," Sam said.

"Are you a representative of the news media?" the second man asked.

"No," Sam said again.

They turned to Fargas. "Are you a law enforcement

official or in the employ of any government department?"

"Talk to me when you lose the—" Fargas began, but stopped when Sam kicked him on the ankle, hard. "No," Fargas said.

They entered a large storeroom lined with unused storage racks. It was dusty, decrepit and smelled faintly of sawdust and machine oil.

Thirty or forty people were milling around a row of computers at one end. Behind them a data projector was casting blue nothing onto a large screen.

So this was Neoh@ck Con.

Everybody wore a disguise or face covering of some kind. Some people wore masks, Buzz Lightyear and Darth Vader being the two most popular. Sam noticed one person had his face entirely swathed in bandages like a mummy with just a slit for his eyes. Others hid their faces with make-up. To their left was a tall, strong-looking punk, his head clean-shaven, his face painted into a grinning skull. He wore torn jeans that seemed to be held together with chains and safety pins, and a leather T-shirt covered in zips. A tattoo of a biohazard symbol on his forehead was not quite concealed by the white face paint of the skull. He stood with a girl in a denim miniskirt and low-cut white vest with tattoos of intertwining dragons down one arm. Her face covering, incongruously, was a lacy wedding veil.

Freaks and geeks, Sam thought. Freaks and geeks.

A few more people drifted in and the convention got underway, not with a fanfare and a formal announcement, but simply in the groups of people that converged around the various computer workstations.

One of the larger groups was congregated around the mummy. Sam heard the word "Telecomerica" mentioned. He motioned for Fargas to follow and they wandered in that direction.

Sam found himself standing behind Skullface Punk, and unable to see, moved to stand behind Rock Chick Bride.

"But there's no way to beat the IPSec on that model firewall without setting off the zone alarm," the mummy was saying. "So even if they'd used malformed TCP packets to exploit a vulnerability in the firewall and made it into the DMZ, they'd have been shut down before they could infiltrate any further."

"That's me 'ole bleedin' point," Skullface said emphatically, stabbing a finger into the air.

He was English, Sam thought, judging by his accent. Maybe even a London cockney.

Skullface continued, "It can't have been an 'ack. It ain't possible. It was an inside job. Some rogue trader with a grudge."

"So if it was an inside job..." a kid in a rubber rooster mask began.

"Then it ain't worth discussing," Skullface said. "Some muppet on the payroll letting go a couple of wet farts ain't what we're here for."

"You don't know it was an inside job," Sam said quietly.

"Ain't no way in from the outside." Skullface half-turned to face Sam. "End of bleedin' story."

"Any network can be hacked," Sam said.

There was a moment's silence.

Rock Chick Bride said, "Oh, he's so cute! Can I keep him?"

Sam glared at her through the C-3PO mask.

"I suppose you could have hacked 'em too, if you'd felt like it." Skullface grinned and there was laughter from somewhere in the crowd.

"If I had to," Sam said.

"Oh, please," Rock Chick Bride said, "I promise I'll look after him!"

"Even if you got past the DMZ, you'd set off the zone alarm," the mummy said.

"Yeah," Sam said, "but what if the hacker used a signal extender to pirate a wireless station and bypass the whole DMZ? Run a network analyser, rainbow-crack the SAM file and he'd have owned the network."

He shut his mouth abruptly.

There was another short silence.

"Come back when you lose the training wheels, muppet," Skullface said.

"Waste of freaking time," Sam said. He whirled and strode off.

He made it almost as far as the door, Fargas at his heels, when Skullface's voice came from behind him. "Hold up, script kiddy."

Sam turned back, his fists clenched as Skullface and Rock Chick Bride approached.

"Back off, duckweed," Fargas said beside him.

Skullface moved close and spoke in a low voice.

"I was just winding you up," he said. "Wanted to see what you got."

"More than you got, ass wipe," Fargas said.

"Just chill, monkey boy," Skullface said, then to Sam: "You could be right about that Telecomerica job."

Sam looked at him for a long moment, then shrugged. "It's just a guess."

"It was a good guess. Better than most of them would be capable of." He jerked his head back behind him. "You want to go to Neoh@ck?"

"Been there, done that," Fargas said, looking around the old warehouse. "Ain't buying the T-shirt."

Skullface made that macabre smile again. "This ain't Neo. This is just the weeding-out party. Just a bunch of muppets who were lucky enough to crack the code in the invite."

Rock Chick Bride moved up beside Sam; a sneer appeared to be permanently attached to her lip.

Skullface continued, "You want to go to the real Neoh@ck, you gotta earn it. Think you're up to it?"

Sam felt his fists unclench. "Where is it held?" he asked, intrigued despite himself.

Rock Chick Bride shook her head. "They'll never get in."

"It ain't held anywhere," Skullface said. "Think about

it. Why would a bunch of serious hackers put on silly masks and compare weenies in an old warehouse? The real convention, Neoh@ck Con, is *online*. Tonight. Starts at nine o'clock. The best of the best from all around the world. You gotta hack your way in to prove you got what it takes."

"Where?" Sam asked again.

"Out of your league is where," Rock Chick Bride said.

Skullface grinned evilly. "We're meeting for dinner. Where the President lives. If you make it, it's going to rock your world."

6. THE WHITE HOUSE

No matter how deep you dug, Sam thought, there always seemed to be a level deeper. The more you knew, the more you realised how little you really knew.

The real Neoh@ck Con was held somewhere inside the White House. One of the most secure networks in the entire world. Just the idea that there was a bunch of hackers so powerful, so skilful, that they actually held their meetings within the White House without anyone knowing, was mind-blowing!

And if he made it, according to Skullface, it was going to rock his world.

He arrived home just after noon and wolfed a quick sandwich before shutting himself away in his room.

Fargas had taken his laptop and headset and headed off home, suddenly having remembered he had some chores to do for his mother. Sam suspected he was really going home to play *Neuro-Doom* and wondered if that might be something to worry about. Game addiction was a huge international problem and they said that neuro-games were far more addictive than normal computer games.

He resolved to give Fargas a call later and see what he was up to.

In the meantime: the White House. Surely an impossible hack, one part of his brain kept saying. They were just kidding you.

But Skullface had sounded serious when he had said it.

He started with an hour on Google.

The computer networks at the White House are managed by the WHCA, the White House Communications Agency, which is itself controlled by the DISA, the Defence Information Systems Agency.

The White House was a part of GovNet, a separate network air gapped from the internet: isolated by the very simple process of having no actual physical connections between GovNet and the internet.

Sam reasoned that through. Theoretically, it was impossible to access an air-gapped system; however, the reality was that a widespread network like GovNet would be almost impossible to air gap one hundred per cent, despite the best efforts of the computer administrators and their security policies. It just took one connection from inside the network to the outside world and the entire air gap was compromised.

DISA controlled ten digital gateways that served the network from three network operations centres. The network covered the White House, Camp David (the presidential retreat), Air Force One, the fleet of presidential helicopters, the presidential limo fleet and the president's cell phone, along with a wide range of other governmental locations.

Emails were routed to a cluster of specialised servers based in the Washington DC network operations (NetOp) centre. From there White House traffic was filtered, monitored and transferred inside GovNet to a secondary email server in the White House itself, where it was rescreened and finally distributed to the various email accounts throughout the building.

The only open connection between the internet-connected email servers in the NetOp centre, and the server in the White House was a two-way email pipe. All other network ports were shut off.

But it was a wire that crossed the air gap.

That would do it. One of Sam's special tricks was a clever bit of software that would break IP packets into tiny bits, attach them to genuine emails and reassemble them at the other end, creating an invisible connection between the two computers that flowed along beneath the constant current of email messages between the two networks.

It was like writing secret messages, one word at a time, underneath stamps on envelopes and posting them one after the other. At the receiving end someone had to assemble the words back into a full sentence.

He called it *Crossfire* for no particular reason.

He slipped his software onto the NetOp email server by launching a Denial of Service (DOS) attack from a small server farm in the Netherlands that he had compromised over a year before.

While the systems and their administrators responded to that, he slid Crossfire quietly onto the server using a variant of the old Metasploit tool.

Now for the email server.

It was protected against power outages by an Uninterruptible Power Supply, a UPS. The UPS was connected to the server by an old-fashioned serial cable, which in emergencies could send a shut down command to the server. Furthermore, the company that installed the UPS monitored it, so they could run diagnostics and respond to any problems in the device.

Sam crept carefully into the network of the UPS supplier and slid slowly down the wire to the UPS device itself.

It wasn't enough to load Crossfire onto the server though; it had to be run. The program had to be executed and he couldn't do that through a serial connection.

He encased Crossfire in a self-executing shell and renamed it to that of a common internal Windows program. Someone inside the White House would unwittingly run the program that would complete the circuit and give Sam access, through the email connection, into the heart of the US Government.

Through the serial connection, he copied the file into the Operating System folder of the email server and closed out of the UPS and the UPS company network.

Now there was nothing more he could do. It was up to the staff at the White House to open the door and let him in.

7. NEOH@CK

He checked his watch a couple of times, not worried, but a little nervous. If Crossfire was detected, then he was sunk. If it simply wasn't activated, then he would miss the convention.

To pass the time he alt-tabbed back to see Ursula.

The next set of neuro-exercises involved loading a program, such as Photoshop, while thinking about that program. Very soon he could open and close programs, activate commands and functions, and even move things around on a page, all without touching the keyboard. Next Ursula asked him to visualise each key on the keyboard in turn, while pressing it. That was easy enough.

A short while later he was in the middle of an exercise that involved him thinking of a word, then seeing it appear on the screen, when a pop-up message alerted him that Crossfire was now active.

"See you soon, Ursula," he whispered, and minimised her again.

* * *

Someone had activated Crossfire, opening up a tiny pathway onto one of the email servers on the White House network.

He slipped Ghillie onto the machine and it lay there for a while, unobserved, but observing.

The amount of data traffic was amazing, but not unexpected for the nerve centre of a world superpower.

Sam did not move at all and just watched for intrusion detectors or security spiders. The spiders were everywhere, constantly crawling through the White House network. They passed over him harmlessly though, without seeing.

He spun a small data-web on one branch of the network, blocking packets from getting through. Not many, and they would get through on the retry, but enough for him to gauge how the network reacted.

The White House network was monitored by special software called *Therminator*. It presented the network as a thermal image, with any problems showing up as hot spots. But there had to be a built-in tolerance level, Sam figured, otherwise every slight networking issue would set off alarm bells.

No alarms went off. No searchlights blared. A small packet loss was within the tolerance of the network, it seemed, and as it should be.

He extended a probe, a clever device that emulated broken TCP-IP packets and simulated data loss, which would be ignored by Therminator. He scanned the disk structure of the big server.

There were over thirty disk drives attached to the machine. He scrolled through the list of drives, wondering where to start.

One caught his eye. A tiny drive, just half a gigabyte. A fraction of the size of the others, which was why he noticed it. It was labelled "NHC".

It took a moment before that clicked.

NHC! Neoh@ck Con! It had to be, he thought, as he accessed the contents of the drive itself.

The hackers had set up their own partition on one of the White House central server's disks, and were using that for their meetings. On the drive there was just a single file. An executable. A program. That would be the online forum software, he guessed.

His watch said it was 8.15. Too early. Not that he minded being early, but there might be risks in logging on too soon. The longer he was logged in, the greater the chance of being caught.

He alt-tabbed to bring the Neuro-Sensor software to the front again, but even as he did so, he realised something strange. For the last twenty minutes he had been crawling around inside the computer network of the White House. He had activated programs, spun data-webs, even written short bursts of code.

But he hadn't touched the mouse or the keyboard at all.

* * *

Ursula had a whole bunch of other exercises to improve his skills, but he was getting impatient, so he bypassed them and loaded the next module.

"Neuro-visualisation," Ursula told him smoothly. "The neuro-sensors in your headset are also transmitters. They not only pick up signals from your brain, but they can feed sounds and images into your brain, by stimulating brainwaves in your visual and audio cortices."

"Cool," Sam said, nervously flicking a glance at his watch. It was 8.16. Just a minute had passed.

"Close your eyes," Ursula said. "I am going to send an image to you now. Nothing fancy, just a red triangle. Relax and allow your brain to receive and interpret the image. If you open your eyes, the feed will automatically shut off. This is a safety mechanism to ensure you do not overload the visual receptors in your brain with information from two different sources."

Sam closed his eyes.

"Visual feed starting now," Ursula said.

A blurry red dot appeared behind Sam's eyes.

"It had better get better than this!" he muttered.

"You should now be seeing a fuzzy red shape," Ursula said. "Focus on it, try and draw it towards you."

Sam focused, imagining himself speeding towards the red nothingness. It began to grow in size.

After a moment it filled almost half of his vision and, although still out of focus, was clearly a large red triangle.

"Concentrate on the triangle, try and bring it sharply

into focus. As it changes, I want you to press the plus and minus keys on your keyboard. If it gets clearer, press plus. If it becomes less distinct, then press minus. When it is perfectly sharp, press the space bar."

Sam waited until the edges were sharp and clear, then pressed the space bar.

"Okay," she said. "Now for colour. I am going to show you a series of colour images. When you see the one that has a red dot at the top, a blue dot at the left, and a green dot on the right, then press the space bar."

It was the first image.

"Good. Now I am going to send you a colour image. If you can identify the image, then type the name on the screen," she said, and added, "with your mind, of course."

Sam opened his eyes for a moment to check his watch (8.53 pm) and when he shut them a huge, clear image of the famous da Vinci painting, *Mona Lisa,* was hanging right in front of him, occupying all of his vision. It was bigger and clearer than he could have ever dreamed possible and he realised that the image was being beamed directly into his visual cortex.

Mona Lisa, he thought and the words appeared over the top of the picture. The bemused smile on the face in the painting broke into a grin and Mona Lisa said, with Ursula's voice, "Congratulations. You are correct. You are now ready to use your neuro-connector to view and operate your computer. Have fun!"

The painting disappeared, replaced by his normal

Windows background and icons. He opened a few programs, and closed them again just to prove he could do it. He opened a word processor and typed a few sentences with his mind. He ran an MP3 file and was astounded to hear the music inside his head. He tried the same with a video and was rewarded by the movie starting to play in a small window.

He closed it and glanced at the clock in the lower right corner of his screen (did you call it a screen when it was inside your head?) and noticed that it was 8.59 pm.

"Dinnertime," he said out loud.

Without touching the mouse, the keyboard, or looking at the LCD screen of his laptop, he ventured back into the electronic corridors of the White House.

He checked the clock in the bottom right corner again. 9.00 pm.

Open, he thought, staring at the file.

It opened.

There was a brief second or two of a standard hourglass then the software took over the whole of his screen, the whole of his *vision*!

It opened into an image, a virtual version of the White House. He was somewhere in the grounds of the big building. It was a sunny day and the grass was green underfoot. In front of him a fountain, surrounded by a low hedge, sprayed virtual water up into the air, digital droplets sparkling in the bright sun before cascading back to earth.

Now, finally, he understood what Skullface had meant. It wasn't just an online forum, it was virtual meeting software, where their avatars would see and talk to each other in a cyberworld. Like *Third Life.* They would probably meet in the Oval Office itself, he thought. No, Skullface said dinner – it would be in the formal dining room.

By thinking himself forward, he began to move, skirting around the side of the fountain towards the front doors.

He moved across a roadway, past the white pillars, up a flight of stairs towards the huge double doors of the White House in an arched entranceway.

He imagined the doors opening, but they did not.

He opened his eyes and tried clicking on the doors with his mouse, but they remained solidly closed.

He closed his eyes again and looked around.

To the right of the doors, conveniently placed at head height on the doorframe, was a black rectangular plastic shape with a white button in the centre.

A doorbell.

Sam chuckled to himself. So simple. The final hurdle was not a hurdle at all.

At the start it had seemed impossible, yet here he was, at the front door of the White House, about to embark on an incredible new adventure. What would he learn? Who would he meet?

He took a deep breath, and clicked on the doorbell.

A sound intruded and he opened his eyes with a start, shutting off the visual/audio feed from the neuro-connector. The White House doors and the doorbell were still there though, staring at him from the laptop screen.

Surely he had just imagined that sound.

He kept his eyes open and tried again, but this time preferring the traditional methods. He reached out and grasped his mouse with his right hand and moved it over to the doorbell.

Drawing in his breath again, he clicked on the button a second time.

And jumped out of his chair with sudden terrible knowledge and fear.

Outside his bedroom, past the kitchen where his mother was working, at the end of the hallway, at the front door of their sixth-floor apartment, the doorbell rang again.

8. KIWI

Sam lay on the lumpy mattress on the metal-framed bunk, staring blankly at the ceiling of his cell.

He felt he was going mad. Three days locked in a cell they called a bedroom. But it had wire mesh on the windows and the door was permanently locked, which seemed more like a prison cell to Sam.

Three days ago he had raced down the hallway to the front door of their apartment. Terrified of opening the door, but even more terrified of his mother opening it first.

The man standing there wore tactical black SWAT-type coveralls and a Kevlar vest. A pistol in a black leather holster was strapped, not to his hip, but halfway down his thigh. He was in his late twenties. Not short, but not tall either. His hair was slicked back in a style reminiscent of old fifties rock'n'rollers, as if to make him taller, and he wore dark aviator-style mirrored glasses which he removed as Sam opened the door.

The man was flanked by two others, in identical uniforms, but with automatic rifles slung across their chests. They stood back from the doorway, against the wall on the opposite side of the hall, and their gaze flicked left and right as if they were expecting trouble.

All three of them wore flesh-coloured earpieces with a curly wire that disappeared around the back of their necks.

Through a half-open door on the other side of the corridor, Louis, the Neanderthal twelve year old, watched wide-eyed.

"Sam Wilson?" the first man asked.

Sam nodded mutely.

"I'm Special Agent Tyler Ranger from the Department of Homeland Security, Cyber Defence Division. I am placing you under arrest on suspicion of government network infiltration and sabotage. You have the right..."

Sam didn't get to hear his rights. Not just then anyway.

"What?" his mother screamed from right behind him. "What is going on? What are you doing? What..." There were quite a lot of "whats" in fact.

None of which phased the men in black at all.

Since then he had been here. Wherever *here* was. It was somewhere near Washington DC, that much he knew. A collection of old-looking buildings surrounded by tall trees and a high razor wire fence, a mile or two from the nearest town.

He had seen it when they had flown over, in the black Learjet emblazoned with Homeland Security logos, and again, up close, through the wire mesh windows of the black Chevy van that had brought him from the small airfield to his new home.

As prisons went, it could have been worse, he thought. The floors were a polished dark wood and the walls were timber panels, although he suspected they covered a more solid, concrete construction. There was a toilet in a cupboard on the left side of the bedroom, and a communal shower block at the end of the hallway.

It wasn't a prison for adults, that much was clear. It was some kind of remand centre or juvie hall for youth offenders. Nobody that he saw through the mesh on the window looked older than eighteen.

There was a beep from the electronic lock on his door and it opened. It was one of the wardens, a hard-faced man with a gut that hung low over his belt, named Brewer.

Brewer looked around the cell before placing a large cardboard box on the floor. It bore a red label with the word "inspected".

He scowled at Sam and left.

Sam got up off the bunk and opened the carton.

On the inside flap he found a huge heart drawn with a thick marker pen and *I love you, Sam,* written in his mother's neat hand.

That was the only communication from his mother in three days.

The carton was full of clothes: shirts, shorts, socks.

Under the first layer of clothes had been his model of Thunderbird 2, carefully wrapped in a couple of T-shirts.

He took it out and placed it on the windowsill.

Below that were some sweaters, although it was too warm for those just yet.

He started to lift them out, then stopped, his fingers nerveless. He let the sweaters slip back into the box, realising that he might be sitting in this same cell as the fall leaves drifted off their branches. As the cold winter winds began to howl across the state, and the first tiny soft snowflakes turned into flurries of white ice.

He had been so sure of himself. So confident of his own cleverness that he hadn't ever really stopped to consider the consequences of his actions. He had charged around the country's networks as if he was playing a computer game.

But it wasn't a game. It was real.

He'd thought he couldn't be caught, and yet the whole time they had been watching him, just waiting to pounce. That uncomfortable feeling he had had inside the Telecomerica network – that had been more than just a case of nerves or indigestion. Thinking he could fool them with a C-3PO mask at the hackers' conference. What a joke that was.

But the joke was on him.

And there were consequences.

And at the moment the consequence was a cell, a *bedroom,* in an unnamed security facility somewhere near the nation's capital.

He turned back to the window, picked up the

Thunderbird model and hurled it against the far wall.

It shattered and fell.

He lay back down on the bed, and cried.

That afternoon he was allowed out for exercise in the courtyard for the first time. It did not meet his expectations of a prison courtyard at all. It had pleasant, grassy park-like grounds, bushy trees and a small pond.

There were about seventy or eighty other inmates, all boys, wandering around the courtyard in groups or pairs, or playing soccer on a flat patch of ground in the centre, using shoes to mark out goalposts.

Others played basketball on a concrete court over by the administration block.

Sam kept to himself in an empty area of the park. He had heard too many horror stories about life in prison to want to get on the wrong side of the wrong people. Right now he didn't even know who the wrong people were.

The sky was that kind of indecisive overcast that could fade away to sunshine or intensify to showers just as quickly.

He sat on the grass, keeping his eyes low, careful not to make eye contact with the other inmates, and contemplated his own stupidity.

"G'day, mate," a voice intruded and he looked up. He hadn't heard the boy approach.

He was about seventeen, in Sam's best guess, and wore a pair of thin, wire-framed glasses. His hair was wild. His mouth was open in a goofy grin that made him look a little soft in the head. Sam wondered if he was.

"Um, hi, I guess," Sam responded. "Australian?"

"Nyew Zilder," the boy said, which Sam took to mean New Zealander. That was a small island of the coast of Australia, he thought, or was that Tasmania?

The boy stuck out his hand. Sam took it and shook it. He seemed harmless enough.

"Jase," the boy said. "They call me Kiwi."

He pronounced it *koy-wee*.

"Kiwi like the fruit?" Sam queried.

"Like the bird," the boy, Jase – Kiwi – said.

"Sorry, no offence," Sam said.

"No worries," Kiwi said.

"I'm Sam," Sam said.

"What are you in for?" Kiwi asked.

"Stuff," Sam said, not wanting to give away too much. "What about you?"

"Armed robbery," Kiwi said.

Sam blinked. With his casual appearance and goofy grin, Kiwi didn't look like a typical armed robber.

"Really?" he asked.

"True as a fart in a suitcase," Kiwi said, although Sam had no idea what he meant. "I robbed a bank in Nebraska, armed with a computer."

Sam laughed. "Computer fraud?"

Kiwi hushed him. "Don't tell any of them." He nodded at the rest of the inmates. "They keep away from me. Think I'm dangerous."

"Sure thing, killer." Sam smiled.

"So what are you in for?" Kiwi asked. "You're cyber too, right? I saw the CDD van when you arrived." He saw Sam's quizzical look and elaborated, "Cyber Defence Division. Homeland Security boofheads."

Sam shrugged. "They reckon I was somewhere I shouldn't have been."

"Where?" Kiwi asked.

"I'm not admitting anything," Sam said.

"Yeah, yeah, same, same, but what did they *accuse* you of breaking in to?" Kiwi asked. He sat down on the grass beside Sam and crossed his legs like a first grader on a teacher's mat.

Sam looked at him and decided that he was an unlikely snitch.

"The White House," he admitted at last.

Kiwi's jaw dropped. "No way."

"That's the accusation," Sam said.

"The White House! That's impossible. You'd never get near it. It's on GovNet; it's air gapped and therminated. You wouldn't have got within a hundred miles."

He wasn't quite as dumb as he looked, Sam decided.

"The White House," he confirmed.

"Oh, that's funny." Kiwi laughed. "How far did you get?"

"Could have peed in the presidential john if I'd wanted to."

"No way of the dragon!" Kiwi breathed.

"How long have you been here?" Sam asked. "How long did you get?"

"Just three years," Kiwi said. "'Cos of my age. Woulda been worse if I'd been older. I got one year here at Recton, then a couple of years upstate. After that I'll be repatriated. Sent home to New Zealand. Kicked out, in other words. How about you?"

"I dunno," Sam said. "I haven't been officially charged with anything yet, as far as I know. I haven't seen a lawyer, haven't been to court. Nothing like that. I haven't even spoken to my mom."

"Right," Kiwi said knowingly. "CDD."

"What does that mean? How long can they keep me here?" Sam asked.

"Long as they want," Kiwi said. "They got me under the Fraud Act – that's criminal. But they would have got you under the Terrorism Act. Since Vegas, if they call it terrorism, they can do what they want with you. You'll stay here till you turn eighteen, then you'll head upstate to a real prison. With the adult prisoners. Good chance that they'll throw away the key and forget you ever existed. Sorry, mate, but I'd rather be in my shoes, if you know what I mean."

Kiwi must have seen the look on Sam's face, as he added quickly, "You should email your mum, let her know that you're okay. There are computers in the library."

"There's a library?" Sam asked.

"Over by the admin block."

"With computers?"

9. THE LIBRARY

The library was old and, if it was possible, even more wooden than the long hallways and bedrooms of the dormitory block.

The tables were scrawled with graffiti, most of it obscene. There was shelf after shelf of books but Sam didn't stop to investigate just yet. First stop was the computer table.

There were four computers in all, separated by wooden partitions. Only the first one was in use. The user was a rat-faced boy with the word *BadAss* tattooed, not professionally, on the back of his neck.

Sam chose the farthest computer.

He sent a quick email to his mom, assuring her that he was okay and not to worry, then browsed around the computer, seeing what was available to the inmates.

It was a standard HP computer, running a Microsoft operating system. But it was locked down tighter than any computer he had ever seen. Net Nanny, WebMarshal, the list went on, all bound into a managed environment so the user couldn't reconfigure the machine in any way.

Internet Explorer was available, but only a restricted list of sites was accessible. Solitaire and Minesweeper were the only games, although one of the allowed websites was a chess site where you could play against people from all over the world.

One way of passing the time.

The prison email program was allowed, as well as a few utilities like calculators and spreadsheets.

Other than that, there was nothing.

Nor was there any way of loading software onto the computer. The keyboard, mouse and screen were the only accessible parts. Everything else was locked away in a solid-looking cupboard below the table.

A sign affixed to the top of each computer warned that any attempt to interfere with the computers would result in the computers being removed.

That would be one way to get yourself noticed, Sam thought, and become highly unpopular with the other inmates. Still...

Sam played solitaire until BadAss left, and kept a careful eye on the door to make sure nobody else came in.

He didn't know where he was and he didn't know how long he would be staying, but he did know that he was sitting in front of a computer. And that computer was connected to the prison network.

And despite the warning sign on the top of the screen, he couldn't resist the temptation.

To have a go.

Just once, to see if it could be done.

Control, alt, delete: the basic reset keys did nothing. That was no surprise.

The spreadsheet program was the key. He was surprised that they allowed it, but that had to be plain ignorance.

Most people just used spreadsheets for basic calculations, but the cells allowed functions, and functions were really tiny programs in their own right.

It was an old trick, but a good one. He opened a spreadsheet and created a function that caused an endless loop. A complex mathematical calculation with no end, just whizzing around and around inside itself going nowhere.

He opened a second spreadsheet page and copied in the same function. Already, the machine was performing like an arthritic snail.

He opened a third page and a fourth. By the tenth the overloaded computer was taking over a minute just to bring up a page, the hourglass spinning frantically as the processor ground its teeth to nothing.

One more page tipped it. The computer froze. It stayed that way for a couple of minutes until the Managed Environment Controller decided that the machine had died (which it had) and started a reboot.

Too easy, Sam thought.

He caught the machine on the reboot and flicked it into Safe Mode, disabling all of the software, including the Managed Environment software. When it had finished restarting, in the subdued colours and low resolution of Safe Mode, he opened the registry file and disabled the Managed Environment completely before restarting the machine again.

This time it booted up normally and when it started, everything worked. The restrictions imposed by the security software were gone. The computer was his.

Quickly, keeping one eye on the door, he wrote a trapdoor, deep in the operating system, so that a certain combination of keys would automatically kill the Managed Environment and give him full control. That way he could return the machine to its normal state, but still use it whenever he felt like it.

So, he thought, let's have a look around.

He accessed one of his drones in Mexico, where he permanently stored a copy of Ghillie and released it into the prison network.

The SAM database was easy and the SysAdmin rights were his within seconds. He strode through the prison network security without breaking his stride.

Everything was there. Menus for the meals, weekly supply orders. Guard rosters (along with their personal details and income details).

Even the codes for the electronic doors.

10. THE WRECK

Recton Hall Juvenile Detention Centre is in Bethesda, Maryland on the shores of the Dalecarlia Reservoir, to the north-west of the nation's capital and just over the Potomac River from the CIA's headquarters in Langley, Virginia. It caters for juvenile offenders up to the age of seventeen.

Like many other juvenile halls, or juvies, Recton takes pride in providing a secure environment that does not feel like a prison.

The high security fence that surrounds the facility is softened, completely hidden in some places, by the tall red maples and river birches planted on both sides of the razor wire.

Inside the perimeter a white picket fence adds a rustic touch and hides a proximity-and-thermal sensor. An observer with an eye for detail would also notice that the tops of the pickets are white painted metal, not wood, and are sharper than you would usually expect for a picket fence. Also that the fence, at four-foot high, is a little taller than usual, just high enough in fact to prevent anyone from casually stepping over it. It has to be climbed. The same innocent-looking fence delineates the area in which the inmates, referred to as guests, are allowed to roam.

Every inch of the ground between the picket fence, and the wire mesh security fence on the outside, is covered by cameras and monitored by motion sensors. There are plenty of blind spots among the trees, but none at all in the four-yard clear space on either side of the fence.

There is only one way in or out of Recton and that is through the "cage", part of the administration block. Large metal gates on the outside and reinforced doors on the inside create a kind of holding area in which all prisoners, visitors, staff and supply vans must be cleared, before proceeding in or out of the facility.

The cage is on the first floor of the administration block, along with the inmate processing centre, the loading dock and the school office. The second floor contains administration offices, storerooms and the armoury, plus the guards' rest area and washroom.

The third floor is the watch-house: the control room that runs Recton, monitoring comings and goings, and the activities of the guests.

Dormitories and classrooms are housed in separate buildings spread throughout the spacious grounds.

Recton Hall, known to guests as "Wrecking Ball", "Rectum" or just "The Wreck" does not house gang members, drug addicts, game addicts or murderers. In the overall scheme of juvenile detention centres, Recton is at the top end. It is the place where white-collar juvenile criminals get sent for crimes like fraud, embezzlement, cybercrime and espionage.

It surprises most people to learn that the biggest category of offenders at Recton is not fraud but espionage. Industrial espionage mostly, plus a limited amount of military or governmental espionage. Generally, the culprits have parents in high-level positions in strategic organisations and are targeted by unscrupulous agents of corporations or foreign countries.

There are a few "common" criminals at the facility, usually because their parents were powerful or wealthy enough to pull the political strings necessary to get them transferred to a "safe" institution like Recton, away from the gangbangers and addicts that fill the halls of the other juvies.

Guests have limited access to a telephone, one per dormitory, although all phone calls are recorded. Cell phones are not allowed and a powerful network jammer ensures that even smuggled-in phones are useless.

All of this Sam found out simply by typing "Recton" into Google.

The trees shivered a little in a late afternoon breeze, and a few loose leaves twirled like butterflies down over the razor wire fence. One leaf caught for a moment on a spike before a stronger gust dislodged it.

A trio of Asian inmates were playing some complicated card game, sitting on the grass near the boundary, just a few yards away. Sam tried to figure out the rules, without staring. It involved a lot of picture cards and the queens seemed especially important, and every few moments one of them would reach over and slap one of the others hard across the face, then they would all fall about laughing.

It made no sense to Sam at all.

He looked back at the fence. So thin, so delicate, yet so vicious with its sharks' teeth of jagged metal.

The idea had been in his mind from the moment he had found the codes for the electronic doors, but actually making the decision to escape was another thing.

On one hand there was an unspecified amount of time in jail. (*Throw away the key*, according to Kiwi.) On the other hand was a life of running and hiding, constantly looking over his shoulder. An outlaw, an outcast, a fugitive.

Would he ever be able to see his mother again? Or Fargas? Would he have to leave the country, sneak over the border into Canada or Mexico and live the rest of his life in some foreign land?

But then he looked around at the razor-topped fences and tried to imagine spending month after month of his life in this one small patch of land, constantly under watch by armed guards.

And worse. On his eighteenth birthday, the transfer to an adult prison. What kind of horrors would that hold, amidst the burglars, murderers and gangsters?

Recton was scary enough. The thought of some unknown adult prison "upstate" was simply terrifying.

Sam saw Kiwi walking over towards him, and stood up.

Together they strolled along the exercise track that ran around the circumference of Recton, a yard or two inside the white picket fence.

He counted his paces, although he was careful not to look like someone who was counting his paces.

It had been two weeks now since he had arrived. Two weeks of limp, flavourless food, communal showers (which he hated) and a horrible claustrophobic feeling every night as the electronic door beeped and locked itself at nine o'clock.

He had put that time to good use though. Noting the routines of the guards. Where their rounds were. Who was scrupulous, who was punctual, who was lazy and did the barest minimum to fulfil their duties.

He had drawn a map of the fences and sketched in the sensors and other hidden alarms that he located on the security system on the admin computer. He had measured distances on the ground, and compared those with the information online, working out times and distances.

He had full run of the computer networks and there was nothing he couldn't find out if he wanted to.

Two weeks of researching, planning, and finally he was ready to go.

All he needed was an accomplice.

Sam casually picked up a stone from the path and

tossed it over the picket fence where it landed among the trees. No alarms sounded. It would take more than a pebble to set off the motion sensors.

"Kiwi," he began, glancing back at the watch-house. "I need your help."

"Yeah, no worries," Kiwi said.

11. PRISON BREAK

Sam was ready at ten to ten, standing just inside the door of his bedroom, waiting for the fire alarm.

He had accessed the fire control system and scheduled a fire drill for ten o'clock, then disabled the line of code in the program that knew it was only a drill.

As far as the computer was concerned, the fire would be real, and it would react accordingly.

His few belongings were shoved into the pockets of his warm jacket.

Everything now relied on Kiwi. He had agreed, a little reluctantly, to Sam's request. If caught, he could wave goodbye to his hopes of serving out his sentence in New Zealand. But he'd agreed anyway.

Seconds ticked away on his watch and the minutes slowly dripped away as well.

Was he prepared for this? he wondered. A life of constantly hiding. A life without his family and friends. A life underground.

The fire alarm sounded just outside the door to his room. A long bell that went on and on.

When a fire alarm went off at Recton, the computers that controlled the facility would automatically unlock all the cell doors to make sure no inmates were trapped inside.

The door in front of him unlocked itself with a beep and the clunk of the electronic latch. Sam was through it and running down the hallway the moment the handle came free in his hand.

He had counted every step between the dormitory and the admin block and knew exactly how much time he had.

He'd make it, as long as he didn't stumble or trip over.

He was flying out of the hallway door into the courtyard even as other doors were opening into the corridor behind him. Frightened, confused voices followed him out of the door.

He made it to the admin block just in time, flattening himself against the side wall as the door opened and three guards came out at a trot.

Three? The roster had said four.

He waited a moment longer to be safe, but no one else emerged.

He keyed in the security code and yanked on the doorhandle. The door opened without question and pulled itself shut behind him.

The guards would have fun trying to get back in. As of right now, the codes had all changed and only Sam knew the new ones.

He had never been in this part of the admin block

before, but knew his way around as if he worked there, from the floor plans he had found on the central server.

He raced up two flights of stairs past the guards' showers and changing rooms, down a short corridor with doors to the armoury and records room, and keyed the code for the door at the far end: the storeroom.

In here were all the belongings of the guests, in numbered cardboard boxes. His number was 5143 and he scanned along the shelves until he found it.

His wallet and cell phone went into his jacket pockets along with a few other odds and ends that he had been carrying when he'd been arrested.

He left the storeroom door open and ran up another flight of stairs to the watch-house.

The first thing he had learned, by studying the security plans for Recton, was that the main gates that formed the outside wall of the cage were not under any kind of computer control. Nor could they be opened manually from within the cage. They could only be opened from the watch-house.

The button for the gates was clearly marked. It was large and black and fitted with a plastic cover so it couldn't be pressed accidentally.

The plastic cover was locked, but three quick blows from a fire-extinguisher smashed the hinges into plastic slivers.

He watched on one of the security monitors as the gates began to grind their way open.

He marked his watch. Plenty of time, but he had better not hang around. The gates would automatically shut after two minutes if left open.

He ran back along the short corridor and headed for the cage.

The gates were wide open by the time he got there. Heavy, metal, and open like a 7-Eleven.

Sam burst through the inner door to the cage and made at least five or six yards towards the gates before he heard a click from behind him.

He faltered, then stopped dead as the low tones of Warden Brewer came from near the door.

"Goin' somewheres?"

Sam stood motionless, breathing heavily in and out, before turning to face Brewer.

The warden's cap was pulled low, casting his face in shadow, but his eyes caught the glare of the incandescent bulbs at the end of the cage and glinted like cat's eyes from under the peak. His fleshy jowls pulled up into a menacing smile, his teeth bared like a wild animal.

Brewer had a gun in his hand. Some kind of pistol. Sleek, black and deadly, and aimed right at Sam's chest. At this range he couldn't miss.

Sam took a step backwards. A step closer to the gates.

"That's about as far's you get," Brewer said, rising off a wooden seat by the delivery dock. "Fire alarm at this time of night seemed just a mite convenient to me. And all the phone lines going dead? Very suspicious."

Sam glanced at his watch. Over a minute was gone already.

Brewer saw the movement. "About a minute left," he said, "before them gates close. After that it won't matter what kind of trickery you got up to in the watch-house. They won't be opening again."

Sam didn't doubt it.

"I guess you 'n' me'll just wait it out," Brewer said. "Seeing as you don't seem to feel much like talking."

Sam remained silent and Brewer continued, "Police'll be here in a minute or two. I dunno how you cut off the phones, but you forgot about the emergency radio."

He must have seen the expression on Sam's face because he whistled softly and said, "You didn't forget about the radio, did you? What'd you do to it? Don't matter, I guess."

All Sam had done to the computerised radio system was to change the frequency. As simple as that. No doubt someone somewhere would have picked up the transmission but not the police or anyone else who would understand what it was.

"Don't matter," Brewer said. "'Cos the fire department gonna be here in a coupla minutes anyways. They'll have their own radios in their trucks, and I don't s'pose you figured out a way to screw up their radios now, did you?"

Sam took another step backwards, a couple of feet closer to the gates. His eye caught the security camera above Brewer's head and a plan started to form in his mind.

"Don't you move," Brewer said, raising the gun, but Sam did move. He raised his hands high in the air and slowly turned around.

"Better," Brewer said. "Now you're getting the idea."

In front of Sam the gates began to close.

He took a step towards them.

"Next step is your last, boy," Brewer said.

"I don't think so." Sam found his voice. "You won't do it."

"I don't think you wanna find out," Brewer said.

"See the camera?" Sam said, nodding towards the camera to the left above the gates. "CNN. Live feed. I wired it right into their network." It wasn't true, but how would Brewer know? He gestured towards the one on the right. "Fox News and the two at the back are BBC. You want to be seen all over the world shooting an unarmed teenager in the back?"

He took another step and there was no shot. He took one more. The gates were a quarter closed now. The gap was narrowing rapidly.

He sensed, rather than saw, Brewer holster the pistol, but he heard the heavy hasty footsteps behind him.

Sam dropped his head and sprinted towards the gates.

Brewer was older, fatter and slower than Sam. Sam would have easily beaten him if he hadn't caught his left shoe behind his right ankle and gone sprawling across the tarmac four or five yards from the gates.

He was up quickly though and actually through the gates when a meaty hand latched onto the collar of his jacket. Sam was stopped dead in his tracks. He turned around to see the sweating, scowling face of Brewer just an arm's length away.

"Gotcha!" Brewer said triumphantly.

"Not unless you want to lose that arm," Sam noted.

It was true. Sam had slipped through the slenderest of gaps and Brewer was too large to get through behind him. The gap had already narrowed even more, and there was no way Brewer would be able to pull Sam back inside.

Only his arm was through the gates now, and the heavy metal edges were closing in fast.

Brewer swore violently and snatched his arm back inside, just as the gates slammed shut.

Sam didn't wait around for any clever repartee. He just ran. He had allowed himself ten minutes to get to the intersection of MacArthur Boulevard and Little Falls Road. He had already used three.

Sam ran. A strong gusty breeze buffeted him, alternately pushing him backwards or helping him along. He stayed off the boulevard with its inconstant stream of headlights and ran on the grass of the reservoir park alongside, staying in the darkness by the high safety fence.

Sweat streamed from his face. His chest ached, his knee also. He must have hurt it when he had tripped inside the cage. No matter. He ignored it and ran.

Kiwi would have sent the "false alarm" message by now. The one thing Sam had needed him to do. It would take only a minute for the fire controller to relay that to the fire trucks and they would turn around at the first place they could, the MacArthur Boulevard and Little Falls Road intersection.

He had to get there first.

Sam ran.

He wondered what kind of confusion he had left behind him at Recton. The codes no longer worked. The phones and radios were inoperable. The cell phone jammer was still operating though; he had made sure of that.

The guards were captives in their own prison, and unable to tell anyone about it.

He would have laughed out loud, if he had had the breath. But he didn't.

He ran.

The flashing red lights of a fire truck appeared along the boulevard in front of him, partly obscured by the trees in the narrow strip of parkland. Even as he watched, the truck slowed and the lights ceased.

It was only a few hundred yards away now, but the

truck slowed further, signalled, and turned left, not right as he had thought, heading back down the other side of MacArthur Boulevard rather than taking the short cut back through Little Falls. No matter. As long as he got there in time.

Eighty yards to go, that was all, and the second truck, a large pumper unit, clearly visible in the glare of the intersection streetlights, turned and moved away in the stream of traffic heading south down the boulevard.

A third fire truck turned and was gone, and the fourth, and the last truck also, signalling and turning while he was still twenty yards away.

The last truck stopped in the through road, giving way to an eighteen-wheeler and a succession of sedans, before making the turn.

Sam caught the truck as it was just starting to move, grabbing a chrome bar with one hand, and swinging himself up onto the back running board, hanging on, barely, as it accelerated away.

Wind whipped at his hair and threatened to knock him off his perch, but he clung tightly to the round metal bar and pulled himself as close as possible to the body of the truck.

There was no traffic behind him, for which he was grateful, as it might be a bit hard to explain what he was doing there if an alert motorist noticed him.

The traffic was light heading back along Dalecarlia Parkway back to Friendly Village, and the trip passed without incident.

He stepped off the back of the truck at the first intersection they came to in the town centre, seeing the lights of a taxi stand at the end of the street.

He heard sirens now, not fire, but police sirens, only a few blocks away, without doubt sounding for him. Brewer must have found a way to raise the alarm.

Sam strolled casually along to the taxi stand, opening the door and sliding into the back seat of the first cab on the stand.

"Where to guv'nor?" the driver asked, sounding just like a London cabbie, or at least what Sam's impression of a London cabbie was like, from TV shows and movies. He had a passing feeling that he had seen this driver before, but that was surely impossible.

"The train station," Sam said calmly. He didn't want to sound like a prisoner on the run, even if he was one.

"Bethesda or Silver Spring?" the driver asked. "Bethesda is closer, but the express goes through Silver Spring."

"Bethesda," Sam answered. He'd checked that out too. The express didn't run this late at night, but Bethesda was on the red line and he could catch a train to Union Station. From there he could disappear anywhere he wanted.

"Rightio, Bethesda it is then, guv," the driver said, turning around to face him.

He was surprisingly young for a cab driver, Sam thought. No more than eighteen and completely bald under a peaked cap. His face was long and thin, but there was a glint of a chuckle in his eyes. Sam had never seen him before in his life, and yet...

Then he got it. It was the voice. The accent, it was unmistakable.

The driver grinned, a slightly macabre, almost demonic, smile, even without the face paint. He tilted back his cap, revealing the tattoo of a biohazard symbol on his forehead.

"Skullface!" Sam cried out and the driver laughed.

"Took your bleedin' time gettin' out, ya muppet," he said. "Another day an' we'd have had to send you home."

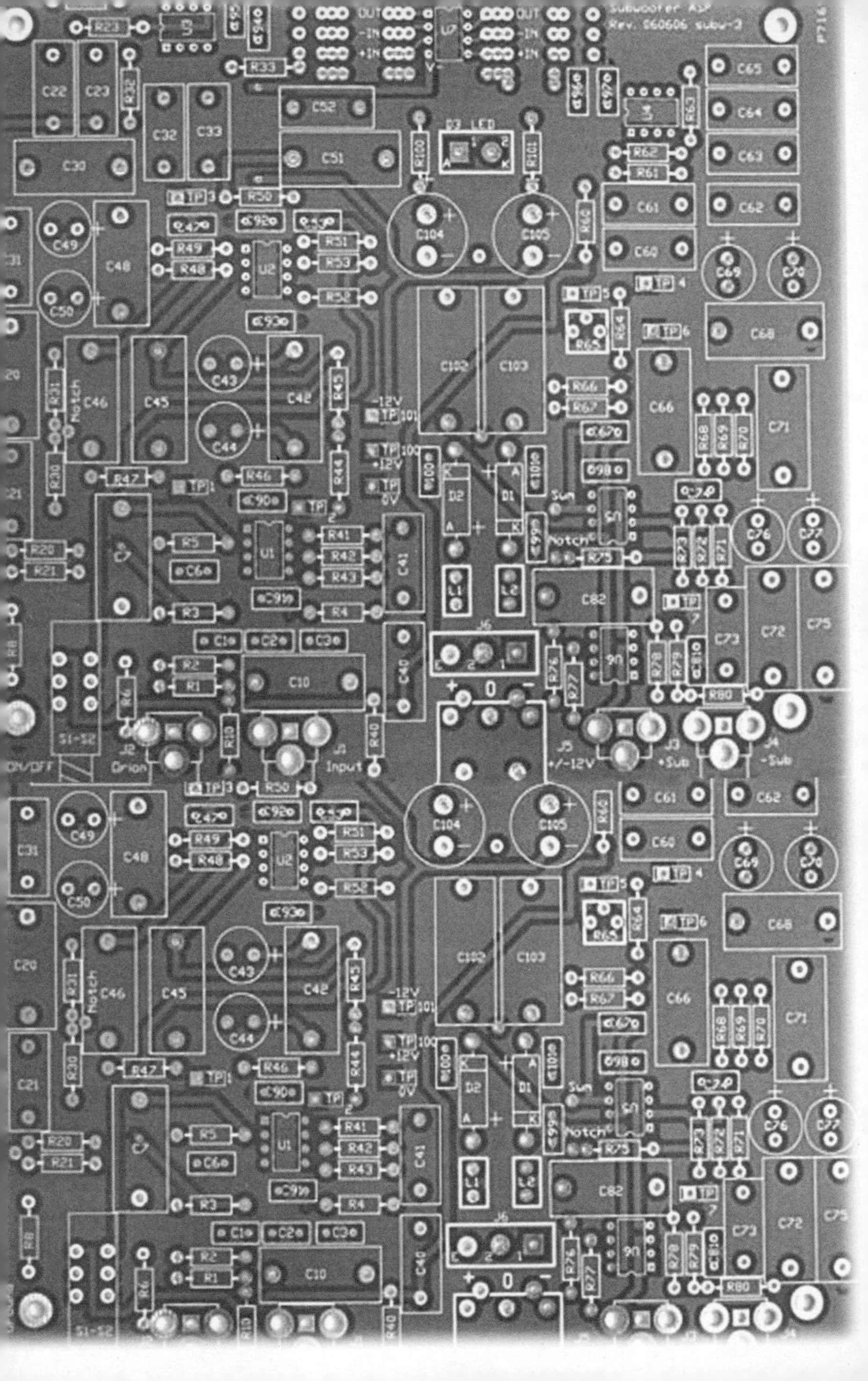
Subwoofer ASP
Rev. 060606 subu-2
Input
Orion
ON/OFF
+/-12V
+Sub
-Sub
Notch
Sum

BOOK TWO
REVELATIONS

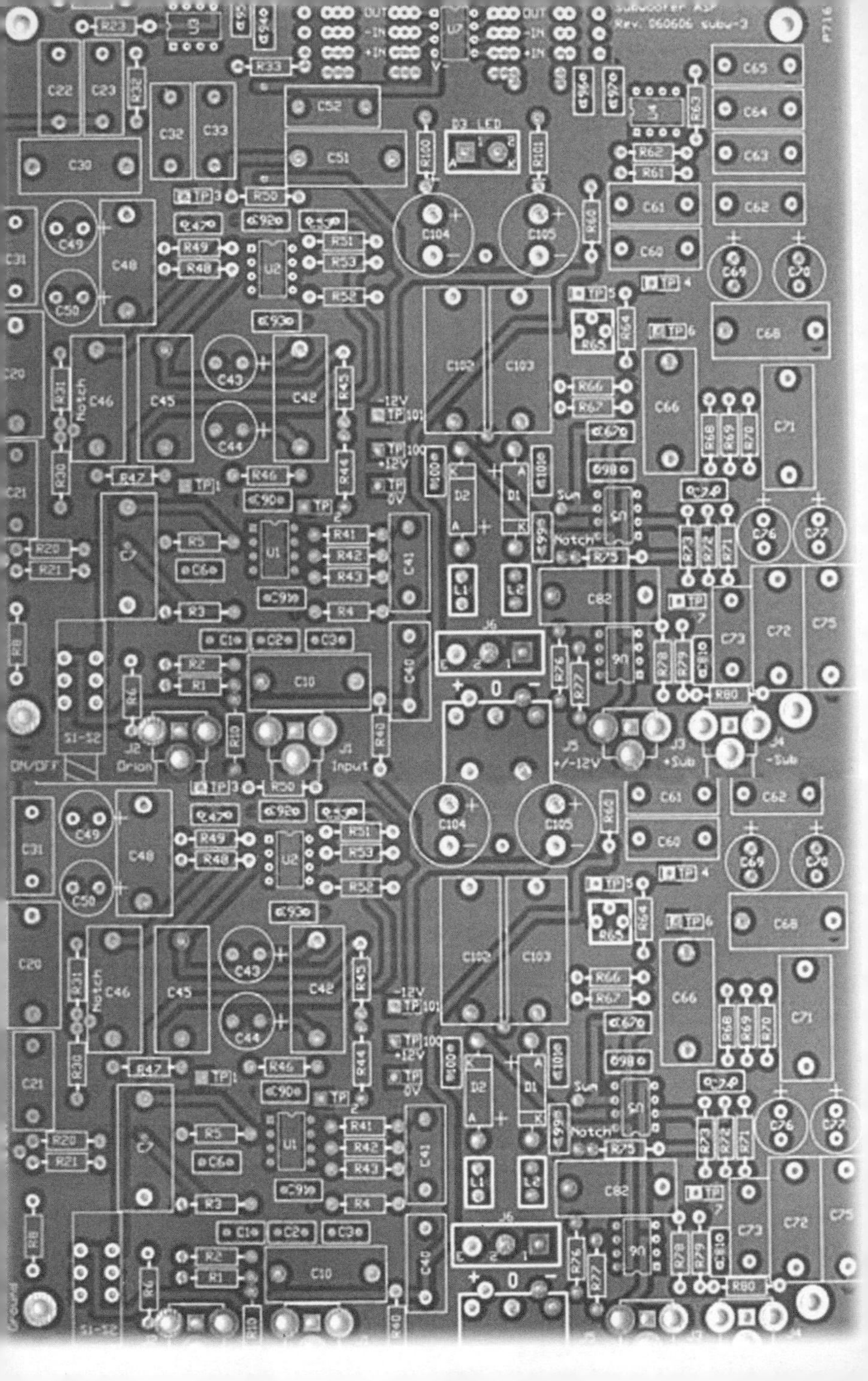

1. SILICON VALLEY

"You're Sam Wilson?"

The man in front of Sam was tall, his back straight, his head erect. Ex-military, Sam thought. A scar ran sideways across his face, crossing just below the bridge of his nose.

"Yes. Yes, sir," Sam managed, trying not to stare at the scar.

"Come with me, son."

Sam stood up from the chair in the waiting area and tried to keep up with the man as he made quick yards down a long, featureless corridor.

A woman was waiting for the man at the end of the corridor, by the open door to an office. She was short and plump and less than five feet tall, but with a huge frizz of orange hair that added another six inches. She glanced briefly at Sam before handing the man a folder.

It was only for a half second but in that time he felt that as though he had just been X-rayed. That her black eyes had burned their way through to his soul.

The tall man opened the folder, reviewing its contents.

"How good is the intel?" he asked the woman.

"As good as it gets," she said. "We just don't know when. It could be this afternoon, or it might not be for months."

The man nodded. "Okay. We'll raise the threat level. Go to lockdown."

"I'll tell the team," the woman said, glancing again at Sam.

"Thanks. I'll be along shortly."

The woman disappeared back along the corridor with the folder as Sam followed the man into the office.

"Sit down, Mr Wilson," he said, taking a seat behind a large desk.

Sam sat on a chair on the other side. A photo of the man in a Marines uniform sat on a bookshelf to his right, confirming the military background. The man in the photo had no scar though.

"My name is John Jaggard. Welcome to Homeland Security," the man said.

"CDD?" Sam ventured and Jaggard nodded.

Cyber Defence Division.

"I don't quite understand why I'm here," Sam said carefully. "Am I in trouble?"

"You should be," Jaggard said, punching something on his keyboard that brought up Sam's file on a screen they could both see. He handed Sam a thick sheaf of papers. "But as it happens, we need people with your skills. We want you to work for us."

"Work for you?"

"That's what I said."

Jaggard smiled. The scar echoed the smile. Sam thought back to the whirlwind of the last few weeks and shook his head, confused.

"But the White House? Neoh@ck Con?"

"There is no Neoh@ck Con," Jaggard said. "Think of it as a job application."

"And Recton Hall?"

"The job interview."

Sam was still having trouble comprehending it all. "What's this?" he asked, holding up the bundle of papers.

"It's a job offer," Jaggard said, although he clearly thought that was obvious. "You can take it or leave it."

"I'm only sixteen," Sam said, thinking they must already know that.

"Sam," Jaggard looked at him appraisingly, "everybody at that meeting in the old warehouse was given the same information. Hack into the White House for the Neoh@ck Convention. You want to know how many of them got through?"

Sam shrugged.

"Just you, Sam."

Sam looked again at the figure on the bottom line of the contract. It seemed extraordinarily generous for an annual salary. Almost too high in fact.

"What does that work out to be per month?" he wondered out loud, trying to do the math. His brain seemed to be running in slow motion.

"That is per month," Jaggard said.

Sam gasped.

"You can take it or leave it," the man said again.

He didn't expand on that, but Sam had the strong sense that if he left it, that would mean a return to Recton.

"If you take it," Jaggard continued, "you're on probation for three months. If you survive the probation ..." He'd said "survive" Sam noted, not "pass" or "succeed". "... then that figure doubles."

"Doubles?" Sam blurted.

"Think we're being overgenerous?" Jaggard and his scar smiled again.

Overgenerous? The amount was *obscene*! Sam thought, but said nothing.

"We pay well," Jaggard said. "We have to, or at least we choose to. We only select the best of the best, so we pay them accordingly. But it goes a little deeper than that. You'll have almost unlimited access inside every Government department and financial institution in the country. We want to remove the temptation to help yourself, and to avoid the possibility of bribery by outside agencies. We feel that if you have more money than you know what to do with, it makes you a little more resilient to corruption."

Sam leaned back in his chair and looked around the office, trying to get his thoughts in order.

Dodge – Skullface – had driven him straight to the same small private airfield just out of Bethesda that he had flown into a few weeks earlier.

The drive hadn't been without incident. A police cruiser had passed them on the main street through Friendly Village and shone a light into the rear of the cab before pulling in behind them. The red and blues had come on.

Dodge reached for his cell phone the moment the cruiser had shown interest, talking quietly into it even as he signalled and pulled over to stop.

Two Bethesda cops stepped out of the cruiser and approached cautiously, weapons drawn, silhouetted in their own headlights. They only made it halfway to the car when they halted and one put a radio to his ear.

That was it. The two officers retraced their steps to the cruiser and switched off the flashing lights, just sitting there.

Dodge flipped his cell phone back in his pocket as he accelerated away from the curb.

These guys had some powerful mojo, Sam thought.

The flight, in the same black Learjet (or at least an identical one), was longer this time, and he had slept on the plane. He woke at the jolt of landing. His watch said six thirty and he would have expected to see the early dawn lightening of the sky, but it was still as dark as tar. That meant they had flown west, into a new time zone. The flight time (they had taken off around midnight) meant California.

Signs on the freeway on the drive in from the airfield confirmed it. San Jose.

Right in the heart of Silicon Valley.

* * *

"Welcome aboard," Jaggard said as Sam finished signing the last of the paperwork. Jaggard stood. "I'll take you through to meet the rest of the team."

"What about my mom?"

Jaggard considered that for a moment and sat back down. "It's all in your contract, but the gist of it is this. For the next three months, as far as your mother is concerned, you're still at Recton. Any emails to your Recton account will be intercepted and relayed here. Any efforts to visit you will be rebuffed. Any legal challenges or official channels she might complain to will turn a deaf ear."

Sam nodded his understanding.

"At the end of the three months, if you survive, then your mother will be fed some cock-and-bull story about you working out a deal with the FBI, and working for them." He looked Sam in the eye. "At no time is your mother, *or anyone else you talk to,* allowed to know about your involvement with the CDD. A network is only as safe as the people who protect it. If the bad guys know who you are, they can compromise you, and if they do that, they can compromise our entire operation, and with it the data infrastructure of this entire country. Is that clear enough for you?"

"Yes, sir," Sam stammered out nervously.

"I'm not trying to frighten you," Jaggard said.

Sam wondered what he'd be saying if he *was* trying to frighten him.

Jaggard continued, "But secrecy is our first line of defence. Let's go."

Jaggard stood and led him through a series of doors that he unlocked with a keycard, into some kind of control centre. The room was circular with workstations arranged in pairs around the outer circumference. Dark tinted windows gave a dimly shaded view of the outside world. A few blocks away he could see the Adobe logo on top of a group of high-rise towers, and across the motorway was a large sports stadium that he thought was the Hewlett Packard Pavilion.

This was Silicon Valley all right.

In the centre of the room giant plasma screens faced in every direction. Some of the screens were security monitors, showing switching views of both the inside and the outside of the building. They surrounded a small, raised octagonal office. Sam couldn't see in, but had a strong feeling that someone was in there, looking out.

There were at least seventy people in the control centre when he arrived, and only a few empty desks. The people sat in pairs, three computer screens to each person.

He saw Dodge sitting at one of the workstations. Dodge looked up briefly as Sam walked in behind Jaggard. The rest of the workers ignored them, intent on their screens. There was a sense of urgency in the room.

It could be this afternoon, or it might not be for months,

Sam recalled the words that the strange woman had said earlier.

Jaggard put two fingers in his mouth and made a piercing whistle. Work stopped.

"Team, I'd like you to meet our new probationer," Jaggard said in a voice that filled the whole of the large room. "This is Sam."

He heard a voice somewhere behind him mutter, "Fresh meat."

Another voice, from across the room, called out, "Two weeks."

"Ten days."

"I give him a month."

Jaggard rolled his eyes. "Sam is the one who pulled off the Telecomerica hack a few weeks ago."

There was a sudden, emphatic silence in the room.

Dodge jumped up from his console and bounded over. He shook Sam's hand. "Welcome aboard," he said and smiled, creasing the biohazard tattoo on his forehead.

He wore denim shorts, raggedly ripped off at the knees from a pair of jeans; steel chains crisscrossed a tight tartan T-shirt; and a skull on a leather strap hung from around his neck.

Jaggard said, "You'll be working closely with Dodge. You've also met Vienna."

Vienna was a short-haired girl with a fierce gleam in her eye. She wore a leather miniskirt and a black T-shirt that read "Who are you and why are you reading my T-shirt?"

But it was the intertwined dragons tattooed on her arm that gave it away. *Rock Chick Bride*!

A succession of others came over to meet him.

"This is Socks, Zombie, Bashful, Gummi Bear." Jaggard introduced each of them in turn.

Sam didn't hear the door open behind him, but noticed Jaggard's glance.

"You're late," Jaggard said.

"A few problems with the paperwork," said a voice he well recognised.

Sam half-turned, his mouth gaping open.

"G'day, mate," Kiwi said.

2. LAST LINE OF DEFENCE

Sam settled down into the chair and looked at the three large monitors in front of him.

An ergonomic keyboard, one of those oddly angled ones that were supposed to be better for your wrists, and a wireless wheel mouse were the only things on the desk in front of him, although a standard microphone headset hung on the side of the central monitor.

He had never got the hang of that style of keyboard and wondered if he could get it changed. It crossed his mind that a neuro-headset could be useful, but it was a little early for that. It was only his first day.

He looked at Dodge, seated to his right. Not so much seated as embedded into the soft leather of the high-backed chair. He looked like a part of the furniture. Like he belonged.

Sam shuffled his backside around a bit, getting used to the chair, which was larger and more comfortable than he was used to. No doubt he was going to end up spending long periods of time in it.

To his left, and to Dodge's right, fabric-covered

partitions separated them from the teams on either side. Dodge's was adorned with stubs from rock concert tickets, including a few backstage passes, while Sam's was empty, although several pinholes and indentations in the fabric showed that some items had recently been removed. He wondered who had owned this seat before him.

"Fire 'er up, and we'll go for a dive," Dodge said, glancing over at him. "I'll show you around."

Dodge put on his headset and Sam followed suit, adjusting the microphone to the level of his mouth. A feeling of trepidation – *would he be up to this?* – was balanced by tremendous excitement at the thought of a whole new world that was about to be revealed to him.

Dodge's voice sounded strong and clear in his ear. "Everything you say is recorded and monitored by both our guys, and Swamp Witch in the middle there." He nodded at the raised octagonal office with the reflective windows in the centre of the room.

"Swamp Witch?"

Dodge laughed. "She's got a proper handle, but nobody ever uses it. Just hope that you don't get to meet her. Official-like, that is."

"Swamp Witch?" Sam asked again.

"Oversight officer. Permanent representative of the Congressional Oversight Committee. The sort of power we have around here, someone's got to make sure we don't abuse it. Know what I mean?"

Sam glanced up at the office, wondering if he was being watched right now.

"Right, follow me," Dodge said. "We'll head out on a short patrol, just to give you the feel of things. I'm on your left screen. Everything I see, you'll see there. Centre screen is you, and your right screen is your overview. Your 'navigation map', some like to call it. Also has most of your scanners, scopes and weapons systems. We're going to head over to the Pentagon, run a sweep through their networks. It's serious stuff over there so no mucking about, right?"

"We're going to hack into the Pentagon?" Sam raised his eyebrows.

"Hack?" Dodge laughed. "You're on the other team now, mate. We've got a backstage pass. Access all areas."

Sam looked at his row of monitors, then back at Dodge. "Before we start, Dodge," he hesitated, "I don't want to sound stupid, but I don't even know what my job is yet. What do I do here?"

Dodge raised an eyebrow. "Sorry, Sam, mate. I thought Jaggard had already run through that with you. You're my new wingman."

"Wingman," Sam said, nodding as if he understood.

"I'm on point. You back me up. I go after the bad guys and you stop them going after me. Got it?"

Sam nodded again.

"After three months, if it works out, then we'll pair up officially until you move on to take point and get your own wingman." Dodge grinned and continued, "Or until one of us burns out. Whichever comes first."

That sounded a little ominous, but Sam didn't pursue it.

"So my only job is to protect you," he said for confirmation.

"I'm the quarterback, you're the linebacker. It's your job to keep the bogeys off my arse while I make the play. Okay?"

"Okay..." Sam said cautiously, "I'll try my best. What about training?"

"This is the training," Dodge said. "On the job. Let's head over to the Pentagon. I'll explain more as we go."

Sam kept an eye on his left screen, watching what Dodge did, and copying him as they slid, undetectably, through the firewalls and outer defences of the country's central military command post.

"It's like the Dark Ages out there," Dodge was saying in his ear. "And we're the knights in shining amour. Everybody builds these highly secure networks, like big castles, for protection, right. But a castle is just a big lump of stone unless there's someone to defend it. We're the soldiers patrolling the battlements."

A vivid picture came into Sam's mind of himself standing atop the high stone parapets of a castle, smoke billowing behind him, heroically resisting the invaders.

"Firewalls, antivirus programs, network spiders, all that is what we call 'passive defence', like the walls of the castle. What we do is called 'active defence'. You remember that old Will Smith movie, *Men in Black*?"

"Sure."

"Well that's us. We're the first, last, and best line of defence against the worst scum of the universe."

Dodge's "short patrol" took the rest of the afternoon, touring around the servers in the massive Pentagon complex. They spent the time examining and testing security systems, prodding and poking everything that could be prodded or poked, to make sure the system was watertight. They were constantly looking out for signs of anything that wasn't as it should be. Watching out for invaders. For people like Sam.

"What's going on at the moment?" Sam asked at one point. "Mr Jaggard said something about raising the alert level."

Dodge nodded.

"There's something big in the wind. A rotten smell in the air. We had some intel through from the Easter Bunny that some kind of attack is in the offing. All pretty sketchy at the moment but we got scouts out in all directions looking for signs."

"Hang on," Sam said, "you get your intel from the Easter Bunny? Why? Was Santa Claus busy?"

Dodge laughed. "The Easter Bunny, Santa Claus, the

Tooth Fairy, call 'em what you like. They don't exist."

"I'm not getting you," Sam said. "Who doesn't exist?"

"In football," Dodge said, "and I don't mean soccer, each side has two teams, right?"

Sam nodded. "Offence and defence." He didn't play or even watch the game himself, but he knew the rules from school.

"Right," Dodge said. "Well, we're the defence."

Sam took his eyes off the screen and looked over at Dodge. "There's an offence?"

"What do you reckon? Do you think the US of A ain't ready to knock over the computer and communications systems of any country it might happen to get into a punching match with? Do you think that bombs and guns are the only kind of warfare there is?"

Sam considered that. "So what you're saying is that there's another unit, a bit like us, but their job is to attack, hack into networks and destroy systems."

"Nope," Dodge said. "They don't exist."

3. LOCKDOWN

The phone woofed, startling him. Sam was lying on the emperor-sized bed in his suite. The television was on and he had almost dozed off in front of a game show. No, not dozed off, just zoned out, his mind free-falling, weightless.

Getting back to the hotel from the CDD building had been a surreal experience. They had finished their shift at three o'clock. A grey van had been waiting for them. A large man in a dark suit with a curly wire coming out of his ear drove the van, and his twin rode shotgun beside him.

The van drove out from the underground car park of the oddly shaped building that was his new workplace, across to the other side of the road, and down into the underground car park of the hotel.

He could have walked there faster.

Another of the curly-eared gentlemen was standing outside the elevators on his floor, and nodded to him curtly when he stepped out.

Vienna got out on his floor also, but turned left, where he turned right.

"See you tomorrow," Sam had said cheerfully, but other than a quick glance back over her shoulder, she had ignored him.

The phone woofed again and Sam reached over to answer it, his brain slowly coming back online.

Jaggard had given him a cell phone and, stuck in the hotel suite, Sam had played around with all the features on it. The phone had a variety of sounds, ranging from buzzes to birds, to Mr Spok from *Star Trek* saying "It's a call, Jim, but not as you know it." Sam had chosen a barking dog, for no good reason.

"This is Sam," he said cautiously.

"Sam, ya muppet," Dodge boomed in his ear. "Feel like a swim? We're going up to the pool."

"I don't have any board shorts..." Sam started to say, but Dodge had already hung up.

The pool was on the roof of the hotel, protected from the wind by a heavy glass wall that ran around three sides. The fourth side was a plain-faced concrete structure that offered shade to one end of the pool and housed the elevators and washrooms.

It looked more like a meandering curved pond than a swimming pool, surrounded by tall palm trees in wooden tubs. When Sam glanced in the pool he was astonished to see dolphins swimming around, then realised that the bottom of the pool was actually a large video screen. From the surface the dolphins seemed remarkably lifelike.

The low afternoon sun hit his face the moment he stepped out onto the roof, and he blinked a couple of times against the glare.

White wicker loungers were arranged in small clusters around the edge of the pool, and it was in one of the clusters, near a barbecue trolley, that Sam found Dodge, Vienna and Kiwi, lying in the sun, drinking soda. Dodge and Kiwi were shirtless, in board shorts and Vienna wore a bikini top and shorts.

The bikini top was a green camouflage pattern with a brass centre ring and straps that...

"Nice view?" Vienna asked, and Sam quickly averted his eyes.

"Sorry, I was just—"

"Yes, you were," Vienna said.

"Grab a lounger," Dodge said. "What kept you?"

"Didn't have any board shorts," Sam replied. "Had to go buy some at the hotel gift shop."

"Shouldn't have bothered," Dodge said immediately. "We're all going skinny-dipping anyway."

Sam looked at the other's faces to see if Dodge was joking, but Kiwi's face was expressionless, and Vienna's held only a slight smirk that gave nothing away.

Dodge was surely just joking, Sam decided. Although they were the only ones there.

Sam slipped his shirt off as he clambered onto an empty lounger next to Dodge.

Dodge gesticulated in the air, a vague hand gesture, and a waiter in a white dinner jacket appeared from a small gazebo.

"What would you like, sir?" the waiter asked Sam.

"Just water, iced," Sam said, and the waiter retreated, returning a moment later with a glass brimming with ice and topped with a lime slice.

Dodge raised his own glass. "To Sam's first day," he said with a big smile that crinkled the tattoo on his forehead.

"To another day of keeping the barbarians at bay," Kiwi said.

Sam sipped at his water. "Do they ever get in?" he asked.

"Sometimes," Dodge said. "Little stuff here and there. We stamp on it right quick."

"Usually without too much damage, and without Joe the Public ever getting wind of it," Kiwi added.

"Usually?" Sam asked.

"Usually," Dodge agreed. "There's only been one serious breach in the last four or five years."

"Really? What was that?" Sam asked.

There was a silence and the leaves of the palm tree above them waved gently in a strengthening afternoon breeze. It was Vienna who finally answered the question.

"You, Sam."

* * *

"Anyone for a swim?" Sam asked a little later, feeling that he had gone from medium-rare to well-done in a short space of time.

"You go," Dodge said. "I'll join you soon."

That same smirk was back on Vienna's face, and Sam wondered why.

Sam walked to the edge of the pool and tested the water with his toe. It was pleasantly cool, not stomach-tightening cold, and he bent his legs ready to dive in.

In an instant the playful dolphins disappeared, replaced by a swarm of writhing, circling sharks.

"Whoa!" Sam yelled, jumping back from the edge. The others howled with laughter. In his hand, Dodge held some kind of remote control.

Sam grinned and shook his head.

He tested the water again with his toe and immediately, the sharks converged, thrashing and writhing in a feeding frenzy, right where his toe was, their white underbellies flashing. A redness spread from the centre of the pack, rippling throughout the pool.

He snatched his toe out again.

"What's wrong with ya?" Kiwi yelled with a grin. "They're not real."

Sam looked again at the pool and decided to postpone his swim anyway. Real or not, it no longer seemed like a pleasant experience.

Vienna made a clucking sound like a chicken as he walked back to the lounger.

Dodge held up the remote device. "Reprogrammed the hotel pool system," he said, laughing.

"Then you go swim in it," Sam said.

"Right you are," Dodge said and jumped up, heading towards the pool.

"I thought you were going skinny-dipping," Sam called after him.

"Right you are!" Dodge said again, stripping off his board shorts and letting them lie where they fell.

He jogged naked towards the pool, then veered off to the left, bounded up onto a lounger that was pushed up against the glass wall and sprang up onto the top of the wall itself.

"Dodge!" Sam cried out, suddenly terrified. On the other side of that wall was a twenty-storey drop. He glanced around at the others, but they seemed calm and relaxed.

"Done this lots of times," Dodge said, balancing, stark-naked on the wall. The glass was topped with a stainless steel rail, Sam saw now, at least six inches wide. Even so, it seemed precarious, considering the drop that was on the other side.

"It's a bit gusty up here," Dodge said, waving his arms about for balance.

"Dodge?" Sam said. "Dodge!"

"Whoooaoo," Dodge yelled, his arms now flailing as he fought for balance on the narrow top edge of the wall. His foot slipped. One moment he was there, the next he was on one leg, leaning backwards out over the drop, far too far. Sam jumped up, rushing towards him, but knowing, with utter horror, that he could never make it in time.

Then, with a twist of his body, Dodge executed a perfect somersault into the pool, landing right in the middle of the shark feeding frenzy.

He came up for air and took a bow in the water.

Sam looked around at the others in shock.

"He does that to all the eggs," Kiwi said and explained, "Probationers. One day he's going to kill himself."

"Why don't you stop him?" Sam asked, his heart pounding.

"If he dies, I get promoted to point," Kiwi said. "In fact, one day I might just push him off the edge myself."

Sam opened his mouth to say something, then saw Kiwi's grin. He laughed. "You're all mad."

"Goes with the job," Vienna said.

Two girls in bikinis emerged from the elevators and made their way to a couple of loungers on the far side of the pool. One was about his age, and the other slightly older. They appeared to be sisters with matching blond hair.

Sam looked back at Dodge, still in the pool.

"Now what are you going to do?" he asked.

"Get out," Dodge said, and did so.

He walked straight past the two girls as if it was perfectly natural, picked up his board shorts, and pulled them on before flopping back down on his lounger.

The two girls stretched out on their loungers and the younger one looked and smiled.

"She just smiled at you, mate," Dodge said. "Go on over and say hello."

"I don't think it was me she was looking at," Sam said.

"Go on," Dodge said.

Sam just laughed and casually glanced over towards the younger girl, trying not to make it obvious that he was looking.

"What's with the doorbell thing, at the White House?" he asked.

"We just do that to freak people out." Kiwi laughed.

"It works," Sam said. "So how come we all live in this fancy hotel?"

"We don't live here," Dodge said. "You're here 'cause you're on probation, and we just moved in for a few weeks 'cause of the threat level."

"I have an apartment over in Milpitas," Kiwi said.

"They keep us close at hand in a crisis 'cause it's quicker, and also so they can protect us better," Dodge added.

"Protect us?" Sam asked.

"If the bad guys got hold of you, it could compromise the whole CDD," Kiwi said.

Sam nodded. John Jaggard had said something similar that morning.

"Now go on over and introduce yourself to Miss Congeniality before she starts to think you're a right numb-nuts," Dodge said.

"Yeah, yeah, soon," Sam said, not moving. "Tell me more. Is there anywhere we can't go? Anywhere off limits?"

"Not much. Some financial stuff. CIA, of course. Some classified government files," Dodge said, rolling over onto his stomach and resting his head on his hands.

"Where they keep the answers to all the big questions," Kiwi said.

"JFK, Roswell, Vegas, stuff like that," Dodge said.

Sam sat up on the lounger and looked over with sudden interest. The assassination of JFK last century was still a cause for speculation and conspiracy theories, even now; the purported crashed alien spaceship at Roswell was regarded as a joke by some, and as gospel by others; while Vegas was often described as the world's biggest unsolved murder.

"Serious?" Sam said. "And you can't get in?"

"I said we weren't allowed to. I didn't say we weren't capable," Dodge said.

"Leave it alone, Dodge," Vienna said. "He's an egg."

Dodge leaned towards Sam and spoke in a low voice. "Do you really want to know who actually killed JFK?"

"Yeah, of course. Doesn't everyone?"

"Not who you'd think," Dodge said enigmatically.

Sam began, "But—"

"Whatever you've read, whatever you've imagined, you're not even close," Dodge cut him off. "Want to know the truth about Roswell?"

"Hell, yeah!"

"Never happened. No spaceship, no dead aliens, nothing. It was a cover-up all right, but not for a crashed UFO. That was just the diversion, to draw attention away from what was really going on, which is even harder to believe."

"What—"

"And Vegas..."

It was strange the names that were given to major tragedies, Sam thought. The World Trade Centre disaster was always known by the date, 9/11, while the explosion three years earlier that had left a radioactive scar on the desert where Las Vegas used to be was known simply as Vegas.

"You want to know who set off that warhead and turned the place into a nuclear crap-hole?" Dodge asked.

"Okay."

"So do they, matey, so do they."

Later, upstairs in his room, Sam tried to watch TV but no shows held his interest.

He worried about the new job, and how he would cope.

He worried about his mom and what she would be thinking.

He worried whether he was worrying too much, and would not be able to sleep.

Eventually though, he must have fallen asleep despite it all, because when he opened his eyes the glowing clock on the nightstand said 02.53.

And the phone was woofing at him again.

4. PEACH BOTTOM

Dodge said, "Sorry, mate, but you're out of bed, right now. One of our sniffers has picked up a nasty smell on the Net, over by the Peach Bottom Atomic Power Station in Pennsylvania. There's been a fifteen per cent rise in data packet transfer over the last two hours. We're going in quiet. Just monitor the activity and decode it, see what's moving around." He hung up the phone without saying goodbye.

A guard in a dark suit and curly earpiece was waiting for him by the elevators. He recognised the man, Special Agent Ranger, he recalled, with the gelled-back hairdo and mirrored glasses. The man who had arrested him.

The glasses were missing but the hair was still the same. *Too cool for school.*

It was the same routine with the grey van: up the ramp, across the road, and down the ramp on the other side, which still seemed a bit silly, but it was not up to him to argue with their procedures.

Dodge was already seated when he entered the control room. He just glanced up as Sam slid into the chair beside him.

"Nothing yet," he said. "Firewall is wound up tighter than a two-bob watch. All the data traffic looks legit, but that don't explain a sudden increase at this time o' the morning."

"I thought all nuke plants were air gapped," Sam said. "Not just firewalled."

"That's right. This ain't coming from the control software. That's a self-contained system. It's from the general admin offices. Jump in behind me and see what you make of it."

Sam picked up the location from his left screen and shot out a probe. As he did that, he scanned the central CDD database for information on Peach Bottom and added in a Google search for good measure.

"It's an older plant," he said. "Two BWR units, whatever they are."

"Boiling Water Reactors," Dodge said, not taking his eyes off the screen. "Most of the modern ones are Pressurised Water Reactors, PWR. Don't matter. What we want to know is what data is leaking outta that site, and who's picking it up."

"It's an inside job," Sam said after a few moments.

"Too early to tell," Dodge said. "Could just as easily be an outside hack. There are some old Windows servers on the LAN so I'm thinking it might be a null session hack."

"No," Sam said, more firmly than he felt. "It's an inside job. I already checked the registry on the old servers and they're set to restrict anonymous access."

"Still don't mean an inside job," Dodge said thoughtfully.

"The data packets are mimicking backup activity," Sam said. "But it's running under a user account, not a machine account, which is suspicious, isn't it? I checked the firewall and it blocks remote logins, so it has to be a direct login, on that computer itself. Someone inside the plant is doing this."

A low voice came from behind them. "What's going on, Dodge?"

It was Jaggard. He was in jeans and an old Spartans sweatshirt and looked as though he had just got out of bed.

"Rogue trader," Dodge said. "Looks like it, anyway."

"An inside job?"

Dodge nodded and gestured at Sam. "Newbie over here picked it up right away. 'Course I would've picked it myself if I'd been proper awake."

He winked and Sam felt a glow of pride.

"What data are they taking?"

"Dunno yet. There's nothing new about the technology there – it's just old BWR stuff. Nothing of use to any foreign power."

"Could they use the information to compromise the plant? Cause a meltdown?"

"Well, it would help. But so would Google."

"Okay, where's the data going?"

"A public server in a small farm in Cleveland. I boxed

it off the moment I traced it. Surrounded it with fishhooks. Anybody goes in there to retrieve the data and I'll reel 'em in like a bluefin tuna."

Jaggard turned to Sam. "Good work, Sam. First day on the job."

"Second," Sam said, pointing to his watch.

Jaggard smiled briefly. "Stay on it. I want to know who wants that info and why."

"We're on it," Dodge said.

"Why don't we scramble the data?" Sam suggested. "In case they manage to retrieve it. In case we've missed something important that we don't want loose in the world."

"What are you suggesting?" Jaggard asked.

"Let me crack the files," Sam said. "Change a few pluses to minuses. A few 'dos' to 'don'ts'. Switch some diagrams around. Randomise it. Whatever. Just enough to make the data worthless if it does slip out, and destroy any ciphers that could be embedded in the text."

"Can you do it without them knowing?" Jaggard asked.

"The kid can fart rainbows," Dodge said, giving Sam a grin.

"Then do it. Don't get spotted or you'll scare them off." Jaggard paused for a moment, thinking. "And get me the name of the insider."

"No problem," Dodge said. "I'll access the security camera footage for the plant."

"Do it. I'll alert Tactical. We'll hold off as long as possible to try to reel in the receivers, but I don't want him out there any longer than necessary."

"Tactical?" Sam asked when Jaggard disappeared.

"Tactical Response Team," Dodge said. "The guys with the dark suits and the big guns."

The main door to the control centre opened and in walked the strange woman Sam had seen the previous day in the corridor. She crabbed sideways across the room, muttering to herself. As she passed his desk, she suddenly turned her head as if she had detected his thoughts and knew he was looking at her. She caught his eyes with that piercing gaze that made Sam feel as though the contents of his brain's hard disk had just been scanned and analysed. She didn't stop but disappeared into the octagonal office in the centre.

Dodge saw Sam looking.

"Swamp Witch," he said.

Tactical were deployed at 5.45 that morning and reached Peach Bottom just before noon. They set up a perimeter around an old weatherboard house on the main street of Delta, a small township just west of the plant site, and home to many of the workers.

It was the residence of Harrison Ellis, an inspector in the Health and Safety office of the plant.

"Wanna watch?" Dodge asked, at about 12.15.

The scrambled data package had been picked up from the Cleveland server about three hours earlier, and they were busy tracing the recipient.

"We can watch?" Sam asked, surprised.

"Let's see what we got." Dodge worked at his keyboard for a moment. "Satellite footage of course, but that's always extreme zoom. I got an ATM camera in a block of shops down the street, but ... no, here's the best view. The house directly opposite has a security cam covering their front yard. It's internet enabled, so I'll just crack the security..."

A picture appeared on his screen of a small town front yard, overgrown with weeds, a trash can waiting to be collected by a low wooden fence with missing palings.

"... and we'll just shift the view angle a bit."

The camera rose and focused on a house on the other side of the street. It zoomed in a little and even as it did so, there was a small puff of smoke from the front window. From nowhere, black-suited figures appeared, swarming into the house.

Not long afterwards, a man dressed in just shorts and an undershirt was led out of the house in handcuffs.

"Got the dirty geezer," Dodge said. "Now let's get back to tracing his buyer. Then we can all get some sleep."

* * *

Half an hour later though, Dodge sat back with a worried expression and Jaggard appeared behind them.

"What is it, Dodge?"

"Got the source," Dodge said. "It's a dead end."

"They get wind of you?" Jaggard asked, looking at Sam.

"Nah, that's not it," Dodge said. "The package got shifted around in a big circle, one server to another, various parts of the world, and ended up back on the server in Cleveland. Then the whole cycle started all over again. Also, Sam hacked into the files and we had a gander at them. It's nothing. Power generation stats for a couple of years, and a bunch of data from their original reactor, which closed down in the 1970s. No use to nobody. No hidden codes, neither."

"What do you make of it then?" Jaggard asked.

"I think they was chucking stones at a wasps' nest," Dodge said. "I think they didn't really want the data at all. They just wanted to see how we reacted, and how fast."

5. VIENNA

The excitement of Sam's first days quickly turned to monotony. It wasn't every day, it seemed, that cyber-terrorists tried to infiltrate nuclear power plants – if in fact that was what they had been doing.

Rather, the average day at the office was one of patrols. Skirting around the battlements of the electronic castles, keeping an eye out for approaching enemies.

As it was for those soldiers in the olden days, Sam thought, the average day was basically very boring. He imagined them trudging back and forth on the walls of the castle, trying to stay alert and vigilant, while hours turned into days, and days turned into weeks. Wearing out boot leather on a well-trodden path, hoping for some excitement to break the monotony, and hoping at the same time that the attack would never come.

Life in the luxurious suite at the Crowne Plaza could not have been easier, if also a little boring. Every meal was provided, with twenty-four-hour room service if he wanted it.

His mother emailed nearly every day, still convinced

that he was imprisoned in some horrible concrete cell, being beaten up by the other inmates.

Sam replied to each email, sitting in the luxurious leather chair at the expensive writing desk by the picture window that gave a spectacular view out over the city, and said nothing to dispel her concerns.

Now and then, just for fun, he went flying.

With some of the new real-time world mapping websites, you could position yourself above any major city and move around, in any direction. Up and down, forwards and backwards, left or right.

Do that with a neuro-headset on and the only way to describe the sensation was that of flying, soaring above buildings, swooping through parks, making like a bird, without ever leaving your chair.

By October, the threat level had been lowered, and the need to be transported across the street in the anonymous grey vans removed. The team was still holed up in the hotel, but the powers that watched over the CDD team members were at last relaxed enough to let them cross the street by themselves.

On November 3, as Sam waited for the elevator, he realised that he was halfway through his probation. Had he done enough? He had felt confident that first week, but since then the endless patrolling had given him few opportunities to prove his value. How could they judge his performance based on routine patrols?

Still, he reasoned, he hadn't done anything to warrant

them throwing him out. He hadn't done anything wrong, or illegal, or stupid.

The elevator doors opened and Vienna was inside. Sam nodded hello to her without speaking and stepped in. Speaking to Vienna was a waste of time, he had come to realise.

The doors opened on the ground floor and she stepped forward first, striding towards the hotel entrance without a glance at him. Kiwi, her wingman, was waiting by the entrance, and they left the hotel together, discussing the merits of neuro-headsets versus keyboards and mice. Vienna apparently was opposed to the new technology, preferring the hands-on feel of the old-fashioned method.

Sam stared after them for a moment without moving, then, just as the elevator doors began to shut in front of him, he put a hand out to stop them, and raced after Vienna and Kiwi.

He caught up with them a few yards along the street.

"Hey, Vienna," he said.

She ignored him.

The street was lined with trees and the fall leaves made a soft carpet underfoot. A VW beetle was parked on the side road ahead of them, and had almost disappeared under the leaves. Sunlight glared through the nearly bare branches of the trees. There was a sudden wind gust and for a moment they were immersed in an orange and yellow fluttering cloud.

Sam walked alongside her and sniffed at his armpits.

"What is it? Did I forget to shower today?" He grinned. "Do I have a big toe growing out of the middle of my forehead?"

Kiwi nodded, putting his thumb to his forehead to illustrate.

"You're an egg. I don't talk to eggs," Vienna said. "Only one in four last the three months. Everyone else might think you're the next big thing, but I think you just got lucky."

Kiwi looked at Sam and shrugged sympathetically, earning a narrowed glance from Vienna for his troubles.

They crossed the road and headed down the ramp to the underground parking area and secure entrance to the CDD building.

"I'm just trying—" Sam began, but Vienna cut him off.

"Right now, you're all that Dodge has to watch his back. If you crash and burn, he's going to get taken down, and if that happens, and the bad guys get past the barricades, then we're all in a deep pile of crap. You'd better stay lucky."

Vienna walked up to the security door and swiped her keycard through the lock.

The outer door opened and they entered the holding area. Vienna waited for the first door to shut before swiping her card at the inner security door.

The doors were linked. The inner one would not open while the outer door was still open, creating a kind of airlock to prevent unauthorised access to the building.

The inner door slid silently open and Vienna headed towards the elevators. Kiwi stopped at a coffee machine and pressed buttons for a hot chocolate.

"So that's why she doesn't like me," Sam said, stopping with him.

The machine whirred and ground its teeth. A paper cup with a pull-out handle dropped down and began to fill.

Kiwi shook his head. "That's not it. Not really. When you got past the defences at Telecomerica, we were watching you the whole time. You were never supposed to get as far as you did. You beat us, big-time."

"So?" Sam asked.

"Who d'you think was on your case?"

6. FARGAS

The hospital corridor seemed to stretch out forever. Sam hurried along it, a slightly crumpled box of Hershey Miniatures clutched tightly in his hand.

The corridor was almost deserted except for an old man in pyjamas who was inching his way towards Sam, using a chrome walking frame. Sam passed him without acknowledgement.

The room was nearly at the end of the corridor. The door was open, but an apricot-coloured curtain covered the entrance. Sam stopped and checked the number on the door before entering. He pushed back the curtain slowly and peered through to double-check that he was in the right place.

The room was large enough for two people, with a central curtain to separate the two beds, although only one was occupied. The walls were white and shiny, except for some stainless steel panels. Various bits of high-tech medical machinery jutted out from the walls. The room smelled strongly of soap and antiseptic.

Fargas lay on the second bed, closer to the window,

with a plastic tube embedded in his arm. The other end of the tube ran up to a plastic bag filled with a clear fluid. He looked gaunt in the sharp light from the window. His head was shaved, although not recently, his long hair replaced by a fuzzy matt of regrowth. He had dark rings around his eyes and bruises in a circular pattern around his head.

"Where'd they drag you up from?" Fargas asked, grinning as Sam entered.

"Mom emailed me," Sam said, trying not to show on his face the shock he was feeling. "I just flew in."

He neglected to mention that it had been on a Government-owned Learjet.

He held out the chocolates and Fargas took them with a hand that twitched constantly.

"Thanks," he said. "They gave you a get-out-of-jail pass, huh?"

"Something like that." Sam smiled briefly.

"It's good to see you, dude. What you been doing?"

"What have *you* been doing, man? What the crap is all this?"

"It's nothing, man. Just being stupid. You know." Fargas avoided his eyes. "Have a seat. How's the job?"

Sam sat on a metal-framed chair with blue vinyl padding that was against the wall by the window. Sunlight hit the back of his head like a blast furnace.

"It's..." Sam paused then asked a little too quickly, "Job?"

"You can fool your mother with that bull about prison,

but you can't fool your best mate. So what are you, some kind of Government spy now?"

"Why do you say that?" Sam asked.

"You're not the only one who knows how to use a computer," Fargas said. "When you disappeared, I started prowling around the internet. To see if I could track you down. Next thing two heavies in black suits turn up on my doorstep telling me to cease and desist."

"What did you do?" Sam asked with sudden concern.

"I ceased," Fargas said. "Then I desisted. But I'm not buying into any story about prison."

"It's complicated," Sam said, and this time it was he who avoided Fargas's eyes.

"Can't talk about it, huh? Where you living now?"

"Out west," Sam said and when Fargas was silent, added, "San Jose."

"Nice."

"How's school?" Sam asked.

"I gave that away. Wasn't getting anywhere. Tell me about San Jose."

"I'm really not supposed to say anything."

"Not even to me?"

"No one," Sam said.

There was an uncomfortable silence.

"I like your new haircut," Sam said.

Fargas rubbed his head. "They reckon you get a better connection. I never noticed any difference though."

Another silence. The sun on the back of Sam's head

was making him feel a bit woozy as if his brain was slowly broiling inside his skull. He moved the chair into the shade of a curtain.

"Why don't you come over to San Jose? Hang out with me," he said.

"You got a job, man. And what am I going to do in Jose?"

"Lot of hot chicks there."

"Dude, I can't get a girl to look at me here. Why do you think some pumped-up, bleach-blond, West Coast chick is gonna pucker up for me?"

"Fargas, there's gotta be better—"

"Better?" Fargas cut him off, sitting up and leaning forward with sudden fire in his eyes. "You *better* than me, dude?"

"No, man—" Sam jumped to his feet, holding his hands up in front of him as if fending off an attack.

"It's okay. I'm just playing with you." Fargas flashed a grin and lay back down. "Of course you're better than me. You got a job. Secret agent man. Got a fancy apartment, I bet. You got a fancy chick too?"

Sam sat back down in his chair. "Come over. Check it out for yourself," he said.

"So I can be a dweeb loser on a different coast? Forget about it. Inside the game, I'm a king."

Sam said nothing for a moment and just looked at Fargas. He said, "That's not real, man."

"Works for me," Fargas said.

"Really?" Sam asked, and it was Fargas's turn to be silent for a moment, staring down at the bedsheets.

"It's exciting," he said eventually. "I started out as a peasant and now I'm a king."

Sam said nothing.

"I guess..." Fargas began, "I guess it started with just an hour or so in the evening. You know, finish my homework and play a bit before bed. And then I started playing *before* my homework. I'd promise myself that I'd play for an hour, then do my work, but I never did. Sometimes I'd play until I fell asleep, at like three or four in the morning. So I set a time for myself. Two hours a day, max. Seven pm till nine pm. But I found that between times, all I was thinking about was the game, so I might as well log on."

Sam shook his head.

"It's really exciting," Fargas said again. "You're running on adrenaline the whole time. You see this beautiful woman enter the room and part of your brain knows that she could just as easily be a ten-year-old boy from New Jersey or some fifty-year-old guy from Australia, but you don't really think about that. You're wondering if she's a princess, or a spy, or an assassin. When you log out, the real world seems flat and grey. No gorgeous women are going to walk in your door and try to kill you. There are no armies to lead on a counterattack against the neighbouring kingdom. Your dad asks you to take out the trash and you look at your stats homework that you haven't done yet, and you just want to climb back inside."

"You hadn't eaten in four days," Sam said. "You were passed out on the floor."

Fargas said, "I'm good at this. Really good. My kingdom is strong and my subjects respect me. All your real-world problems, in there, they just disappear. The worst thing that could happen to you is that you might die and have to start over."

"I'll move back. Forget the job. We'll hang out like we used to," Sam said.

Fargas looked him in the eye for a while, then broke the gaze. He laughed. "No, man. I'm all right. I was just blowing off steam. I kicked it. I'm not going back in again. The king is dead. Long live the next king."

"True?"

"Yeah, man. Those games are dangerous. I can't believe they're still legal."

"What are you going to do?" Sam asked.

"Got a good shot at a job with Truck-Rite. My uncle organised it. Just a storeman, but someday I could end up a driver."

"Cool. Big rigs?"

"Ten four, good buddy," Fargas said. "Might get a coast to coast and come and see you, after all."

Sam thought about that for a moment. He had the feeling that it would never happen.

"No, come to San Jose," he said in a no-arguments tone. "I know some people there. I can get you a good job."

He wasn't sure if that was true, but the amount he was earning, he could pay Fargas's wages himself if he had to.

"No—"

"It's not a suggestion," Sam said. "You can stay where I'm staying till you get a place of your own. It'll be cool."

"They're going to keep me here for a week," Fargas said, glancing up at the IV bottle.

"As soon as you're out, let me know," Sam said. "I'll organise the plane ticket."

Fargas's eyes wandered around the ward for a moment, then finally settled back on Sam.

"Okay," he said, and there was a lift in his voice. "Okay, yeah, let's do that. It'll be cool."

"It'll be cool," Sam echoed with a smile. "I'll see you in a week or so."

7. SHARKS

The Sharks' wing scraped tightly around the back of the net, cut inside the defender and flicked a reverse shot past the goalie's outstretched glove into the net.

The blind man in front of Sam roared with excitement and leaped to his feet.

Sam checked the scoreboard. That put the San Jose Sharks ahead of the Anaheim Ducks with just two minutes to go. It was his first ice hockey game and it was pretty exciting stuff.

One of the Ducks' players had taken offence to something though, and had jammed the Sharks' centre up against the fence, pummelling him with heavy blows.

The Shark took it for a moment, then responded with a deep uppercut that caught the Duck under his chin, cracking his head backwards and knocking him flat on his back on the ice.

The blind man thrust a fist in the air, almost as excited by the fisticuffs as by the goal, but all his jumping around must have upset his neuro-headset, as he sat down again quickly and made some adjustments to it.

The man's cameras were built into heavy framed glasses, feeding the image to a portable receiver on his belt, then directly into his neuro-headset.

With neuro, blind people could see; deaf people could hear. Some said it was the greatest step forward since the invention of language itself. They were even producing neuro-caps now that let you see in the dark, access street maps, or just listen to music.

Sam had heard that the portable neuro-sets could also pick up the video feed from the TV cameras, so the man would have instant access to all the camera angles, slow-mo replays and high shots that the TV audience at home saw.

"Why don't we use neuro at CDD?" Sam asked.

Dodge half-turned his head, keeping his eyes on the ice.

"You figure it out," he said.

"Been trying," Sam said. "Doesn't make any sense to me. I can work much faster on my laptop back in the hotel with my neuro-set than I can in the office using a keyboard and mouse."

The Ducks had two quick shots at the Sharks' goal, but their quick-handed goalie deflected them both, keeping the Sharks in front.

"Okay, see that man three rows in front of us?" Dodge asked, pointing discreetly.

The man was tall and balding, sitting next to two young boys who were probably his sons. On the other side of the boys a woman, perhaps the man's wife, was engrossed in the game. The man, however, had his cell phone concealed in his lap.

"Yeah."

"Texting away on his cell phone, in the middle of an exciting ice hockey game. What could be so important to keep him from watching the game?"

"Beats me," Sam said.

"Let's find out."

Dodge produced his cell phone and slid up the front panel to reveal the miniature keyboard underneath. He tapped a few keys then aimed the stubby aerial of the phone right at the man.

"Blue rifle, built in," he said. "I'm bluesnarfing his cell."

He showed the man's cell phone number to Sam.

"From his phone company, I'll get his home address and find out his internet service provider."

Sam watched, intrigued, as Dodge worked. A moment later he held up the phone triumphantly. "Got him."

"Okay, he's got three computers on his home LAN. A laptop, a desktop, and one other that I think is his sons'. Let me check his emails and chat history," Dodge said.

Sam looked on with interest.

"Interesting, he's recently deleted a whole bunch of chat history. Let's recover that and see what it says."

Dodge looked up after a moment. "I suspected as much. He's having an affair. Probably chatting to his girlfriend right now. Right in front of his wife, the dirty geezer."

"Let's have a look then," Sam said.

"Too right."

Dodge pressed a few more keys, then held his phone up for Sam to see. "Here are his last few texts."

Sam's eyes widened. Dodge was right. The man was texting his girlfriend, in intimate, flowery language, with his wife sitting three seats along.

"Watch this," Dodge said, and worked away for a moment.

A sudden roar of laughter came from the crowd and Sam followed the movement of heads towards the huge electronic scoreboard.

In the space for messages and announcements, the man's texts, sent and received, were now slowly scrolling up the screen as he typed them.

U R da luv of my lyf

I cnt wait 2 CU & run my fngrs thru yr hair

I wnt 2 kss U rite now

On it went, getting steamier by the line.

The man was still texting, unaware that every word was being displayed in huge letters to everyone in the stadium, including his wife.

The woman looked at the scoreboard, then at her husband, noticing the cell phone. She reached over and snatched it off him in a deft movement, comparing the screen of the phone to the scoreboard.

The man started to whimper something, but his wife

wasn't having a bar of it. She grabbed the boys' hands and stormed off, the man, red faced, trailing in her wake.

The crowd erupted into hoots and cheers.

"And that is why we don't use neuro," Dodge said with a smug smile.

Sam looked at the retreating family, then turned back to Dodge and raised an eyebrow.

"Took me thirty seconds to find out everything worth knowing about that guy," Dodge said. "We can hack into anything. You plug your brain into a computer, who's to say that someone can't hack into that too?"

"You're joking."

"Serious as a heart attack. The headsets have got a special neuro-firewall, specifically to prevent it. They even have a term for it. *Brain intrusion.* But since when has a firewall bothered people like you and me? There's no way that the Oversight Committee is going to—"

Dodge's cell phone emitted an urgent bleeping noise. A half second later, Sam's started woofing.

"Bleedin' hell," Dodge said. "It's begun."

8. THE RAID

"Here they come," Dodge said. "And they're coming in heavy."

"Listen up," Jaggard said, from the centre of the room. "This is no stealthy, crawling, under-the-wire incursion. It's a full-on cyberattack, and the targets are nuclear reactor sites."

"We're covering Peach Bottom," Dodge said. "Since we know it best. We're going in battle group formation, Vienna and Kiwi are covering our ten, with Zombie and Gummi in reserve. Stay on my tail and keep those bugs off my arse."

Sam glued his eyes to the screens and wished for his neuro-headset, despite what Dodge had said. The keyboard and mouse were just too slow and cumbersome.

"What are they after?" Vienna's voice sounded in his ear. "They can't bridge the air gap, we already checked that."

"Maybe they know something we don't," Sock's raspy voice said.

Dodge said, "They're after something, or they wouldn't be coming in this hot and hard. Let's kick them in the bollocks first of all, then try and figure out their game plan."

"Where are they coming from?" Vienna asked.

"Working on it," Kiwi replied.

"I'm going to try and take back the main router," Dodge said. "As soon as I hit them, their bugs are going to be all over me. Sam, I'm depending on you."

"I'm there," Sam said in a quiet voice.

"Vienna, you lead with a diversionary attack on the internet gateway," Dodge said. "Make them think we're coming in through the roof. Stay sharp."

Sam kept one eye on his left monitor, following what Dodge was doing, and the other on his scanners, on the right. They had drilled and drilled over exactly this scenario, running simulations and game plays against their simulator computer, and against each other.

But this was no game. This was real.

Dodge was going in to root out the malicious code on the main router, but in doing so he was exposing himself to attack. Sam's job was to cut that attack off at the knees.

"There you are, you slimy prat," Dodge said. "Big mother of a candiru fish, hiding in the swap-file. I'm going to hit it with a depth charge. Vienna, Zombie, get on the nodes around me and watch for wrigglers."

Sam watched as the swap-file dissolved, crumbling in on itself as the depth charge imploded in its midst.

Flashing red lights appeared immediately on his TCP scopes.

"I got predators," he shouted.

"Keep them off me," Dodge yelled back. "I've got corruptions everywhere; I gotta stay on this."

The hackers were honing in on the source of the depth charge: Dodge. Predator programs, designed to trace Dodge's signal back to its source and attack it there. Sam keyed his weapons systems, readying a freeze-bot. Whatever server the predator was on, the bot would freeze the central processor, running the CPU around in circles until it was barely alive. Once the server was frozen he could scan the drive, find and analyse the predator, which would be ice bound, unable to shape-shift and easy to detect. Once he had its genetic structure – its central code – he would feed that into the proximity detectors of his sidewinders.

The lights on his scope flashed brilliant red as one of the predators streaked across the screen, honing in on Dodge's code trail.

"Ouch!" Dodge cried. "Something just bit me. Switching nodes now."

"Sorry, Dodge," Sam said. "Had to let him bite to see where he was coming from."

He hurled the freeze-bot at the predator, a nasty, writhing malicious bit of code that had burrowed into an email server in Kentucky. He isolated the code quickly, and scanned it in, analysing it line by line himself, not just relying on the automated code scanners built into his system.

"Hurry it up, Sam," Dodge said. "I'm getting more nibbles here."

"Almost got it," Sam said, feeding the digital DNA of the creature into his master weapons control. "Okay, code's in the wire, fellas. Lock and load, let's blast these guys out of the sky."

"Got it," Gummi and Kiwi both said, as they loaded their warheads with the information.

"I got crawlers all over the place," Vienna said. "I'm going to need a big cold can of whoop-ass down here."

Sam focused on the red predator alerts on his scope, tracing the trail through the complex nodes of the internet, narrowing down the location of the intruders.

The one he was chasing disappeared, flitting out through an open port before he could hit it.

"Hold still, you mongrel," he said to himself, as he fired a sidewinder through the same port. There was a flash on his scope as he did so. "Got you!"

"Good work, Sam," said Dodge. "But there's plenty more where that came from."

The sidewinder was one of the most basic of weapons, but highly effective.

Its proximity fuse meant that if it even got close to a predator, it would explode, simply wiping all the data off the RAM sector where the predator code was. It could cause havoc for the owner of that computer, but that's what backups were for, right?

Sam fired off a few more sidewinders in the general

direction of the other predators, hoping he might get lucky. The missiles were coded for the DNA of the predator and would just circle around, in an ever-increasing spiral, trying to home in on the signature. If they didn't find it, they would eventually self-destruct.

"Bullseye!" Gummi Bear's voice came into his ear, and one of the red dots disappeared from his scope. Sam hammered a stream of sidewinders into the offices of a small ISP in New York and was rewarded with a series of flashes as the missiles took out their targets.

"I got the source!" Kiwi shouted. "It's right here in the States. Chicago. Server cluster in a warehouse registered to a shipping company. Looks like it was purpose-built for the attack."

"Main router is clear," Dodge said. "And inoculated. How's the rest of the network?"

"Getting there," Vienna said.

Zombie added, "Is the air gap holding?"

"Don't know," Dodge said. "Somebody get on a landline to the site. Check with their techs if there's anything suspicious in the wagon circle."

"You should see this place," Kiwi said. "It's swarming like a wasps' nest."

Sam saw it too. He unleashed a string of sidewinders into the heart of the cluster, but even as he did so, his scope exploded into a fireworks display of coloured sparks.

"Oh, crap!" he said.

"What's going on, Sam?" Dodge asked.

"It's like a zoo down here," Sam said. "And I think we just fell into the snake pit. There's got to be a million of them."

"Stay calm," Vienna said. "Scan them, read them, shut them down. They'll come in waves, but there can't be that many different kinds."

"There are too many," Gummi Bear yelled. "We can't hold them!"

"You got the address of the warehouse?" Dodge asked.

"I got it," Kiwi shouted.

"Take out their power, now. Get into the nearest substation and kill their powerlines. Take out the whole block if you have to. Vienna, notify Chicago PD and get the location to Tactical."

Sam slashed his way into the storm of predators. There were all types: vipers, rabid dogs, shooters, blockers, vampires and other kinds he had never seen before.

One by one, he said to himself. *Take them one by one.*

"Power's out," Kiwi yelled. "But they're still streaming! They must be on UPS."

"Let me have a go at it," Sam called.

"Okay, Sam, it's yours."

He scanned the warehouse with a heat sensor, ignoring the haze of marauders buzzing through the networks around him. The UPS showed up clearly and he ran its signature through a pattern-matching program, comparing it to an equipment database.

"It's an HVC9001," Sam said. "It's got Power Line Networking. I can take this baby out. Kiwi, I need the power back on for a moment. Can you do it?"

"Just say when."

"Hang on ... hang on... Okay, now! Count to three then shut it off."

The 9001 had built-in Power Line Networking, enabling it to communicate directly through the power cables. Sam grabbed the latest firmware updates from the HVC download site and modified the code, just slightly, before updating the firmware on the motherboard.

"Give it ten seconds, then pump it with all the juice you can. I took out the voltage limiter."

Dodge breathed, "It'll go sky-high!"

"Gonna give them a mother of a power spike," Kiwi called out. "In three, two, one – take that, you code suckers!"

The red-hot core at the centre of the storm on Sam's scope blinked once, and disappeared. He could just imagine what the overloaded spike of electricity had done to the UPS system without a voltage limiter in place to protect it. At the very least it would have melted down. With luck there might have been an explosion.

The swarms of predators still circled, but aimlessly, without intelligence behind them to direct them.

"Good work, team," Dodge said. "Let's clean this up. I want those predators classified, neutralised and stuck on a bulletin board in the lunchroom before those filthy geezers can pick themselves up off the floor and try again."

Sam grinned. He had done well. He knew that. New kid on the block and he had...

A movement caught his eye and he half-turned, just in time to see a black command window appear and disappear on his left-side screen.

"Dodge," he said in a voice that was not as steady as it should have been.

"What is it, Sam?"

"I think I just got infiltrated."

"Not possible. Not in here."

"But—"

Sam was cut off by a shout from the other side of the room.

"I got a blue screen of death over here. What's going on?"

"Crap! Me too," Vienna said. "I just got wiped."

Sam looked around and saw Jaggard sprinting across the room towards them.

"Shut them down," he shouted. "Shut them down, now!"

9. VICTORIA

Victoria Dean hated her hair. As a child she had loved its tight curls, but as an adult it left her with just two options: cut it short, or let it grow into a black mop. There were hair straighteners, but they took too long, and straightening perms, but they were too expensive. She settled for the mop.

When she was nervous, or stressed, she would wind her fingers into the tight curls and pull at them gently, as if trying to straighten them.

When she was extremely stressed she would tug at them until it hurt.

In the high pressure, and mostly male, world of air traffic control, she pulled at her hair a lot, and worried if it would make her go bald.

Today all their computers were offline and her hair hurt.

"Get them down," Taylor, her shift supervisor, said again from behind her shoulder. "Every one of them. I want those birds sitting on the ground until we regain control of our own system."

Taylor, a small grey man in a dark grey suit, wasn't

talking to her directly. He was addressing the room. But he was right by her shoulder which made her feel as though she was the only one not doing her best to achieve the impossible.

They had one hundred and seventeen planes either on approach, or inbound, when the computers went haywire. She was responsible for eight of those. Over eleven hundred souls.

There had been several moments of panic as some of the planes had obeyed nonsensical messages on their onboard computer systems, fed from the ground, but most pilots had the sense to check with their flight controller first, and did not deviate.

The challenge now was to get those planes on the ground using just old-fashioned voice instruction. They trained for that, sure, but to actually use it was a whole new ball game.

She pressed the foot switch to activate her radio.

"Singapore SQ12 Airbus inbound, I have you cleared for final approach on runway two five right, please confirm visual, over," she said into her radio.

The voice came back in her ear, with barely a trace of static, and a slight Malaysian accent, "SQ 12 on visual approach for runway two five right. I have a US Airlines Boeing 777 just clearing two five right for the taxiway, over."

"Roger that. The triple seven will be clear before you land, over."

"Roger, and thanks for your help, LAX Control. We have a full load, over."

"Welcome to LA, SQ12," Victoria signed off.

"LAX Control, this is Southwest 3567 from Albany, New York, over."

Victoria glanced at her charts and her progress strips.

"Southwest 3567, continue your holding pattern, expect an approach for two five left, but we've got a bunch of internationals waiting and they're lower on fuel, over."

"LAX Control, this is Southwest 3567. Our UAS just got triggered. Please confirm the reason for this, over."

Victoria involuntarily looked up out of the windows, scanning the sky for the plane.

"Please repeat your last, Southwest 3567, over," she said with a sudden rasp in her voice.

"Southwest 3567 confirming activation of in-flight UAS. We have no reason to believe there are any unfriendlies on board. Please advise if you are aware of a situation, over."

"Damn," she said. "Taylor!"

The UAS or Uninterruptible Autopilot System was a Federal requirement in all commercial passenger jets that flew over American soil. Developed after the 9/11 attacks it allowed ground-based flight controllers to assume control of an aircraft, flying and landing the plane using the autopilot and auto-landing system. Once activated, there was no way of retaking control from within the plane.

Taylor was at her right shoulder in a second.

"What have you got, Dean?"

"UAS on Southwest 3567 just got activated. A Boeing 787. Did we do that?"

"Not on my instruction," he spoke rapidly into a hand-held radio. "Are we activating any UASs on any of the planes, Simon?"

The voice sounded thin and tinny through the small speaker in the hand-held. "Ah, that's a negative, Taylor. We have been instructed to avoid all computerised systems until further notice."

"Where are they?" Taylor asked, picking up a pair of binoculars off the desk.

"Southwest 3567, please confirm your course and altitude, over," Victoria said.

The reply came immediately and the captain's voice was calm, even curious, rather than worried. "This is Southwest 3567. We are currently passing flight level three two zero and heading three zero zero. Where are you taking us, Control? We don't have the fuel for a long flight, over."

"They're heading for Santa Barbara, maybe Lompoc Airport," Victoria said.

"Lompoc is a single runway commuter airfield. They can't handle a 787," Taylor said.

"Well after that," Victoria said. "It's straight out to sea."

Her head hurt, and she realised that for the last few minutes she had been tearing at her hair.

"What the hell is going on?" Taylor asked.

"We got bogies in the wire," Dodge shouted. "Inside the building!"

"Shut it down," Jaggard said calmly. "They're all over us."

"We were the target," Vienna yelled. "Everything else was just a diversion. They were going after us all along. How the hell did they get through our firewalls?"

"Isolate the building," Jaggard said. "Shut it down and sterilise it. Bring it back up when we're clear."

"I'm still okay," Dodge said. "I'm staying up, see if I can battle it out."

"I'm with you," Sam said. "I got infiltrated but I saw it as it happened and blocked the intrusion before they could get a foothold."

"Don't risk it," Jaggard said. "Shut everything down, isolate the building and we'll disinfect—" His cell phone rang, an urgent *pip, pip, pip.* He grabbed at it and listened intently. When he hung up his face seemed a shade or two whiter than before.

"They're after the planes," he said. "Air Traffic Control in Los Angeles has just lost its flight control systems."

"How did they get in there?" Sam asked.

"Through here," Dodge said quietly. "Once they busted us wide open they got access to all areas. Wherever we can go, they can go."

Jaggard swore violently behind them.

"We can't shut down now," Dodge said with uncharacteristic vehemence. "By the time we get back up, this country will be a scrap heap."

Sam concentrated on his screens. Oily black fingers dripping with poison were sliding through the network around him. He built a protective screen surrounding his and Dodge's computers, a wall of code, and lobbed fragmentation grenades over it at the intruders whenever they impinged, scrambling the data on the disk sectors they were occupying. So far it was holding.

"I want to know how they got in," Jaggard was shouting. "Who's still up?"

"I'm on it," Socks called out from across the room. "Zombie is keeping me together, just."

"Get into that firewall," Jaggard ordered. "Find out how they breached it."

"Shoot! Blue screen of death." Bashful's voice sounded to his left. "I'm gone. Sorry, guys."

"Dodge, you gotta find out what they're using," Jaggard said. "I want its DNA and I want it now."

"I'm on it," Dodge said. "Shut up and let me do it."

"There's a gaping big tunnel under the firewall," Socks shouted. "That's how they got in."

"How the hell did they get a tunnel through our firewall?" Jaggard asked. "It's supposed to be invincible!"

"It's in the firmware," Socks called back. "Looks like an exploit."

"Can't be an exploit!" Jaggard said. "Must be a bug."

"Nope, it's a trapdoor," Socks said. "It's deliberate, not bad coding."

A trapdoor in the firewall, Sam thought, as he hurled

a frag grenade at a murky pool of the intruder's code. How could they get a trapdoor in the firmware for the firewall?

"When was the last firmware upgrade?" Dodge asked, his eyes intent on the screen.

"Five days ago," Jaggard answered, then said, "Damn! It must be an inside job."

He punched some numbers on his cell phone and started barking commands.

"Still on the same course?" Taylor asked, behind Victoria.

"I'll find out," she said, but the radio pre-empted her.

"LAX Control, this is Southwest 3567, advising of a course change. Turning right to nor'-east six zero."

"They're heading back inland," Taylor said. His face reflected in the inactive radar screen in front of her was grave. "Where are they going?"

Victoria plotted the course change on the chart with a pencil and a plastic ruler.

"If they stay on this course..."

"Yes?"

"San Jose," she said.

Those with fried workstations gathered around behind Dodge and Sam, watching their battle against the intruder code. The group was getting bigger. Socks was trying to revert the firmware on the firewall, but the intruders had taken control of that too. He was trying to hack back into it, so far without success.

"They want us out of the picture, so they can use our access to rip through the heart of this country," Jaggard said behind them. "We're looking at a potential China syndrome, guys, and we need some answers."

China syndrome was a term that had originally come from the nuclear industry and referred to a catastrophic meltdown, supposedly a meltdown that would go all the way to China.

A meltdown of the country's computer and data infrastructure was too frightening to contemplate.

"Okay, what do we know?" Jaggard asked. "They launched a diversionary attack on a series of nuclear plants, and while we were busy with that they opened a trapdoor in our firewall and snuck in. They're in the system and they've got control, but as long as we can keep them busy here, we can limit the damage they can do outside."

"I don't know how much longer we can hold them," Dodge said through gritted teeth. "Every time I get my hands around them, they just disappear and I'm left with a handful of dust."

"They're recoding on the fly," Sam said.

"Not possible," Dodge said. "Nobody is that fast!"

"Tell *them* that," Sam said flatly.

Jaggard said, "I want Cheyenne Mountain powered

up now, but do not, repeat, do not, bring it online until we can confirm that the firewall there is secure. And get hold of air transport, I want all the jets fuelled and sitting on the runway now. Team, we're going to move out to the backup control centre at Cheyenne. We'll resume the fight from there. Dodge and Socks, you and your wingmen are going to keep them busy here. Cover the retreat. Okay, move it people."

The group dispersed as Jaggard's cell phone rang.

"Jaggard." He listened intently for a moment, interrupting only to say, "Heading where?"

When he clicked off the phone his face seemed pale, but he kept a professional calm.

"Everybody out, right now. Emergency evacuation procedure. That means now. And it means everybody." He was looking at Dodge and Sam.

"What is it, guv?" Dodge asked.

"Air Traffic Control have a 787 under remote ground control, UAS. Ninety-two passengers, heading for San Jose. We have to assume it's under the control of the hackers."

"What!"

"I think we're the target."

Vienna's voice sounded from over by the door. "Keycard is not working. They've recoded the locks."

"What!" Jaggard spun around towards her.

"The freaking doors are jammed," she said in a voice just teetering over into panic. "We can't get out."

10. UAS

"How long have we got?" Dodge asked calmly.

Jaggard didn't answer but pressed keys on his phone. "Put me through to LAX Control. I want the controller of that Southwest plane."

While he waited for the connection he called out, "Leave the intruders, Socks, you're on the door codes. Find out what they did and undo it, or just find some way to open them."

"On it," Socks said.

"Dodge, you too, leave the intruders alone. Nothing we can do about them anyway. Get over to LAX and try and shut down the UAS system."

"Can't do that, guv," Dodge said. "I'm all over this guy at the moment. He's having to recode constantly to keep away from me. I take the pressure off and he'll wipe our arses."

"If you don't get over to LAX, you're going to get your ass wiped by a 787," Jaggard said. He listened to his phone for a second then pressed a key. A voice came from the overhead speakers.

"This is Victoria Dean. Who am I talking to?"

"Victoria, this is John Jaggard at Homeland Security in San Jose. We believe we may be the target of your rogue 787."

There was a short silence and Sam thought he heard "Damn," faintly at the other end.

"Victoria, how long have we got before the plane gets here?"

Her voice came back with urgency. "You better get out of there now, sir, because he's real close."

"How close?"

"You in the centre of town?"

"We're near the airport."

"Then I give you less than five minutes, no more. You better be leaving, sir."

"We wish we could," Jaggard said under his breath, then more loudly. "Victoria, do you know where in the building the UAS computers are located?"

"I believe so, yes, sir."

"Victoria, I want you to get there now and shut them down. Pull out power cables if you have to, smash them up, I don't care. Just take that system offline any way you can. If you can shut down the UAS, the plane will return control to the pilot."

There was a muffled conversation at the other end of the phone then her voice came through clearly. "I'm heading there now, sir."

* * *

Taylor ran along next to her, out of breath after just a few steps. Somewhere along the way he had discarded his suit jacket and his tie was loosened into a loop, like a hangman's knot, Victoria thought.

Her phone was in her pocket, on speakerphone, and she could hear Jaggard issuing terse orders from its tinny speaker.

UAS was a small, unmanned office next to the central computer room. It was down one floor at the end of a long, dimly lit corridor. Human beings seldom came here except for repair and maintenance work. The corridor seemed endless although it couldn't have been more than sixty yards.

She beat Taylor to the door, but he was right behind her, despite his laboured breathing. She slammed her security card into the slot by the door and jerked on the handle, but it did not open. The light stayed red.

"Try mine," Taylor said, handing her his supervisor's card. Victoria snapped a glance at her watch. Maybe three minutes left, if they were lucky. She slid Taylor's card into the slot.

The light remained a steady constant red.

"They must have been expecting us," Dodge said. "They've locked down our access."

"Can you get in?" Jaggard asked.

"I think so," Dodge said. "It's a Linux system. I'm going to crash the shell with a buffer overflow and get in via the rhosts file."

"Do you have time for that?" Jaggard asked.

"No choice. Sam, you gotta keep this bug off my tail for a bit longer, mate."

"Doing my best," Sam said.

"Move aside." It was Vienna's voice. She moved next to Sam, nudging him with her body, reaching out for his keyboard.

Sam blasted a wide swathe through a pile of crawling fungus on the doorstep of Dodge's workstation.

"I'm a little busy right now," he said, lining up his next shot.

"Get out of the way, Sam." To Jaggard she said, "Dodge is our only hope. If they get him, we are all dead. Dead as in cemetery, not as in reboot your system. Sam hasn't got the experience."

"Sam is the only thing keeping me alive," Dodge said. "You stay right there, mate."

"Vienna's right," Jaggard said. "Sam's only been on the job for a couple of months. I don't care what kind of hot shot he is. Move aside, Sam, and that is an order."

"Sam stays." A thin, wiry voice came from behind Jaggard and, without even looking, Sam knew whom it belonged to.

Swamp Witch.

She continued, "He's our best hope right now; the

intruders are too fast."

"I'm in," Dodge said, and a moment later. "Oh, oh!"

"What is it?" Jaggard asked.

"UAS has its own firewall, inside the system. It's heavily protected and they've locked us out of that too."

"Can you break it?" Jaggard asked. There was a note in his voice that hadn't been there before, Sam thought. It sounded a lot like despair.

"I don't think we have the time," Dodge said.

Next to him, Vienna glanced upwards and Sam couldn't help but follow her gaze. Through the large, rounded, tinted windows of the control centre, high in the sky he could see an airplane.

"Smash it!" Victoria cried as Taylor pounded on the doorframe with the butt of a large fire-extinguisher. It left red paint on the door, but otherwise made little impression.

"Give it to me," she said, and didn't wait for him to agree, snatching the heavy fire-extinguisher away from him.

She moved to the right and ignored the lock, pounding instead on the hinge side of the door with huge crashing blows, holding the extinguisher high above her head. Each blow sent shock waves through her arms, juddering into her spine, but she kept at it.

Suddenly, there was a crack and the top of the door gave way slightly.

"God, I hope we're not too late," she cried and switched to the bottom hinge.

The intruder was everywhere now, crawling in and out of the systems like a creeping black vine. It was all Sam could do to keep Dodge and himself alive. The shape of the airplane was clearly distinguishable in the sky by the eastern tower of the Adobe buildings.

"Give me half an hour and I could bust this wide open," Dodge said, his eyes focused on his screen.

He hasn't seen the plane yet, Sam thought.

"We don't have half an hour," Jaggard said evenly.

"I know," Dodge said.

"DOS attack!" Sam said. "Hit 'em with a DOS attack."

Denial of Service was a common attack used by vandal hackers, saturating the target server with so many simultaneous connections and requests that it would slow to a crawl.

"That won't get us in." Vienna's voice was loud and unsteady.

"What's your thinking?" Jaggard asked, but Sam could see that Dodge had already worked it out, and was scurrying to set it up.

"Just do it," Sam said.

"Kid's a genius," Dodge said. "DOS attack will clog up the routers, slow down the transmission signal. If we slow it down enough, it should have the same effect as shutting down the servers."

Sam ripped a jagged hole in the code of one of the branches of the intruder, but it grew back even as he did it.

"Come on, come on," Dodge muttered, stabbing at the keyboard.

"Too late," Vienna yelled.

Sam looked up. The nose of the plane seemed to fill the window.

He braced himself for the impact, knowing it would do no good.

The hinge gave way with a final shudder and Victoria kicked the door to one side, dropping the fire-extinguisher and barging into the UAS room.

A long row of metal server racks stared at her, each one alive with flashing lights, blinking and winking behind the fine metal grille of the doors.

The power cables came in through the top, she realised, and traced them back quickly with her eyes to where they disappeared into the top of a large, wall-mounted UPS system.

The mains switch on the UPS was locked in the on position with a heavy brass padlock.

"You got a key?" Victoria demanded.

Taylor shook his head.

"Then get out of the way, and pass me that goddamn fire-extinguisher."

The tinny voices from the phone in her pocket abruptly vanished, replaced by a roaring static.

"Jaggard?" she asked, as Taylor passed her the fire-extinguisher. There was no sound but the static.

She pounded desperately on the padlock with the heavy red cylinder. The shiny metal loop buckled, but held.

"Jaggard? Are you there?" she yelled. "Jaggard?"

11. BIGGER FISH

The explosion didn't happen. The momentary burst of brick and glass before everything turned to oblivion didn't occur, although Sam saw it clearly in his mind's eye all the same.

The entire building shook and several windows shattered under the shock wave, but the plane passed over their heads with a deafening roar.

Through the opposite window Sam saw the nose of the plane rise high above the tail. It skimmed above the roof of the Park Centre Plaza, narrowly avoiding the tall buildings in an adjacent block, and clawed its way back into the sky.

"Jaggard, are you still there?" the voice of the air traffic controller sounded from the overhead speakers as the roar subsided. They could hear bangs and crashes in the background.

"Only just," Jaggard answered.

"How close is the plane?"

"It missed," Jaggard said. "Pilot got control back."

"Thank God for that," Victoria said. "We've just broken

into the cabinet. We're about to kill the power. That'll stop them from trying again."

Sam found he was still staring out of the far windows at the shrinking shape of the Boeing. He forced his eyes back to his screen, to find it empty.

All he had now was the blue screen of death. He looked across at Dodge's computer, but his screen was the same.

"Okay, people, we're still alive," Jaggard called out, clapping his hands together. "But if we don't get our act together then pretty soon this country is going to go China syndrome. You still up, Socks?"

"Barely," Socks muttered. "Still trying to get into the security door system, though and..." He trailed off, staring at his screen. "What the hell?"

"What is it, Socks?"

"I'm back," he said. "Just like that. Fully operational."

"How?" Jaggard asked.

"Something just ate the intruder."

There was complete silence in the room.

"Say that again."

"I don't know how else to describe it. One minute I was getting smothered by the big mother and the next minute this big black nothing raced out of nowhere and tore it to shreds, gobbled it up."

"A big black nothing raced out of nowhere and gobbled it up?" Jaggard said. "Please try not to be so technical."

"There's always a bigger fish," Dodge said.

There was a flash in front of Sam and his central screen

suddenly flickered back into life, followed by his left and right screens.

"I'm back," he said in astonishment.

"Me too," Dodge said.

The group dispersed around the room and there was a chorus of agreement as one by one their systems came back online.

"Where's the intruder?" Jaggard asked.

"No sign of it," Dodge said a moment or two later. "Just fragments of code lying around on the hard drives."

"Just fragments?"

"Yeah," Dodge said. "Looks like they've been *chewed.*"

The silence in the room was absolute.

Dodge had called up the footage from a security camera on the roof of the hotel opposite, and put it up on the large central screens. They watched the jet airplane get closer and closer to the CDD building, pulling up at the last minute and clearing the roof by less than ten yards.

"So do we know anything at all?" Jaggard asked.

"I know we were surrounded but the cavalry arrived in the nick of time," Socks said.

"The cavalry?" Dodge jumped to his feet. "We *are* the cavalry! The first, last and best line of defence, right? But these guys took us apart and then someone went through them like a bad curry. We weren't even on the same page."

"Sit down, Dodge," Jaggard said. "Let's stay focused on this. Who are the bad guys? Who are the good guys who saved us?"

"The phantom of the internet," Socks muttered.

"And how can a bunch of terrorist hackers beat us at our own game?" Jaggard asked.

"The terrorists had neuro-connections," Sam said.

Jaggard shook his head. "There's no way of knowing that."

"They had neuro," Sam repeated. "I was running on the edge, flying by wire and it still wasn't fast enough. They had to be using neuro."

"He's right, guv," Dodge said. "Had to be neuro."

"Well if they were using neuro," Socks asked, "what the hell was the phantom using?"

Vienna looked up from her console. "Boss, I've traced lines in and out of the Chicago data centre. I got a vid-cam feed. I think the terrorists were monitoring the place from a secondary location."

"Can you back-trace it?" Jaggard asked.

"Yes, it's also in Chicago. I'm narrowing down the exact location now."

"Okay, I want Tactical teams en route. Dodge, you too. Check out a field kit and take Sam with you. As soon as Tactical have secured the location, I want you two to get inside their workstations. Find out how they managed to stick it to us so royally. Expect booby traps, self-destruct sequences and suicide pills. And see if you can find any clues to the identity of this ... phantom."

The phantom, Sam thought. A ghost in the machine. Except it wasn't a ghost. Someone was roaming around the internet with powers they could only dream of.

"What about the neuro?" he asked. "If we can't keep up with the bad guys, this will just be the start."

Swamp Witch, who had been hovering at the back of the group, moved forwards, the team parting to make a path for her, out of respect, or fear, Sam didn't know.

"We can't afford to be compromised like that again," she said. "I'll discuss neuro-headsets with the Oversight Committee."

Vienna was standing just outside the door when Sam went to leave. He steeled himself for the assault.

"Vienna," he started, "I'm sorry about what happened—"

"It's fine," she said, "I just wanted to say thanks. I panicked and you didn't. Simple as that."

To his surprise she reached out and gave him a quick hug. It was cold, awkward, and devoid of feeling, but he felt she was stretching outside her comfort zone even for that.

"Um, you're welcome," he said.

12. FIRST CLASS

The Airbus seemed to Sam to be the size of a hotel. He was amazed that it could get off the ground, and was secretly glad when it did, although he feigned complete nonchalance as the nose lifted and the rumble of the runway ceased.

According to the information tucked in with the in-flight magazines, the plane was as long as sixteen elephants standing trunk to tail. He struggled for a moment to visualise that, and eventually decided that it was quite a herd. Certainly more than the only other plane he had ever been on which was the CDD Learjet. That couldn't have been much more than a couple of elephants long at most.

Special Agent Ranger had met them in the car park entrance of the building as they had hurried to leave.

"You're on a commercial flight," he'd said. "Leaving at ten pm. We've only got two Learjets available and we're using them both for Tactical. I'll see you in Chicago."

Sitting now in the luxury of the huge plane, Sam let his mind wander. He wondered if "elephants" were the international standard for measuring planes, and also whether they were Indian elephants, or African elephants, which he seemed to remember were bigger.

The field kits travelled with them, in the overhead lockers, as Dodge refused to entrust them to the baggage handlers.

They had special tags that got them through airport security unopened, so Sam had not yet seen what was inside them.

The Airbus finished climbing and flattened out into a smooth and level flight. An illuminated seatbelt sign switched off with a quiet ping.

Sam looked around. There were just four seats in this part of the first class cabin. Two of them, on the other side of a frosted glass panel, were occupied by a couple of important-looking executives, or maybe diplomats. If they wondered what a couple of teenagers were doing in the other half of the cabin, they didn't show it by look or gesture.

The flight attendant, a pleasant lady with dark hair pulled back in a tight bun, was suddenly at his side. He hadn't notice her approach.

"Would you like a headset, sir?" she asked. "We have regular or neuro."

Sam tried to remember the last time he had been called "sir" and couldn't. He smiled and shook his head. She asked Dodge the same question and got the same answer, then moved over to the other side of the cabin.

Dodge stood up and extracted his field kit – a

silver briefcase with a digital lock – from the luggage compartment.

"It's your first field mission," Dodge said. "So I'd better show you the ropes."

Dodge showed him the key-code and opened the briefcase.

Inside the case was a collection of tools, some of which Sam recognised at once, and others which he could not identify.

"Right," Dodge said, "we'll start with the disclone."

He pulled out a black device with a long cable attached. The cable disappeared into a slot inside the briefcase. "Before we touch a thing we clone their hard disk. Tactical will have already rendered the computer casing safe, removed any explosives or other booby traps—"

"Explosives?" Sam asked nervously.

"Pretty common," Dodge said. "To destroy any evidence on the hard drives. But don't worry about that – Tactical are specialists at that kind of thing. Once they've finished taking out the terrorists and dealing with any physical booby traps, then we go in. And the first thing we do is clone the drive, so that if there are any software destructs or suicide code, then we get a second chance at it. Remove the drive from the computer, plug it in to the disclone, and it will mirror the contents, bit for bit, byte for byte on an internal drive in the briefcase. Clear?"

"Clear," Sam said.

Dodge went through the rest of the gear in the case,

explaining the use and the operation of each device. It took about half an hour, and was far more interesting, Sam thought, than any in-flight movie.

The cabin attendant – her name badge said "Marie" – brought them some refreshments at one stage, just a soda and a choice of profiteroles. Dodge closed the case while she hovered, and opened it again when she left.

"So what do you think about the phantom?" Sam asked, when the lesson was over. "What's your theory?"

"The beast of the moors." Dodge grinned. "The hound of the Baskervilles."

"Eh?"

"Gummi Bear will tell you that there's some kind of creature roaming the network, a monster, a demon from the depths of the internet."

"More of an angel than a demon," Sam said.

"Ain't that the truth," Dodge said. "Another theory is that it's a coding freak. Someone with immense power and skills."

"Are there really people like that?" Sam asked. "Coding freaks?"

"There are. I've met two of them – well," he wavered, "one for definite and one I'm not sure about yet."

"Who?" Sam asked eagerly.

"Swamp Witch," Dodge said. "She's a freak."

"What do you mean?"

"In this business we do our best work before the age of twenty-two. After that the brain begins to slow down, partly from the pressure and partly from old age.

"At twenty-two?"

"Yup. But every now and then a person comes along who doesn't burn out, and whose mind stays razor sharp year after year. A freak of nature. A natural. Someone who can do this stuff without thinking, without training. That's Swamp Witch. They say she can do magic."

"So could she be the phantom?"

"Don't think I ain't thought about it," Dodge said. "If there's anyone who could throw some lizard gizzards in a boiling pot and make a magic potion, it's her. But she was right behind us when it happened. She couldn't have done it."

"Who else then?"

"Maybe there's another agency out there. Someone like us."

"The Easter Bunny?" Sam asked.

"Could be," Dodge said. "Or maybe our counterparts in another country."

"Nothing quite adds up, when I think about it," Sam said. "It's hard to believe that another country could be that far ahead of us."

"What're you saying?" Dodge asked.

"I have my own theory."

"Go on."

"Well, the intruder code disintegrated and we're all assuming that it got blasted by someone. But what if it just self-destructed?"

"Why suddenly self-destruct when you've just won the battle?"

"Unless the person who hit the self-destruct button was there in the room with us at the time."

"Are you serious?"

"Dodge, you can't mention this to anyone inside the CDD," Sam said. "No one, okay?"

"Okay," Dodge agreed, looking at him closely.

"What if the terrorists had an insider at CDD? They'd know all our procedures; they'd know our response patterns; how we react; what we'd be likely to do; even what defence mechanisms we have at our disposal. It's certainly more likely than some fantasy about a phantom on the internet."

"But this insider didn't know about the plane?"

"Yep – that's my theory," Sam said. "Maybe the plane attack had two goals. To eliminate us, and also to silence the insider. The only person who could identify the terrorists."

"So when the insider realised what was going on, he or she hit the self-destruct key," Dodge said. "Why the delay though? Cut it a bit fine. If we hadn't DOSed the UAS, then we'd be toast by now, and so would the insider. Why wait until the last minute?"

"I'm not sure," Sam said.

Dodge said, "If it was one of us, then who?"

"I don't know," Sam admitted.

"The security cams would have recorded everything.

I'll call Jaggard and ask him to review the footage."

He reached for the airphone.

Sam put a hand on his arm, stopping him. "If there's a traitor inside CDD," he said, picking his words carefully, "how do you know it's not Jaggard?"

"I don't. How do you know it's not me?"

"I don't. But I didn't know who else to talk to."

"Okay, we'll check it ourselves when we get back. I'll hack into the security system so that we don't have to formally request access."

Sam nodded. "That's what I was thinking."

"I can't believe it's Jaggard though," Dodge said. "I've known him a long time."

"Who then? Kiwi? Vienna? Gummi?"

Dodge said, "I don't know. There's no reason to suspect any of them. Nor Socks or Zombie."

"Or even Swamp Witch," Sam said slowly.

The plane banked slightly, and through the window Sam could see a dark scar on the desert: a ruined city, crushed and blackened buildings emanating out from a huge crater.

Dodge saw him looking.

"Vegas," Dodge said. "Not easy to look at, is it?"

Sam shook his head.

"Better get some kip," Dodge said. "It might be your last chance for a while."

* * *

The seat folded flat and was surprisingly comfortable, although quite narrow and not quite long enough for Sam's legs.

He couldn't sleep though, and after a while he asked Marie for a neuro-headset and watched old cowboy movies inside his head as the sixteen-elephant-long flying hotel glided smoothly over darkened Midwest states.

Later, in the dim light of the cabin, with the rush of the wind outside just a warm cocoon of noise enveloping him, he remembered to ask.

"Dodge. You still awake?"

"Am now."

"Sorry."

"Don't be. What is it?"

"You said you had met two freaks in your life. One was Swamp Witch. Who was the other?"

"You," Dodge replied sleepily. "Goodnight, Sam."

13. CHICAGO

Dark men emerged from dark cars as they approached an intersection, just a block from the river, guns strapped across their chests. Chicago PD SWAT officers, according to the badges and markings on their uniforms.

They checked Dodge's and Sam's IDs then directed them to a small cafe on the next block.

Dim blue lights placed on tables gave them just enough light to see by, without showing through the heavy drapes that were pulled across all the windows.

A figure in Tactical coveralls hurried over. A black face mask hung low around his neck.

"We're just finalising our operational plans," Ranger said. "Please join us."

They followed him to a large hand-drawn diagram spread out on a table.

"Okay, guys, here's the situation. The tangos are in an apartment, in a block on the other side of the street. About thirty yards north of us. The apartment is on the third floor."

There were at least sixteen Tactical troops gathered

around the table, and other chairs and tables had been stacked against the walls to make room.

Ranger continued, "Police have sealed off a four-block perimeter. The river is also being patrolled, in case they should escape and make it that far."

He looked around at Dodge and Sam, and Sam had the feeling that he had already been through this, and was doing it again just for their benefit.

"Are you sure these are the terrorists that attacked us?" Sam asked.

"Vienna traced a video link from the server farm that launched the diversionary attack," Ranger said. "It led right here. Solid enough for you?"

Sam nodded.

Ranger said, "Thermal imaging shows us two targets inside the apartment, currently sitting at computers. They haven't moved from the computers since we've been monitoring them, no toilet breaks, no food, nothing. This suggests they're in the middle of something."

"Any activity on the wire over at CDD?" Dodge asked.

"No, nothing yet. But we want to get in there and shut them down as soon as we can. We have a sniffer pipe pulling air in from the apartment and analysis shows traces of both cordite and ammonia, so it's a safe assumption that they've got both weapons and explosives in there."

He turned to the diagram, drawn in marker pens on a large sheet of paper on the table in front of them and illuminated with flashlights at each corner.

"The apartment block is roughly square in shape, with a central courtyard. The target apartment is on the far side. There's an interior balcony off the apartment that hangs over the courtyard. That's going to be our primary entry point. We'll rappel in from the roof and hit the windows with a glass crusher from one of the apartments opposite. We'll take out the front door simultaneously. Flashbang grenades from the window, and from the door glycerol fog canisters. We'll take out the power before we go in, of course, but they'll have a backup power supply, so our main objective is to disconnect the tangos from their computers before they have a chance to do any damage. We're using handguns, not automatic weapons. First round in the chamber will be a puffer, after that the hard stuff. Questions?"

Lots, thought Sam, who hadn't understood half of it, but didn't want to appear stupid and ask.

A bleeping came from Ranger's belt and he pulled out a cell phone, reading the screen before announcing, "Okay, team, we have operational confirmation from CDD HQ. Plan is approved; we are good to go. You know your positions."

Ranger picked up a neuro-headset from a table and positioned it carefully on his head.

"Dodge, Sam. There's a couple of spare headsets on the far table, next to the monitors," he said. "If you want to come for the ride."

"I thought CDD didn't use neuro," Sam said to Dodge.

"We don't," Dodge said. "But Tactical make their own rules. They're been using neuro for years for nonverbal communication. Talking to each other during missions without actually making a sound. Now they're fully equipped with video and audio feeds. Gear up – this'll blow your mind."

The Tactical version of a neuro-headset was unlike any others Sam had seen. It consisted of a rubberised wire framework which held the sensors. It was malleable enough to be shaped into position on your head, rather than being tightly compressed onto your skull. A short cable led to a compact receptor unit with a radio aerial.

"Don't switch it on yet," Dodge said. "You'll want to be sitting down first."

"Sitting down?"

"With the audio and video feeds it's just like being there. But you'll need to sit down, otherwise you'll end up falling over. You'll be seeing what they see, in real time, and your body will tend to react."

"Okay," Sam said.

"You'll probably end up falling off the chair in any case," Dodge said. "But at least it's not so far to fall."

Ranger came over. "Any last questions?"

"What's our entry point?" Dodge asked.

"Stay here till I tell you," Ranger said. "Then head across the road, thirty yards to the north, to the reddish-coloured door. Take the stairs, not the elevator – the power will be out – to the third floor. Our guys'll meet you at the top of the stairs. Wear these." He handed them both a small round device with a metal clip. "Infra-red strobes. Just in case they don't recognise you in the dark."

Ranger moved away and sat at a long table that was covered in screens and other equipment. He produced a thick nylon strap, a little like a seatbelt, from somewhere, and strapped himself to the chair, placing both hands firmly on the table. In the dim light Sam could not see Ranger close his eyes, but knew that he had, from the sudden shift in the posture of his body.

Dodge put on his headset and Sam followed suit. The moment he shut his eyes, a grid appeared with sixteen thumbnail videos, one for each member of the Tactical team.

Some of the videos showed the roof of the building. Another showed the balcony of the apartment from across the interior courtyard. Others showed dark interior passageways.

He selected one of those and it expanded to fill his vision, leaving just a few control icons at the bottom of the screen. As he watched, an arm reached up in front of the camera and a leather-gloved hand unscrewed a light bulb in a ceiling fitting. When the bulb went out, the hand stopped, leaving the bulb in the fitting. It was too dark to see more than vague outlines in the corridor now and he selected "Night Vision" from the control icons at the bottom. His world turned into a strange, green glowing video game as the viewpoint moved further down the corridor.

He clicked on a grid icon and was rewarded by the thumbnail videos again. He selected one of the rooftop soldiers and found himself on a low parapet-style roof where a small group of soldiers was readying ropes and strong metal clips.

"Move to strike positions." Ranger's voice sounded in his head. "Okay, we have final mission confirmation from CDD HQ. Targets are confirmed. Weapons free. Ready to breach. On my go, stand by, stand by..."

The view in Sam's head swung around wildly as the soldier clambered over the parapet, looking down into the courtyard and glancing up at the night sky as he did so.

There was a loud thud somewhere nearby and a sharp pain in his elbow. Sam opened his eyes to find himself lying on the floor.

"Cut the power," Ranger said. "And go."

14. THE APARTMENT

Sam closed his eyes again, but stayed on the floor – at least he couldn't fall any further. The image from the soldier's camera flickered back into vivid green life.

The side of the building turned into a blur and the rope slithered through the fingers in front of his face. He could hear a zizzing sound and realised it was the rope. He was on full audio, as well as video feed.

A voice shouted, "Go! Go! Go!"

Large glass sliding doors approached rapidly, leading in from the balcony.

Ranger's voice in his head, "Glass crusher, now!"

There was a loud explosion and the doors shattered into a thousand tiny fragments, a rain of strange green confetti in the night vision colours.

From inside the apartment came flashes of lightning and a sound of thunder that Sam could hear with his own ears from across the street, as well as through the neuro-set.

Then he was on the balcony and rolling forward through the pulverised doors, rising up, a pistol at eye level seeking targets.

More voices all around him.

"Clear left!"

"Hallway clear!"

"Friendlies to your right."

There were two figures in this room, lolling backwards in their chairs, as if unconscious, knocked out, surely from the stun of the flashbangs.

The computers in front of them were on, the screens glowing greenly in the night vision viewer, but the figures made no attempt to reach for the keyboards.

There was something about the shape of their heads though ... neuro-headsets! Just as Sam had predicted.

Cut the cables, he willed the soldiers. Kill the connections before they can wipe the computers. One of the figures appeared large in his view and a glint of metal flashed from the end of a pair of cutters as the cables at the back of the headset were disconnected.

From the terrorist there was no movement, no sign of resistance. Nothing, in fact, at all.

"Room one clear," a voice sounded, then, "Room three clear, two tangos neutralised."

Why had the terrorists not moved?

The soldier secured the man's hands behind the chair with PlastiCuffs. He moved to the computer and began scanning the case with a hand-held device. Sam didn't have to be told to know he was looking for explosives.

"Something's wrong." It was Ranger's voice, and Sam

opened his eyes to see him looking at them. "Someone's beaten us to it."

"What do you mean?" Dodge asked.

"The terrorists were already down before we got here. They're unconscious. They're barely alive. Someone's been here before us."

"What happened to them?" Sam asked.

"We don't know yet," Ranger replied. "They've been gassed, poisoned, something. Ten to one, whoever did this has also been into the computers. Get in there now and see if they left us any scraps."

The lights were back on by the time Dodge and Sam entered the apartment. Faded wallpaper peeled back from the walls. There might have been carpet once, but it was long gone, and grimy floorboards were covered only by a hard-knotted, but threadbare, rug.

Some jackets, and other indeterminate clothing, hung from a row of wooden pegs inside the door and a faded photograph of a sailing ship hung lopsidedly in front of the door.

The two dark figures they had seen were stretched out on the ground receiving medical attention from the soldiers. Their computers were in pieces on the table.

"Any explosives?" Dodge asked the first soldier he saw.

"None," the man said.

"I thought we sniffed out ammonia?" Dodge said.

"We did, but it wasn't explosives," the man said, and didn't elaborate.

As per his instructions, Sam cloned the drive before starting the computer up and analysing the hard drive.

It took him just a minute to confirm the extent of the disaster. The computer was wiped clean. The operating system was there, and some basic programs, but nothing else. It was as if it had just been taken out of the box. There was a scattering of code fragments near the boot sector of the disk, but it was garbage.

"This has been wiped," Dodge said.

"Same here," Sam murmured.

"Bleedin' hell, what're we going to tell Jaggard?" Dodge asked in a loud voice, then leaned over, talking quietly for Sam's ears only. "Who else knew the location of the terrorists, do you think?" he asked.

"The insider!" Sam realised with shock.

"And who knew we were on our way here?" Dodge pursed his lips and answered his own question. "Same person."

"You think the insider did this?"

"If it is an insider, then it all adds up," Dodge said. "They would have done this to clean up any traces that might have led us back to them."

"Then it's not just one person," Sam said. "They must have had people on the ground here in Chicago."

"Not only that," Dodge said, "but they were able to get in here right under the noses of the Chicago PD, and get out again without being seen."

15. SWAMP WITCH

The octagonal office in the centre of the CDD control centre had been known as the swamp ever since the centre was established, and nobody really knew why.

The first inhabitant, a college professor, balding on top but with long grey hair pulled back in a ponytail, had been known as "The Thing from the Swamp" by the CDD team.

He had been followed by "Swamp Creature", "Swampy", and most recently by "Swamp Witch".

Small, rotund and with a shock of bright orange hair, the name seemed to suit, and although Isabel Donald knew full well of her nickname, the current on-site representative of the Congressional Oversight Committee never complained.

Her references were impeccable, her rise through the ranks of the CIA's IT department remarkable, and her abilities quite unique.

All in all there was no reason to suspect that she could be actively working against the CDD from the inside.

No reason at all, Sam thought.

"Here," Dodge said, tapping the screen of his laptop.

Dodge's room at the Crowne Plaza was identical to Sam's in every luxurious way, although a lot less tidy. Sam yawned and tried to focus his eyes. He had slept very little on the Airbus on the way to Chicago and not at all on the way back.

"Here's Swamp Witch," Dodge said, "appearing behind you and telling Vienna to pull her head in."

"That's not quite what she said," Sam said.

Dodge ignored him. "Right, switch to the overhead camera and we should see where she appeared from."

The data from six different video cameras had been copied onto a memory stick and plugged into the USB3 slot of Sam's laptop. All of the CDD team could be easily identified, intensely working away at their workstations until one by one they threw their hands in the air, giving up as their computers died with the horrible blue screen of death. They congregated behind Dodge and Sam, or Socks and Zombie.

"And we find out about the plane ... here," Dodge said.

The sudden movement and look of panic was unmistakable. Sam felt his palms begin to sweat, just watching the video.

But as far as Sam could see, none of them left the room. No one accessed a computer. No one had the opportunity to hit any kind of self-destruct button on the intruder code.

Except for Swamp Witch. The keeper of the gates. The watcher of the watchers. The guardian of the truth. She was nowhere in sight.

"She stays in her office right up till the last minute," Sam said, running the video forwards and backwards as Swamp Witch emerged and scampered down the slight slope towards their workstations. "Maybe she was just fighting them, the same as we were. Came out when her machine got wiped, like the rest."

"Or maybe not," Dodge said.

"You can't really think that she is our insider," Sam said. "She has security clearance that goes beyond the moon."

"Don't mean nothing," Dodge said. "Maybe she's just pulled the wool over a lot of people's eyes for a long time."

"It still doesn't feel right to me," Sam said.

"Give me a better option," Dodge said.

Sam couldn't. He shrugged. "Now what?"

"We need some proof," Dodge said. "We can't just go accusing the Oversight rep of treason without something a bit stronger than this. I think we need to get into her computer."

"You mean hack in?"

"Nah, ya muppet, you think she wouldn't notice that? We need to get into the swamp when she's not around and clone her hard drive. Then we can analyse it at our leisure back here."

"Security cams would see us," Sam said cautiously.

"Yeah, but nobody reviews the footage unless there is a problem," Dodge said. "So let's not cause a problem."

"I think we should let Jaggard know," Sam said. "That

way, if we're caught, at least one person will know what we were doing."

"If we ask Jaggard, he'll say no. If we then go and do it, we'll be out on our arses," Dodge said.

"Probably be out on our 'arses' anyway," Sam said.

"Maybe," Dodge said. "But it's always easier to apologise later than to ask for permission up-front."

"When?" Sam asked.

"Sooner the better," Dodge said. "How about tomorrow? If you can cover me, I'll try and slip into her office when she's not there."

"Won't it be locked?" Sam asked.

"That will be the least of our worries," Dodge said.

"Any progress?" Jaggard asked, and his tone was not chirpy. He leaned forward on his elbows, staring across the desk at Sam and Dodge. He had called them into his office the moment they arrived at work.

"Nothing yet," Dodge answered for them. "We put the terrorists' hard drives through every kind of test, including spectro-magnetic analysis and we got nothing. They're as clean as the day they were manufactured."

"Is it possible that someone replaced the drives?"

Dodge shook his head. "Forensic examination of the screws and the cable ends says no. These are the original drives. They have just been zeroed."

Jaggard nodded. "That pretty much describes their owners as well. Zeroed."

"What do you mean?" Sam asked. "What's wrong with them?"

"We're not yet sure," Jaggard answered. "They are both in a deep coma. Looks like a massive brain aneurysm. The problem is that the CAT scans don't show any evidence of it. Whoever did this to them has access to drugs or some kind of radiation equipment that we can't begin to imagine."

"Would the CIA have that kind of stuff?" Dodge asked.

"I don't know," Jaggard said. "You want to run over there and ask them?"

"What about the neuro-headsets?" Sam asked. "Any chance you could induce some kind of brainwave that could cause this kind of damage?"

"First thing we thought of," Jaggard said. "Had experts running tests on them all day. Worst they've come up with so far is to induce a mild headache by overloading the audio channels."

"So they're safe?" Dodge asked.

"Better be," Jaggard said, "considering the Oversight Committee has taken Swamp Witch's advice and is insisting that we start training on neuro, effective immediately."

"Cool!" Sam couldn't help blurting it out.

"You won't be so happy when your brain explodes," Dodge said.

"We'll all be on them," Jaggard said. "Here and at Cheyenne. We're not going to get caught out again."

Jaggard pushed a copy of the local paper, the *San Jose Mercury News*, across the desk to Sam.

"You heard about this spam thing?"

Dodge nodded, but Sam shook his head.

"Happened while you were in Chicago."

"SPAM CANNED" was the newspaper headline.

Sam scanned the article quickly. Apparently, a gradual reduction in the amount of spam around the world had turned suddenly into a full-blown collapse.

"Spam servers around the world have been targeted and shut down," Jaggard said. "I want you on it. Find out who's behind the attacks."

"Who cares?" Dodge said with a laugh. "They're spammers. Let 'em burn."

"The day before it was online gaming sites," Jaggard said.

"You think the attacks are related?" Sam asked.

"Possibly, probably, who knows?" Jaggard said. "What I want to know is what's next? What are they planning for tomorrow? As long as they're doing good deeds then nobody really cares. But what defines good? As they – whoever 'they' are – see it. What if they decided at election time that they didn't like one particular candidate, would they crash all the support websites? Worse, would they hack the election software and rig the election?"

"Now you're giving me ideas," Dodge said.

Jaggard ignored him. "And I especially want to know whether it's related to the Chicago terrorists."

"What makes you think that?" Sam said.

"I don't know. Maybe just the timing," Jaggard replied. "We have three separate incidents occurring within three days, and in each case we have no idea how it happened, or who did it. Vienna and Kiwi are already looking into the gaming sites. I want you two on the spammers. If there is a link to the terrorists, or that 'phantom', then I want to know asap."

"On to it, guv," Dodge said, and they both got up to leave.

"Stay for a moment, Sam," Jaggard said.

Sam sat back down slowly.

Jaggard waited until Dodge had left then said, "I need to talk to you."

"Is it my probation?" Sam asked.

Jaggard shook his head. "That's not going to be a problem. We need you around."

Sam said nothing, looking closely at Jaggard. He kept his face emotionless, although inside him a warm surge of pride was competing with a sudden, inexplicable fear.

"Your mother has been in contact," Jaggard said. "A message relayed by the authorities in New York."

"Is she all right?" Sam asked, the fear growing rapidly.

"She's fine," Jaggard said. "It's not about her. It concerns a Derek Fargas."

"Fargas?" Sam mentally kicked himself. He had meant to get in touch with Fargas, but hadn't yet got around to it. The business with the terrorists and the phantom had simply got in the way. Fargas would understand though. Surely? Once Sam was able to explain.

"How well did you know him?" Jaggard asked.

Sam opened his mouth to reply, then shut it again quickly.

Jaggard hadn't said, "How well *do* you know him?"

He'd said "did".

When Sam arrived at his desk, his new CDD-issue neuro-headset was sitting in a plain cardboard box next to his keyboard. He sat and just stared at it for a while. The headsets were the thin rubber-coated wire mesh style that they had used in Chicago. Looking closely at it he saw it was a Neuro-Sensor Pro 3.1. A big step forward from the 1.2-version headset he had scored from Telecomerica. Glancing around, Sam saw that about half of the team was already wearing them.

Bashful and Gummi Bear, to his left, were staring at nothing with their eyes shut and laughing their heads off over some shared private joke. Socks was wearing his, although Zombie seemed to be having difficulty with the shape of his and kept taking it off, making small adjustments to the wires and putting it back on.

"Are you all right?" Dodge asked.

"I'm okay," Sam said, but he wasn't okay. The news about Fargas felt like a kick in the chest, a crushing, winding blow. Was he responsible for what had happened?

"You look pale," Dodge said.

"It's nothing," Sam said. "Let's get on with it."

They spent most of the shift digging around in the dark alleyways of the internet, where the gamers, spammers, scammers and phishers lived.

Places they expected to find full of seedy little servers and malformed code were empty. The dingy bars and backstreets were deserted.

It was as if the barnacles on the dark underbelly of the internet had been scraped off.

What did it; who did it; how they did it; were questions without answers.

Fargas intruded constantly on his thoughts, and several times he found himself blinking back tears. Once he caught Dodge looking at him strangely, but Dodge said nothing, which suited Sam just fine.

Sam kept an eye on his watch as the afternoon progressed, ever conscious of the time. Dodge was casual about it, but breaking into the office of the Oversight rep was no laughing matter. If caught, he could end up back in Recton. Or worse.

He needn't have worried.

Just after 3.30, with the shadows from the windows starting to spread long grey fingers across the room, there was a paralysing scream from the centre of the room.

"What the...?" Dodge began.

The scream continued on and on, an ancient primordial sound that reeked of every kind of terror and black despair, then just as suddenly cut off.

"Get Jaggard," Dodge said. "That came from the swamp." He was already running up the slope to the central octagonal office.

Sam pressed the emergency alert button on his keyboard and ran after Dodge.

The door was locked, but before they could even think about finding someone with a keycard that would open it, the door opened by itself and something that used to be Swamp Witch staggered out.

She made just one tottering step before collapsing to her knees, then slumping over, twisting onto her back as she did so, half in and half out of the door.

Whatever it was inside her that had made that scream, was gone, vanished from her body as if it had never existed. Her face was calm and still. She looked up at Sam and Dodge with the cherubic questioning innocence of a newborn baby.

16. THE PHANTOM

The paramedics took Swamp Witch out on a stretcher, her breathing shallow, her eyes empty. John Jaggard went with them, holding her hand as if she was his child.

The intense laser beam stare was now just a soft wash of moonlight. The piercing intelligence had been replaced by the vacuous mind of an infant.

Sam had hardly known her, and certainly wouldn't have been one to put his hand up and say that he liked her. But there was something about that happening to someone he knew, something about it happening right in front of him, that made it shocking in ways he couldn't fully comprehend. And coming right on the heels of the news about Fargas, it seemed almost too much to deal with.

"Well, I guess she wasn't the insider," Dodge said in a vague attempt at humour.

The main doors closed behind the paramedic team and after a moment or two, people around the room began to turn back to their screens. Getting back to their work, or just discussing what had happened.

"Come with me," Dodge said, picking up the silver field kit that was still sitting under his desk.

Sam started to ask where he was going, but it was unnecessary. Dodge was heading for the swamp.

He rose on shaky legs and followed. By the time he got there Dodge had already plugged in the kit and was cloning the data from the tall tower workstation beneath Swamp Witch's desk.

It smelled a bit dank in the swamp, Sam thought, or was that just his imagination? In the centre was an L-shaped desk where she worked. The big windows gave a perfect view of the entire control centre, while a series of screens arranged in a circle on the outer circumference of the office showed what various members of the team were working on.

The first two screens he looked at showed the contents of his and Dodge's workstations and he felt slightly uncomfortable, knowing that someone had been watching his every keystroke throughout the afternoon.

Swamp Witch was clearly the kind of person who liked to work in a mess. There were scraps of paper in piles everywhere, along with books, pens and scattered Blu-rays.

"I've got her drive," Dodge said very slowly. "But it won't matter."

"Why?" asked Sam.

"Because I can already tell you what's on it," Dodge said. "Absolutely bleedin' nothing. It's been wiped clean. Just like Chicago."

Sam hardly heard. He was too busy looking at what he hadn't seen on his first glance around the office. On the floor, by her chair, half-hanging by a cable from the desk, was a neuro-headset.

"Who could do this?" Sam asked, shaking his head. "Inside this room. This is supposed to be a heavily guarded, top-secret Government facility. But someone just reached inside and squeezed her brain like a grape."

"Get back to the workstation," Dodge said. "I'll be there in a minute."

Kiwi was just walking in as Sam returned to his own desk, and was looking around, aware that something was going on.

"What just happened in here?" he asked.

"Swamp Witch," Sam said, "some kind of seizure, or stroke, or something."

What else could he say, really? What else did he know for sure?

"Oh." Kiwi looked shocked and unsure what to say. He put on his headset and plugged in. After a moment he said, as if it was somehow important, "Vienna's on her way."

When Dodge sat down at his desk there was an edge to his jawline. He pulled his neuro-headset down over his biohazard tattoo and looked at Sam with narrowed eyes.

"What are you doing?" Sam asked.

"I'm going after them," he said. "Right now. Are you with me?"

"What do you mean?"

"I mean that whoever messed with Swamp Witch cannot have blasted their way into this room, through all our security, without leaving traces."

"Dodge." Sam looked down and spoke quietly. "I don't think it's safe. Don't ask me how, but I think the neuro-headsets have something to do with it."

"I'm sure of it," Dodge agreed, "and I'm just as sure that it's the only way we're going to be able to keep up with these guys. Now I'm going after them. Are you with me or not?"

"What if they do to you what they did to Swamp Witch?" Sam blurted.

"They won't," Dodge said darkly.

"How do you know?"

"Because you are going to protect me, wingman."

Sam stared at him for a moment, then strapped on his headset. "Hit it," he said.

They started in the swamp, breaching security with callous disregard for protocol. They swept through the interior network with their scanners blazing, illuminating every nook and cranny of the structure. Sam ran his scopes at full power, checking and rechecking Dodge's system every few fractions of a second.

"Code fragments," Dodge's voice said inside Sam's head. "Chewed up and spat out. Same stuff we saw after the terrorists attacked us. Same stuff we saw in Chicago."

"Why leave it lying around?" Sam asked. "Why not wipe up the traces?"

"I don't know," Dodge said. "Am I still clean?"

"As a whistle," Sam said.

"I want to check out the firewalls," Dodge said. "Try and find out how they got in. Stay with me."

"No problem," Sam said.

The firewalls were solid. No holes, no tunnels, not even a small data leak.

"So they disabled part of the security and enabled it again when they left?" Sam suggested.

"I don't think so," Dodge said. "These aren't toys, and they're overlapping protective fields so you'd have to crack two firewalls simultaneously. Impossible unless you had a tunnel like the terrorists used, and that has been filled in and welded shut."

"How then?"

"I don't know," Dodge said. "Maybe they just passed through the firewalls, like ghosts passing through a solid wall."

"You're not suggesting ghosts?" Sam almost laughed.

"No, that's not what I mean," Dodge said. "It's possible, theoretically possible, to bypass any software on any system, if you're able to program on the fly in machine code."

"Theoretically," Sam said, running a security check on Dodge's CPU cycles. "But a few days ago you were saying it was impossible to program in real time. Nobody could write low-level machine code on the fly."

"Which is why we've never considered it before," Dodge agreed. "But what if somebody could? Some genius. Some freak."

"Still not possible," Sam said. "Machine code is different from machine to machine. The CPU in the routers use different addressing and bit and byte order from the firewalls, and they are different from the servers. You'd have to be coding them all simultaneously."

"If you're free tomorrow, my grandma needs an egg-sucking lesson," Dodge said. "Let's head out of the building, I am going to release some search spiders and hunt for more of that chewed code. See if the phantom has left a trail."

"Dodge, think this through," Sam said. "The phantom wipes out the terrorists. So the phantom is on our side, right?"

"You'd guess so, wouldn't you," Dodge said.

"Then someone wipes out the spammers and the gamers."

"Did the world a favour."

"Then someone wipes out Swamp Witch," Sam said carefully.

"And you think it's the phantom doing it all?" Dodge said. "But why help us fight the terrorists, then attack us? Whose side is the phantom really on?"

"It's own," Sam said. "Maybe it had its own reasons

for taking out the terrorists. As for Swamp Witch, maybe she just went digging a little too deep and stumbled onto something she wasn't supposed to. Maybe the phantom was just protecting itself. Protecting its identity."

Dodge nodded. "First, delete all the incriminating evidence in her computer. Then delete all the incriminating evidence in her brain."

"The phantom is probably watching us right now," Sam said.

"Probably."

"That's what you want," Sam realised. "You want to be attacked! You're poking a stick into the hornet's nest trying to stir up some trouble."

"And when it comes, we'll be able to see where it's coming from," Dodge said.

"You're relying on me to protect you!" Sam said with horror.

"Isn't that what you get paid for?"

"Dodge, the phantom swatted Swamp Witch like a fly. It's too risky."

"No," Dodge said. "I'm going now while the trail is still hot, and..." He broke off, staring at his screen.

"What have you got?" Sam asked.

"Returns from the spiders. That chewed-looking code. They're finding it all over the place."

"How could that be?" Sam asked.

"I don't know. Maybe the phantom is hiding in the machine code, trolling along the lower levels of the internet like some big-arsed shark cruising around the ocean. But when it breaks surface, that's where it's leaving the crushed remains of the code. Maybe if we analyse the pattern of code fragment sites, we can find the source, track its location."

"This is nuts," Sam said. "Let's at least wait until Vienna gets in. She and Kiwi can help me cover your backside while you go do your bait-dangling thing."

"I'm not going to let this trail get cold."

"Dodge, I'm serious. It's not just the internet firewalls the phantom is breaking through; it's getting through neuro-firewalls as well. Into your brain!"

Dodge shook his head, concentrating on his centre screen.

"No way. I'm getting out of here," Sam said, reaching for his headset. "Seriously, the phantom probably knows what we're thinking, right now. It knows we're after it and–"

A million bolts of lightning flashed behind his eyes. A searing pain ripped at his temples. A spasm of pain pulsed through his arms which jerked wildly, flicking the headset from his scalp. It clattered onto the floor by his chair.

"Get your headset off, now!" Sam shrieked, turning to Dodge.

Dodge's eyes were white, turned upwards in his skull. His hands were claws gripping the arms of his chair, and the tendons in his neck strained as his head thrust backwards. His mouth opened in a cruel, demonic grin and he began to scream.

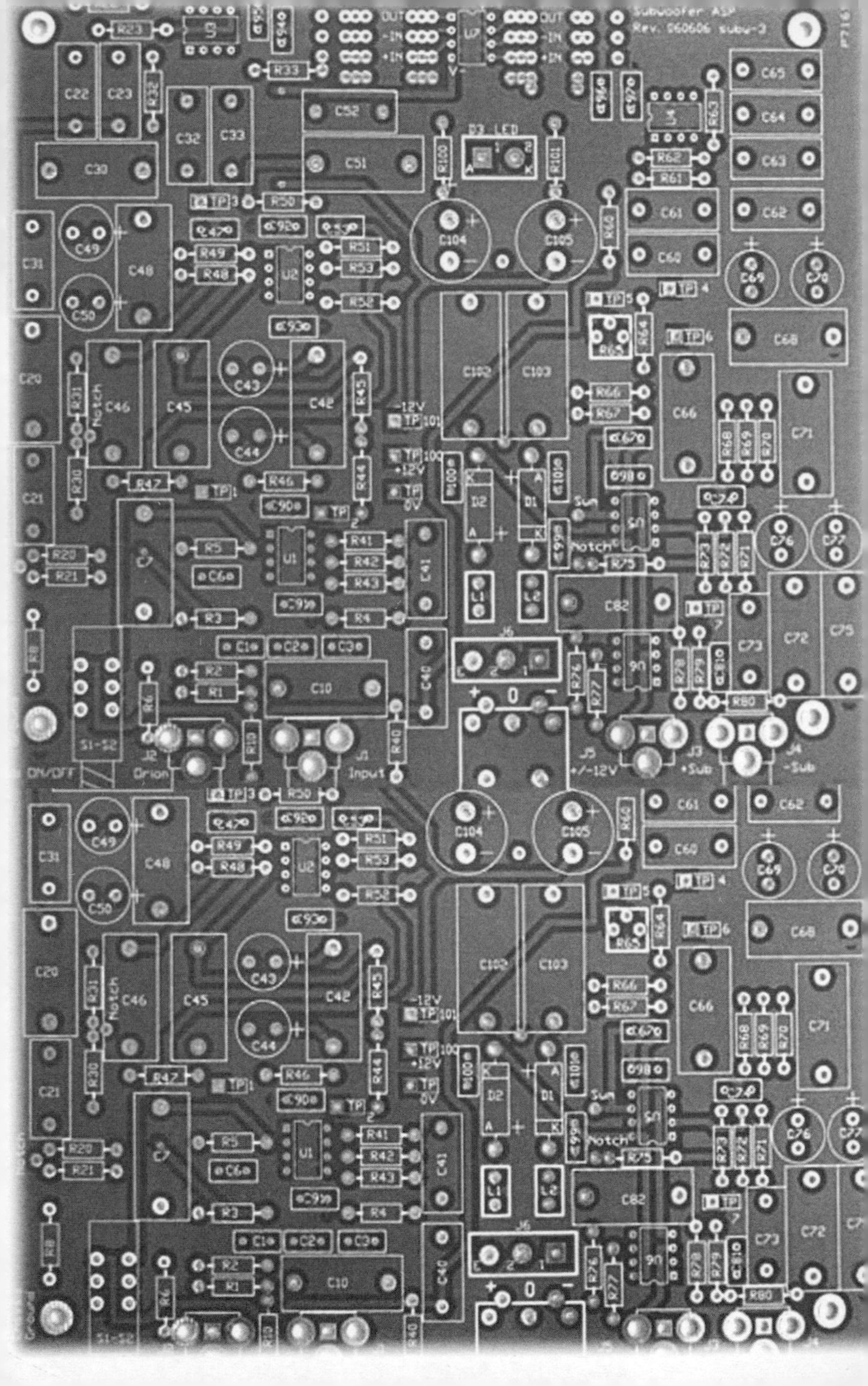
Subwoofer ASP
Rev. 060606 subu-3
ON/OFF
Orion
Input
+/-12V
+Sub
-Sub

BOOK THREE
WISDOM

1. RANGER

Special Agent Tyler Ranger of the CDD Tactical Response Team checked that the men's room was empty before dampening his comb and restoring his hair to its normal wavy style. He kept a small tube of hair gel in his pocket and ran a little through his hair with his fingers. The training session was over, but the neuro-sets always left his hair squashed and lifeless which didn't look cool.

Ranger enjoyed looking cool. But it wasn't cool to be seen making yourself look cool, which is why he checked the washroom first, before combing his hair up and back.

He stepped back from the mirror, turning to the left and right to check his profile.

His cell phone intruded with a high-pitched alert.

He slipped his comb back into the pocket of his coverall and ran for the door, just flicking a quick glance sideways as he did so to catch the image in the mirror: a man of action, running into danger.

Cuthbertson, the watch officer, met Ranger at the door. "It's a full team scramble."

"What's the alert?" Ranger asked.

"Something going on in the main control centre," Cuthbertson said.

Ranger strapped on his weapons kit and crossed to the operations computer.

"Arthur Philip Dodgerson and Sam Robert Wilson," he read off the screen. "Dodge and Sam. Surely not. I've known Dodge for years."

"I don't know what they've been up to," Cuthbertson said, "but Jaggard wants us to bring them in, and to do it now."

"Okay. Where is the team?" Ranger asked.

"Already assembling in the Go Room."

"Good. Let's take these guys down now, and worry about what they've been up to later. Lock down their keycards so they can't get out."

Ranger picked his neuro-headset up off his desk and pulled it firmly down over his head, squashing his hair.

This doesn't make any sense, he thought. He plugged his neuro-headset into the waistband receptor unit and switched it on, immediately immersing himself in the flurry of questions and messages flying back and forth from his team.

"This is Ranger," he communicated. "I want a team of four. Sergeant Hutchens, you pick three others. We go in two minutes."

There were confirmations from the team.

Surely not Dodge? The other kid was new, and maybe hiding something, but not Dodge. No way.

There seemed to be something wrong with the headset and he repositioned it slightly on his head. There was a buzzing, low and annoying, inside his head, as if a blowfly had flitted in one ear and was trying to find a way out.

He checked the connection at the receptor unit, but it was firm. The buzzing continued, a tickling at the base of his brain. He shook his head trying to clear it and after a moment it faded.

He checked the position of his headset again and retrieved his side-arm from the equipment locker.

What had he been thinking about?

Dodge and Sam, of course. Sam had looked shifty from the start, he remembered. And several times he had caught him accessing unauthorised information.

Why hadn't he remembered that before? The memory was vivid, with the clarity and focus of a dream you had just woken up from.

And Dodge. He had always had his suspicions about Dodge with his bald head and tattoos. He was too anti-authority. He could not be trusted.

Ranger checked his weapon and headed for the Go Room.

2. JAGGARD

John Jaggard stared at the alert message on the screen in front of him. A seize and detain notice for Dodge and Sam. What was that about?

According to the screen he was the one who had given the order. But he hadn't. Unless he was going mad. It had been a mad kind of an afternoon, but he'd know if he had given an order like that!

He'd *remember* something like that.

According to the notes on the action command, Dodge and Sam were implicated in the attack on Swamp Witch. But they hadn't been involved as far as he knew.

He would have remembered something like that too.

The terrorists were back. That was the only solution that made sense. They were back and they were using the system, his system, to issue fake orders.

A flashing alert on his computer screen warned him of an incoming message. Urgent. A neuro-communication. He grappled with the headset, still not used to the technology. He plugged it in and waited for the message.

And then he remembered everything.

3. ESCAPE

Sam launched himself off his chair, his arm stretched out in front of him. His fingertips caught the thick black cable that extended from the base of Dodge's skull, wrenching it sideways.

Dodge's head snapped to the side. The screaming became a strangulated gurgle as his windpipe choked. There was a cracking sound from the plug in the receptor unit and the casing fractured, pulling the plug from the socket.

The horrible strangled screaming sound stopped.

Sam hit the ground on an angle and there was a crack from his shoulder and a twist of pain that ran from his neck to his rib cage.

Dodge's head snapped back, then lolled forwards onto his chest.

Sam got back to his feet, ignoring the pain that shot through his body, and lifted Dodge's head with his hand.

"Dodge!" he shouted.

Dodge's eyes moved towards Sam, but he said nothing.

His eyes were dull but not vacant like Swamp Witch's had been.

That was a good thing, wasn't it?

"What the hell did you do that for?"

Sam looked up. It was Kiwi's voice. He had risen to his feet and was staring.

Around the room everybody was staring, their faces pale.

"It wasn't me, it was–" Sam broke off.

Kiwi was still wearing his neuro-headset. If he told Kiwi the truth, then Kiwi might become a target.

"Take off your headset," Sam ordered. "Now."

Kiwi raised an eyebrow and said, "Why? And what have you done to Dodge?"

"I didn't do anything," Sam pleaded. "It was ... a headset malfunction. Get yours off – now. The same thing happened to Swamp Witch earlier."

Kiwi's other eyebrow raised in an expression of shock and he reached for his temples. He grasped the headset and that's where his hands stayed. His eyes suddenly shifted up and to the left as if remembering something. His shocked expression eased.

"Kiwi!" Sam shouted.

Kiwi looked back at him. "It was you all along, wasn't it?"

"No, Kiwi, it's—"

"All these attacks and weird stuff, it all happened after you arrived."

"Kiwi, listen to me, take off your neuro-set!"

Kiwi stuck out a hand, pointing a finger at Sam like a schoolboy telling on his classmate. "It was him all along," he shouted to the room. "Sam's the one doing all this."

"Kiwi!"

"I saw you coming out of the swamp, just before Swamp Witch started screaming." He looked confused for a second, then said, "That's right, I saw you. I remember, I saw you."

"I was never in the swamp before..."

On one of the overhead security monitors, a movement caught Sam's eye. Special Agent Ranger, followed by four of his soldiers, was running across the atrium from their offices on the other side. There could only be one place they were heading.

He looked back at Kiwi. There was a glazed look in his eyes and when he looked at Socks, on the other side, the same look was there.

Around the circular room people were fixing him with accusatory stares. Every one of them wore a neuro-headset.

"Can you hear me, Dodge?" Sam said, holding Dodge's chin and shaking his head slightly. Dodge said nothing, but his eyes narrowed and his brow furrowed. He had at least heard the question.

"We've got to get out of here now," Sam said. "Can you walk?"

Dodge didn't reply. Sam put his arms under Dodge's

shoulders and began to lift, but as he did so Dodge stood up under his own steam.

"Okay, come on," Sam cried, and started to run towards the doors. Below in the atrium, the soldiers disappeared from sight as they entered the stairwell up to the control centre.

He glanced back. Dodge was standing motionless, right where Sam had left him.

"Come on, Dodge!" Sam shouted.

Dodge didn't move.

Sam ran back and put Dodge's arm around his shoulders, trying to drag him towards the door. There was no need. As soon as he started walking, Dodge started walking too, as if someone had pressed a switch.

Sam steered him towards the double doors. Just as they got there, Kiwi stepped in front of them. His neuro-set was still in place, but the cable hung loose, idly swinging below his thighs.

"Kiwi, thank God," Sam cried. "Now give me a hand with Dodge."

"I know what you did," Kiwi spat, barring their way. "And I know who you are. You're going nowhere."

Sam looked at Kiwi's glazed eyes. Somehow Kiwi had been got at. Fed false information, directly into his brain. Sam said, "It's not true, Kiwi. Whatever you think you know, it never happened."

"I know what I saw," Kiwi said, unmoving.

"Oh, crap," Sam said and, without warning, pushed

Dodge right at Kiwi. Kiwi stumbled backwards under the weight of him and Sam slid his keycard through the reader.

Nothing happened. The door remained locked.

"Crap!" Sam said again. They had shut off his keycard. Dodge's too, no doubt.

Kiwi was struggling to push Dodge off him and Sam saw his keycard on a long curly wire attached to his belt.

Sam shoved Dodge forwards again, sending both of them crashing against the wall, then grabbed at the keycard and wrenched. The keycard, curly wire still attached, came away in his hand.

Desperately, he swiped it through the reader, and the doors opened.

He could hear running bootsteps.

He pulled Dodge off Kiwi and thrust him through the doors, like some oversized puppet.

A hand pulled on his shoulder and he swung around instinctively, his fist connecting with Kiwi's face.

Kiwi jolted backwards, blood spurting from his nose.

Sam ran through the doors and grabbed hold of Dodge. Like an automaton, Dodge had walked across to the far side of the corridor and simply stopped, waiting for the next command to execute.

Ranger ran across the atrium at the head of his men.

"Hurry it up," he shouted, and sprinted for the stairway.

He took them two at a time.

There was a small landing between each floor, which made four flights of stairs in all, but he was barely sweating when he reached the top.

He snapped his keycard off his belt and flicked it at the reader in a casual, cool gesture, like a card shark spinning a card from the deck.

The keycard caught the edge of the reader and flipped out of his hand into the stairwell below.

"Keycard, now." Ranger raised his hand and snapped his fingers. There was a brief pause and a card was thrust into his hand.

The bootsteps were on the landing at the top of the stairwell now. Behind Sam the doors to the control centre started to close automatically.

He turned Dodge in the opposite direction and steered him around the corner at the end of the passageway just as the stairwell door opened.

In this part of the corridor was a service elevator that nobody used.

Sam stabbed at the buttons frantically. The elevator was on the lower level and there was a whirr as the motors turned and it started to rise.

* * *

The double glass doors to the control centre opened and Ranger ran inside to a scene of chaos.

Kiwi lay on the ground in front of him, blood pouring from his nose. The others were spread around the room in various stages of shock.

Dodge and Sam's desks were empty.

"Which way?" Ranger shouted. Several people shrugged their shoulders.

Ranger thought quickly.

The door to the left led to the stairwell and past that, the washrooms and rest area. That was a dead end. To the right lay ... the service elevator!

"On me!" he yelled and raced back to the doors. They had closed and he lost half a second swiping the keycard through them.

Ranger made the end of the corridor in three lunging footsteps, and turned in time to see the doors of the elevator starting to close.

He dived forwards at full stretch.

His fingers impacted on solid metal.

The elevator began to descend.

Ranger picked himself up and returned to the corridor, racing for the stairs.

Kiwi stood in the doorway of the control centre, highly agitated.

"They've got my keycard," Kiwi shouted, gesturing at his belt. "They got my keycard!"

"They've got Kiwi's keycard," Ranger echoed back to his command post. "Lock it down, now."

Sam bundled Dodge out of the elevator in the basement. He put his shoulder under Dodge's arm again and tried to run. Dodge ran with him, somehow responding to the physical stimulus, although his face was blank and he did not speak.

They emerged in the entrance lobby, the stairwell to their left. In front of them was the airlock – the secure area, packed with sniffer and scanning equipment. Sam swiped Kiwi's keycard and the door opened. He pushed Dodge through and somehow they stumbled across to the outer door. He slid the keycard into that reader. The light changed to green, but before the doors could open it quickly snapped back to red.

He swiped the card again, but this time the light stayed resolutely red. Again he swiped it with the same result. From the corridor behind him he heard the sound of boots.

4. VIENNA

The doors slid open and Vienna was there, her keycard in her hand, a look of surprise and concern growing on her face as she saw Dodge.

"What's wrong with him?" she asked.

Vienna stared. Sam stared back, unsure what to say.

The airlock doors began to slide closed between them. Sam stepped forwards, blocking the doors with his foot. The inner door behind him would not open until the outer door was shut.

"We've been attacked again," he said.

"What? When?"

"Just now. Someone hacked into the building and attacked Swamp Witch, wiped her brain like the terrorists in Chicago, then tried to do the same to Dodge."

There was a hammering from the doors behind them.

"What the hell is going on?" Vienna asked. She took a few steps backwards, retreating into the parking area.

"Have you been on a neuro-connection today?" Sam asked.

"No," she said. "Why?"

"Dodge is in trouble," Sam said. "He's hurt and we need to get him to a hospital."

"No," Vienna said, regaining a little composure. "I don't know what you've done, but let's talk to Jaggard and sort it–"

"Listen to me, Vienna," Sam hissed. "The hackers have got inside the firewalls, and they've got through the neuro-firewalls. They've done ... something, I don't know what. They're manipulating Kiwi and Socks and Tactical and God knows who else. Help me get Dodge out of here and I'll tell you everything I know."

"Sam—"

"Vienna, Dodge is going to die unless you help me get him out of here now."

She started to say something to that, but stopped and stared at him intently for a moment.

Finally, she grabbed one of Dodge's arms. "Let's get him into one of the vans."

"You take him," Sam said.

The hammering from the inner door was getting louder, but it was supposed to be bulletproof and he knew it wouldn't open until the outer door shut. He ripped off his jacket and rolled it into a ball, wedging it into the doorway as the outer door began to shut. Unable to close properly, it slid open again.

Vienna was already pushing Dodge into the van. He was compliant, malleable, but said nothing. Sam ran to the van.

"I'll drive," Vienna shouted. "You get in the back with Dodge."

Vienna raced to the driver's side. "Put his seatbelt on," she added. "Yours too. Where are we going?"

"Right now, anywhere out of here."

Vienna hit the gas as Sam was still buckling Dodge's seatbelt. The van lurched forwards with a squealing noise and through the back windows he could see a cloud of black rubber smoke.

The sharp acceleration slammed him into the seat next to Dodge, and he grasped wildly for his own seatbelt, nearly falling out of his seat as the van careered around a concrete column towards the exit ramp.

Sam cried out. "They've shut the blast gates!"

Heavy metal, bombproof gates were trundling across the top of the ramp, shutting off the late afternoon sunshine.

"Not yet they haven't," Vienna said, and floored the gas pedal. The black and yellow barrier arm at the exit crumpled like paper and Vienna veered to the right, towards the rapidly closing gap. The edge of the gate scraped paint from the side of the van as they burst through into the sweet daylight outside.

"Where are we going?" she shouted. "We don't have long before they shut us down."

All government vehicles were fitted with the LoJack system that allowed them to be tracked by satellite, and remotely shut down if they were stolen.

Vienna spun out onto San Carlos Street, just about collecting a trio of middle-aged women in a BMW sedan. There were thuds and crashes from underneath as she bounced the vehicle over the light rail tracks in the centre of the road and the van leaned – surely on two wheels, Sam thought – as they twisted left onto the roadway heading east.

"Take the freeway," Sam said, getting an idea. "Head for the Great Mall. Maybe we can lose ourselves in the crowds."

In the CDD lobby Ranger raged at the closed interior door of the airlock.

"Ranger, it's Control."

"Go ahead, Control," he neuroed the response.

"Van four just left the car park at speed."

"Copy that. I need you to open the inner airlock doors and override the security system."

"Can't be done, sir. It's a mechanical system, not electronic. When one door is open it breaks the circuit."

Ranger grabbed the radio off his belt and keyed the mike.

"McTurck, it's Ranger, come in."

A voice responded almost immediately. "McTurck."

"Are you still on duty in the hotel lobby?"

"Yes, sir."

"Come over to the CDD underground car park, right now, we have a situation."

"On my way."

Ranger neuroed back to the command centre. "Get the blast doors back open so McTurck can get in. And locate van four on the LoJack, but don't shut it down yet. Wait till we get to it, otherwise they'll abscond on foot. And get an alert out to the police. Tell them we have two fugitives, one who appears to be semi-conscious. Give them a description of Dodge and Sam. Tell them not to apprehend them if spotted. I'd rather keep this in-house."

"Copy that," the confirmation came back from control.

"Where do you think they are headed?" one of his men asked.

"I don't know," Ranger replied. "And probably neither do they." A thought struck him and he mentally hit the neuro-communication button again. "Stay off the radio, use only neuro or cell phones. They'll be monitoring the radio in the van."

"There's a neuro-headset in the van too," Control pointed out. "They could be monitoring our neuro too."

"They won't be," Ranger said firmly, not even really sure how he knew that.

A sudden image intruded on his vision. A security cam feed from the parking garage. It was Vienna, helping Dodge into the van. Who had fed him the image, he could not tell.

"We are looking for three fugitives," he neuroed. "Vienna Smith is assisting them."

But where had that image come from?

Dodge's head had lolled forward, but when Sam lifted it, it stayed up.

"How long has it been?" Vienna shouted back without looking around.

"What?"

"Since we left CDD, you egg!"

Sam checked his watch. What time had they left? "At least five, maybe ten minutes," he guessed.

"Then why haven't they shut us down?" Vienna wondered. "It takes five minutes max to locate a vehicle on the LoJack and kill the engine. We've got to get off the freeway. Hang on!"

She shot across a couple of lanes without signalling, cutting in front of a delivery truck which delivered its annoyance with a blast on an air horn.

As they spun around the long looping off-ramp, she said, "We have to lose this van now and leg it to the mall. They know our exact location."

"It's not going to work," Sam said. "If they know where we are, it won't take them long to find us after we leave the van."

"I know," Vienna agreed.

In front of them a tow truck with a large orange towing arm and a mangy-looking dog standing upright on the tray turned on its hazard lights, and drifted to the side of the road.

"What time is it?" Vienna asked urgently. "I may have an idea."

"Four fifteen," Sam said.

To their right a small Mitsubishi car was parked on the side of the road, the only car on the roadway. A few yards before it a large sign proclaimed "No parking, 4 PM TO 6 PM Mon-Fri".

The tow truck, its lights flashing, pulled over to the curb in front of the car and began to back towards it.

Vienna signalled and cut over to the right as well, sliding to the curb with a squeal of brakes, just in front of the Mitsubishi.

"Get Dodge out now," she said. "And leave your cell phone, and his, in the van."

Sam slid the door open, and guided Dodge out of the van. A blast of cold air hit him. He wrapped his arms around himself and wished he had kept his jacket.

The tow truck driver was halfway out of his cab by now. A big hairy biker of a man. "Hey!" he yelled at them.

"Government plates," Vienna called back, and flipped him the bird. She grabbed Dodge's hand and began to walk briskly towards the huge shopping mall at the end of the avenue.

* * *

"Special Agent Ranger, this is Cuthbertson in Control."

"Go ahead, Control."

"The van has stopped, I repeat the van has stopped on the Montague Expressway."

Ranger cursed. They must have already escaped on foot. That would make things harder.

"Hold on a second," the voice sounded again in his head, "they're on the move again."

Sam and Vienna walked swiftly along Falcon Drive to the huge outdoor parking lot of the mall, Dodge trotting between them. Security cameras on tall poles were scattered around the area.

"Don't look up," Vienna said. "Just keep moving. The facial recognition software can't ping you if you don't look up."

That was easy, Sam thought. The wind was bitter, scything around the sides of the building, and it was natural to hunker down and shove your hands in your pockets.

Vienna led them away from the entrance to the mall, and around the side to a service lane.

She stopped at the entrance to the lane and scanned the walls of the surrounding buildings. "Two security cameras," she said.

"Where?" Sam asked.

She pointed them out. "They rotate to cover the whole

lane. When this near one is pointed away from us, run to the wall right below the camera, before it swings back and catches us. Do you think Dodge can do that?"

"Let's find out," Sam said.

The service lane was a long road, with concrete walls lining both sides. Nestled into the walls were large roll-up doors and smaller access doors. One or two of them were open, revealing loading docks inside. Signs next to each door gave the names of the retailers. Walmart, Borders, Sears.

"Okay," Vienna said, watching the camera. "Now!"

They each grabbed Dodge by an arm and hauled him along as they ran into the lane. They slammed into the wall beneath the camera just as it turned back the way they had come.

"See the Walmart door?" Vienna asked.

"Uh-huh."

Walmart was on the opposite side of the lane. The roll-up door was shut, but the access door next to it was open a couple of inches, propped open with a block of wood.

"Wait for the camera to swing back again," Vienna said, looking straight up at the camera. "Move!"

They tore across the alleyway to the door, pulling it shut behind them.

Inside it seemed dark. Long overhead fluorescents filled the area with a flickering alien glow, but after the sunlight outside it took their eyes a moment to adjust. The dock looked deserted.

They moved through into the warehouse of the big department store. Floor-to-ceiling shelving systems held every imaginable kind of product in flat, utilitarian racks. There were people moving around in here, but by carefully picking rows they were able to move through the warehouse without being spotted. A doorway on one side, near the entrance to the store itself, led into a dusty disused storeroom.

"Stay here. I'll be back shortly," Vienna said and turned to leave.

"Vienna?" Dodge asked faintly.

5. THE GREAT MALL

Ranger slammed the dashboard with the flat of his hand. "Come on!" he said to the driver for the third time in the last sixty seconds.

The van veered around the corner into South Abel Street, tyres smoking. The siren screamed at other traffic to stay out of their way.

"Ranger, it's Control. The van has turned onto the Nimitz Freeway."

Ranger thought about that for a moment. "Stupid kids. Okay, shut it down. We're just about there, and the next exit is not until California Circle. They'll be trapped on the freeway. Shut it down now."

"Confirming that, shutting down van four, now."

"Okay, all units, listen up," Ranger said, finally feeling that he was recovering control of the situation. "We're stopping the van on the freeway. Red Two, I want your team to keep moving over to California Circle and come in through the exit. Block them from getting out that way. We'll come up behind them."

"Ranger, it's Control again, we may have a problem."

"Go ahead."

"I've engaged the remote shutdown, but the van is still moving, sir."

Damn! Those hacker-kids must have found a way to disable the LoJack mechanism. He'd thought that was supposed to be impossible.

Vienna was back in a few moments with a couple of Walmart plastic shopping bags, packed with items.

"We won't have long," she said. "They'll backtrack from where we parked the van and find us on the parking lot cameras. We have to keep moving before they can close in on our trail."

"I hope you paid cash," Sam said, looking at the shopping bags.

She shook her head and rolled her eyes. "No, I used my credit card. Egg."

She pulled out some jackets and caps from the shopping bags. "We need to change our appearance. Just enough to fool the security cameras in store."

She handed Sam a long black Halloween witch's wig.

"You're kidding," Sam said.

"Don't worry about it," she said. "Up close it's obvious, but on the security cams they won't be able to tell. Here, stick this on too." She passed him a fake goatee.

She also put on a long black wig and pulled a short,

curly blond one down over Dodge's head, topping it off with an outsized baseball cap. She covered his black T-shirt with a padded nylon zippered jacket that Dodge wouldn't have been seen dead wearing under any normal circumstances.

"He looks like a cross between a clown and a rap artist," Sam muttered.

He pulled his wig on, and attached the fake beard around his mouth. Vienna passed him a knitted hat and a nondescript windbreaker, both of which he put on.

"You're not exactly the bachelor of the year yourself," Vienna said with a quick grin.

"I think you're enjoying this," Sam said.

"Having the time of my life," Vienna said, but the grin was gone. "Where do we go once we get into the mall? You got any ideas?"

Sam shook his head. "Not yet."

"Well, you'd better figure out something soon," Vienna said. "It won't take Tactical long to work out where we went."

"Maybe we can get down to the parking levels and borrow a car," Sam said.

"Maybe." Vienna didn't seem convinced.

Sam looked at Dodge. His eyes still seemed soft and vacant and since that one word, *Vienna*, he had not spoken.

"There will be cameras everywhere," Vienna said. "We'll try to stay in a crowd as much as possible. Make sure you never look directly at a camera. If you can't help it, put your hands in front of your face and pretend you're sneezing."

"Okay."

"Ready?"

"Ready."

From fifty yards away, through the growing crush of peak-hour traffic, Ranger could see the problem. They might have shut down the van, but the van was attached to the back of an A & A Towing tow truck.

The siren and lights made a path for them through the lanes and he pulled up alongside the truck, ordering the driver to pull over with the van's loudspeaker.

He was out of the van and up on the running board of the tow truck before it had even come to a halt.

"Where did you pick this up?" he shouted at the driver, although he was pretty sure he already knew.

The mall was bustling with shoppers and it was easy to lose themselves in the thick of the crowd. To his left Sam noticed a store with a huge, three-dimensional model of a neuro-headset displayed in the window. The name of the store was "Neuro-Tick", emblazoned on the wall above the store windows. The store's slogan underneath proclaimed: *Your store for everything Neuro.*

A few yards in front, Vienna was walking with her arm around Dodge, and his around hers. Her head was on his shoulder and his head rested on hers. To a casual viewer it looked like any boyfriend and girlfriend, with no indication that one of the couple was just a few notches above brain dead.

A girl in a white T-shirt walked towards him, wearing a neuro-cap – a baseball cap with a built in neuro-set – chatting animatedly to a friend walking next to her. Sam quickly pretended to sneeze, covering his face with his hands until she was gone.

He increased his pace, moving past Vienna and Dodge and muttering out of the corner of his mouth as he did so, "It's not just cameras we need to worry about. Keep away from anyone wearing neuro."

Vienna said nothing, but he knew she had heard. He stopped and looked in a store window for a moment to let them get back in front.

A young couple walked past wearing matching neuro-caps. They were smiling at each other, sharing secret thoughts. They did not glance at him; they were too besotted in each other. Sam felt that he had blinked and the whole world had turned neuro. Three months ago neuro-sets were a rare sight, but now everybody had them.

A security guard on a raised walkway was staring straight at him. Was that uniform cap a neuro-set too? Sam wondered.

The man looked away. It was not.

Vienna stopped in her tracks and turned towards Dodge, as if having a conversation with him, although Sam knew that was not possible. Not yet. He moved closer and glanced idly around the mall, paying no attention to them.

"ATM ahead," Vienna said. "Wait till someone goes to use it – that'll block the security camera."

"Okay," Sam said.

"Where are we heading?" Vienna asked. "Any ideas yet?"

"I'm not sure," Sam said. "But I know we have to keep moving."

Vienna nodded slightly, to let him know that she had heard. After a moment a large woman with a child in a stroller, and two more in tow, walked up to the ATM and inserted a card. Vienna started walking at once with Dodge. Sam counted to three, then followed her. They repeated the procedure at two more ATMs as they made their way towards the large centre court of the mall.

A sign caught his eye in a corridor that led off to the left.

Sam quickened his step and passed Vienna, whispering as he did so, "Follow me."

6. THE SEARCH

Ranger shut his eyes and flicked through the images that were neuro-feeding into his brain from Control. "That's got to be them walking through the parking lot."

The three figures were quite unmistakable.

"Here they are again, at the north-western end of the lot," Sergeant Hutchens said from the driver's seat. "And after that, nothing. Where did they go to?"

"They're in the mall somewhere. Nowhere else to go."

"But the entrance cameras didn't pick them up," Hutchens said. "Nor did any of the security cameras in the service areas."

"They're in the mall," Ranger said again, certain of it. "These kids know every trick in the book. If anyone can fool a security camera, they can. We're going in. Get mall security to man the exits while we sweep the mall. Bring in the police to maintain a cordon around the entire area."

"Mall security," Agent Amberly said from the rear of the van, handing Ranger a phone. "Duty manager, Bruce Gordon."

Ranger took the phone. "Gordon, my name is Special Agent Ranger from Homeland Security. Here is the situation. We have three fugitives hiding somewhere in the mall. We're sending you photos and descriptions. One of them may be semi-conscious. I want you to move all your security staff immediately to the exits. Circulate the photos to their cell phones. Also make your team aware that my men will be arriving shortly to begin a search. I want every exit covered, including trade and freight entrances. Make sure they can't get out. Any questions so far?"

Ranger looked casually around at the men in the van, relishing the feeling of power. The go-to guy. The man in charge.

"Okay, Gordon, thank you for your cooperation. We'll be picking up the feed from your security cameras, but it would help us if you could also watch your monitors closely."

He handed the cell back to Amberly. "Okay, let's move in. Handguns only and keep them in your holsters. The kids are not armed and we don't want to panic the public. Hutchens, can you assemble the units into search teams? Standard two by four."

Ranger stepped out of the van into the long shadows of the low afternoon sun and stretched, rolling his shoulders around to loosen them up, as he waited for the teams to assemble.

* * *

It was dark outside. Two hours of searching and nothing. Was it possible that they had slipped through his fingers again?

Ranger stood on the mezzanine and looked down over the first-floor shoppers. No. Somewhere in this huge complex, they were hiding. The exits were covered and the police had an outer cordon around that. There was no way out.

Hutchens appeared at the top of the escalator and jogged over.

"Anything?" Ranger asked.

"Nothing. We've been through all the storerooms, warehouses, washrooms, janitor's closets, everywhere."

"They're here somewhere," Ranger said. "Bring in a dog team; see if they can pick up the scent. Get something personal from their desks at CDD."

He punched a button on his cell phone.

"Gordon, it's Ranger. Anything suspicious?"

Gordon's voice sounded a little harassed through the cell phone. "No, sir. I'm closely monitoring every camera in the building myself, and I'll let you know at once if I see any trace of your three missing agents."

"Thanks, Gordon," Ranger said and rang off.

An uneasy feeling settled in his stomach, as if he'd eaten something that disagreed with him, but that wasn't it. Something troubled him about that call. He drummed his fingers on the polished wood railing of the mezzanine floor, thinking. How had Gordon known the fugitives were CDD agents? He hadn't mentioned that, had he?

"We have a positive identification on the girl," Hutchens said, interrupting his thoughts.

"Where and when?"

"An hour or so ago. A store assistant at Walmart remembers her. Paid cash."

"What did she buy?"

"Wigs, fake beards, that kind of thing."

Disguises!

"Send me pictures of the clothes now," Ranger said and waited a second or two while Hutchens flashed through images. "Control?"

"Control here."

"Feed me through the central mall cameras, last two hours, ten second intervals, two per second."

"On its way."

Ranger shut his eyes and waited for the images to arrive. The centre of the mall appeared in his vision and he watched carefully. There! A young couple: a blond male and a female with long black hair, cuddling each other as they walked through the mall. Behind them a male in a windbreaker and a woollen hat. That had to be Sam.

He traced their progress through the mall then lost them in a crush of shoppers. He tried a different camera angle, without success. And another.

Where were they?

He alerted his teams and picked up the phone to call Gordon again.

7. THE PHANTOM

Sam watched Dodge sleep. Even the sound of the ringing phone did not disturb him at all. His face was peaceful. He lay curled in a ball on the floor of the office.

"Security, Gordon." The security officer answered the call on speakerphone, as Sam had instructed.

"Gordon, it's Ranger again. New information. The fugitives have changed their appearance, using wigs and beards. They have also changed their clothing." Ranger went on to describe their outfits and appearance. Gordon noted it all down carefully, all the time staring at the people that were being described.

"Okay, got that," Gordon said at last. "Anything else?"

"No, that's it for now. Keep us informed."

Gordon hung up the phone.

"Good boy," Vienna said pleasantly, aiming Gordon's own gun at him.

Their CDD security IDs had got them through the door, and Vienna had swiftly relieved Gordon of his side-arm.

Gordon must have been in his fifties, Sam thought, and

looked as though he had been doing this job all his life. His stomach hung heavy over a straining belt and if his nose reflected the state of his liver, then his liver was in real trouble. His complexion was ruddy, and his uniform wouldn't recognise an iron. He hadn't been happy when Vienna had taken his gun, and he looked less happy every minute.

Dodge stirred and snorted in his sleep. Sam looked at the tattoo on his forehead and hoped that wasn't too close to the truth. Was Dodge's brain now just a biohazardous wasteland?

"Should I wake him up?" Sam asked. "Isn't it bad for people who have concussion, or something, to sleep?"

"Let him sleep," Vienna said. "That concussion thing is just a myth. Right now his brain is trying to repair itself. Let's just hope that when he wakes up he's okay."

"And if he isn't?"

She didn't reply.

Ranger retraced the steps of the three fugitive CDD agents through the main thoroughfare of the mall, stopping every few paces to close his eyes and compare the neuro-fed images from the security cameras with his surroundings.

Hutchens, a pace in front, ran interference, cutting a path for him through the crowd. Not that it took much doing: the black combat suits and helmets acted as a natural defoliant, a crowd repellent.

The dogs had picked up the trail of the fugitives in the rear storeroom of Walmart, but had lost it in the heavily trafficked main thoroughfare.

"Right here," Ranger said. "This is the last image we have of them. After that they move out of range of the camera, and they don't appear on the next one."

He looked to the left and the right. To the right, a jewellery store with a huge fake diamond rotating slowly in the window joined onto a clothing store for teenagers.

"We've looked everywhere," Hutchens said. "Storerooms, changing rooms, everywhere. And there are no rear exits."

"Come with me," Ranger said. "I want to pay a visit to our friend Gordon in security."

"Where the bleedin' hell are we?"

Sam jumped. He had almost nodded off. He spun around to see Dodge sitting up, looking around with suspicion and concern.

"Dodge! You're awake!" he said with huge relief in his voice.

"And the sky is blue and the Bears are going to win the World Series," Dodge said. "Is it 'state the bleedin' obvious day' today or are you just practising for stupid school?"

"Tell me your name," Sam said, peering as deeply as he could into Dodge's eyes, not sure what he was looking for. He tried to remember the questions they asked on TV shows to see if a person was properly conscious.

"Fozzie Bear, what's yours? Ya muppet."

"How many fingers am I holding up?" Sam asked, holding up three.

"I dunno. How many fingers am I holding up?" Dodge replied, holding up just one middle finger. "Now where the bleedin' hell are we?"

"Security centre at the Great Mall," Vienna said from her chair at the control panel. The pistol sat on the desk in front of her, right by her hand. It still pointed at the guard.

"Why?" Dodge asked.

"What's the last thing you remember?" Sam asked.

Dodge furrowed his brow. "We were at CDD. Working. On the trail of the phantom. We..." he faltered.

"Let me fill in the blanks," Sam said, and spent the next few minutes doing so.

"Who's Ursula?" Vienna asked when he had finished. "You mentioned her a couple of times in your sleep."

Dodge shook his head and got to his feet. He seemed a little shaky, and swayed back and forth, finally holding onto the wall to steady himself.

"Ursula," he said vaguely, shaking his head. "I don't know. But I know who's doing this. I must have worked out most of it just before I got zapped. Figured out the rest while I was sleeping, I guess."

"You know who the phantom is?" Sam asked.

"There is no phantom," Dodge said. "There are no

hackers, or terrorists, apart from those two that got wiped out."

"Then who is it?" Sam asked.

"Who's doing this?" Vienna asked almost simultaneously.

"We are," Dodge said.

8. EXIT STRATEGY

"Lie back down," Sam said. "I don't think you're quite ready to be standing up."

"I'm fine," Dodge said, although he swayed a bit on his feet as he said it.

"Explain," Vienna said.

"It's us. Not you, me and Sam here, but just about everyone else. Everyone with a neuro-connection that is."

"I'm still not getting it," Vienna said, although Sam was starting to.

Dodge said, "They introduced neuro-connections, what, a year ago? The take-up has been phenomenal. Faster than cell phones. And in the last few months sales have gone off the charts. There are millions of people neuro-connected all over the world."

"So?"

"So what happens when you join millions of brains together? What do you get?"

"I don't know," Sam said.

"Nobody knows," Dodge said.

"Are you suggesting that all these connected brains

are somehow working together?" Vienna asked.

"Maybe. Some kind of collective consciousness," Dodge said.

"I thought the neuro-firewalls were supposed to isolate us," Sam said.

"Did they isolate Swamp Witch?" Dodge asked.

There was silence.

"And it's more than that," Dodge said. "The millions of brains are not just connected to each other, but to the internet itself. This 'consciousness' has access to every computer in the world, almost. To every bit and byte of human knowledge. Its eyes are every security cam; every spy satellite; every live neuro-headset."

"A meta-system," Vienna said. "That's what you're talking about. But who's Ursula?"

"She's a sim. One of the training instructors from the neuro-headset software," Sam said. "Haven't you done your training yet?"

"Only just got the headset," Vienna said.

Sam said, "I think Dodge must have associated her in his mind with this 'meta-system'. While he was sleeping."

"Why attack Swamp Witch?" Vienna asked. "Why attack you?"

"My best guess," Dodge said, "is that this meta-system, let's call it Ursula for now, has a very basic, almost childlike, concept of good and bad, of right and wrong. She knew the terrorists were bad so she erased them, like we would erase a computer virus if we found it on our hard drive. Spam, gaming, the same. It's bad, so delete it."

"And Swamp Witch? Was she bad?" Vienna asked.

"She was a threat," Sam said.

Dodge agreed. "Ursula is only a few months old, remember. Just a child in a dark room with a stick. If she feels fear, she hits out at what scares her."

"Even human beings? You said she had a sense of right and wrong," Vienna said.

"I'm not sure she understands what human beings are," Dodge said. "To her, Swamp Witch was just a bug in the code."

"And she got debugged," Sam added.

"Have you guys had your meds today?" Gordon shook his head, disbelieving.

"You still here?" Vienna asked in a surprised tone.

Gordon rolled his eyes and rattled the handcuff that was fastening him to his desk.

"So what now?" Sam asked.

"I don't know," Vienna said. "There's nowhere to run and there's nowhere to hide. If this meta-system – Ursula – exists, then there's no escape from her. She has access to the network–"

"She *is* the network," Dodge said. "She..." His voice thickened and trailed off. He shut his eyes and swayed from side to side.

"Dodge!"

Dodge's eyes opened, but they were blank and unseeing, as before. With an effort, they slowly focused and Sam could see the consciousness returning.

"Are you so sure that she's bad?" Vienna asked. "It seems to me that you're basing a lot of assumptions on what happened to Swamp Witch."

Dodge shook his head. "Today she erased someone she saw as a threat. Yesterday it was spammers and phishers. The day before she targeted gaming sites. Who's to say that tomorrow it won't be based on race or religion? Or height. Human beings have all kinds of prejudices. How many people does it take to feel strongly about something before their collective consciousness, Ursula, decides that it is bad and gets rid of it?"

"We have to warn the public," Sam said. "Tell them not to use their neuro-connections."

"That could cause a panic," Vienna said.

"The more people that plug in, the more powerful she is," Sam said. "We've got to warn them."

"What we have to do," Vienna said, "is to find a way out of here, before they figure out where we are."

Dodge fingered the skull hanging from a chain around his neck and said, "I think it's time to open the crypt."

9. THE CRYPT

"I call it 'the Plague'. It's a crypto-virus," Dodge whispered. "I think it's our only chance."

They were huddled in a far corner of the room, out of earshot of Gordon.

"A crypto-virus?" asked Sam.

Vienna said, "I read a bit of the work that Young and Yung did in the field."

Dodge said, "The Plague is an encrypting virus."

He took off his skull necklace and pulled off the jaw, revealing a USB3 plug underneath.

"This is the nastiest, deadliest, most poisonous bit of code you will ever dream of. I wrote it about two years ago and have been refining it ever since. I keep it with me, hoping that I will never be in such a desperate situation that I might have to think about using it."

"Like now," Vienna said.

Dodge nodded. "The Plague encrypts everything it finds. Secure 2048-bit encryption. The virus can still read it, as it has the decryption key built in, but nothing else can. The machine becomes totally unusable, except by the virus. It replicates and spreads. It operates at the micro-code level, even below machine code, so it doesn't matter what operating system is on the computer. If it encounters a firewall, it encrypts that too and passes through it. Backup files, everything."

"Dodge," Vienna said slowly, "you know that if that got released into the wild, it would destroy the computer infrastructure of the entire country."

"The entire world," Dodge said. "It was far too dangerous to ever think about releasing, so I rewrote it. I built in a safeguard. A time limit. After twenty-four hours it reverses. It starts decrypting. It spreads the same way as before, but decrypts everything it finds."

"What's your plan?" Vienna asked.

"Simple," Dodge replied. "Release the virus through the computers here in this room. Give it an hour or so to spread, and then get the hell out of the city while the networks are all shut down. We'll have a twenty-four-hour window to get clear, before it all starts up again."

"Then what?" Vienna asked.

"I don't know," Dodge admitted.

"Can you rewrite the code?" Sam asked. "Remove the time limit?"

Dodge nodded, but said, "That's far too dangerous though. What if it got loose?"

"What if we set it loose?" Sam said. "What if we unleashed the full version against Ursula?"

Vienna gasped.

"You'll kick the world back to the Stone Age," Dodge whispered.

"The world will survive that," Sam said. "But I don't think it will survive Ursula."

"But we still have to get out of here, and it's crawling with Tactical and surrounded by the police," Vienna said.

"I've been thinking about that," Sam said. "And I may have a plan. But even if we can escape from the mall, we'll only have twenty-four hours! And then if we get out of San Jose, Ursula has eyes and ears everywhere. Where can we possibly hide out while you modify the virus?"

"That's easy," Dodge said, glancing over to make sure Gordon could not hear them. "The safest place on earth. Built to withstand any kind of attack, including chemical or nuclear."

"Where?" Sam asked.

"Cheyenne Mountain," said Vienna.

"Agent Ranger, it's Control." The voice sounded alarmed.

Ranger stopped halfway down the hallway towards the security office."Go ahead, Control."

"PD reports a helicopter approaching the mall, appears to be coming in to land on the rooftop helipad."

"The roof!" Hutchens swore violently.

"Get everybody up there now," Ranger said calmly. "Maintain the mall security guards at the exits, but I want all agents to converge on the roof. What kind of chopper is it, Control?"

"PD reports a charter bird. 'California Choppers'."

"Get hold of their office, immediately. Find out who booked it and see if you can stop it from touching down. Also get a police chopper in the air, tell them to shadow the target until we advise further."

"Copy that."

"Let's get up there," Hutchens said, turning to leave.

"You go," Ranger said. "Find them and hold them. I still want to talk to Gordon."

"Okay, that's it. The file's uploaded to the main computer system at CNN," Sam said. "At seven pm exactly it takes over the teleprompter software. As soon as it finishes executing, it'll infect the system with the Plague. From there it should spread rapidly."

"Shame we won't be here to watch it," Vienna said, watching the security monitors carefully. "Tactical are all heading for the roof. We need to move, now. Before they figure out that the chopper is just a diversion."

"Are you okay, Dodge?" Sam asked. Dodge had that vacant look in his eyes again, and was starting to sway.

"Now please, Mr Gordon," Vienna said.

Gordon gave her a dirty look but picked up his radio. "Reid, Carson, report in."

A voice came back immediately. "All clear here, sir."

Gordon sighed before keying the radio and continuing, "Okay. Looks like they've located the fugitives on the roof. I want you to get over to the central elevators and secure the base of the roof elevator. Make sure they can't come down that way."

"What about the entrance, sir?"

"The police will cover it from outside. I need you at the elevators, now."

"On our way, sir."

"And so are we," Vienna said. "Thanks for all your help."

Gordon just grunted.

Sam said, "Whatever you think of us, you need to avoid using a neuro-headset. You put your life at risk if you do."

"Whatever," Gordon grunted again, but Sam had a feeling that he would take that piece of advice at least.

Vienna put Gordon's gun out of sight in her jacket and took his radio. She picked up the telephone that was on the desk in front of him and wrenched out the handset. A rack on the wall yielded a couple of long, heavy security flashlights.

"It's almost seven – let's go," Sam said, opening the door.

He took one step into the corridor and stopped, staring into the steady eyes and even steadier pistol of Special Agent Ranger.

"Or not," Ranger said.

10. CNN

Ben O'Hara shuffled the papers on the news desk in front of him and smiled studiously and professionally at the camera. The red light on top of the camera was not yet on, but it was only a matter of seconds away, and he didn't want to be caught with a frown or a blank expression when the world tuned in to see his newscast. The papers he was holding were blank. They were a prop, put there by the studio crew to make him look studious and professional.

The floor manager said, "In five, four..." She closed her mouth and held up three fingers, then two, then one.

The light turned red and she pointed at Ben.

"Good evening," Ben said, in his richest, bulletin-opening voice. "And welcome to *CNN Evening News*. In breaking news tonight..." Even as he read the words from the teleprompter, his mind was telling him that there was a problem. There had been no breaking news when they had rehearsed the bulletin just ten minutes ago. If there was now, the news director would have warned him, would have whispered into the tiny earphone that was clipped into his right ear. He had no choice but to continue though.

The words on that screen were the words of CNN and a billion people were waiting for him to deliver them.

"A dangerous computer virus has been identified and tracked across the globe."

What the hell...?

"Known as the 'neuro-virus' this hitherto unknown virus has been described as extremely dangerous by security analysts. It spreads through neuro-connections, infecting human brains through neuro-headsets. Once infected, a person may start to exhibit strange behaviour. The public are asked to watch out for this symptom in neuro-users. There is no known cure for this virus, and all computer users are asked to avoid using neuro-headsets for the conceivable future."

He had a neuro-headset in his office. Why hadn't he been warned about this?

"Users are also advised to expect a massive denial and cover-up of the virus as neuro technology corporations look to safeguard their investments. The Government is also expected to deny the existence of this destructive new virus which experts warn may also be able to infect and destroy ordinary computer networks."

He saw movement from the corner of his eye and glanced over at the floor manager, who was making an urgent throat-cutting gesture at him.

"Cut to break!" A voice shouted in his earphone.

"I'm Ben O'Hara, you're watching CNN, and we'll be back after this short message." When the red light went out he said, not very studiously or professionally, "What the hell is going on?"

"Story's a fake," the news director said in his ear. "Somebody hacked into our teleprompter system and planted it. We've got everybody from Telecomerica to the Pentagon on the line denying it."

But the story said they would deny it, didn't it?

The voice in his ear continued, "We're back in two or three minutes with a retraction. They're just drafting it now. It'll be keyed up on the teleprompter when we go back. The key points are that there is no such virus; it is just a hoax. There is no danger either to neuro-connections or to ordinary computer networks. The Pentagon is sending over a specialist for us to interview and—"

The voice cut off, replace by a high-pitched electronic whine that stung his ear. Ben tore out the earphone with a cry and left it dangling from his collar.

He looked up at the control booth to see the news director gesticulating furiously. The red light on the camera began to flash and he tore his attention back to the teleprompter computer. It was filled with gibberish.

Overhead the studio lights suddenly went out.

11. CAPTURE

Ranger kept his gun level, and steady.

Sam stood in the doorway and stared at him, his mouth, and his eyes, wide open.

"Where's Dodge?" Ranger asked.

Vienna's eyes flicked to the side and Ranger nudged the door open a bit wider with his boot.

Dodge stood to one side, staring off at nothing, his eyes vacant and a strand of drool hanging from the corner of his mouth.

"Shame," Ranger said. "He was a good kid. Maybe the doc can fix him up when we get you back to CDD."

"You know that'll never happen," Vienna spat at him. "You saw what happened to Swamp Witch. That's what's going to happen to all three of us if you take us back in."

"Save the dramatics for the trial," Ranger said calmly. "Now turn around and face the wall."

They did, except for Dodge, who stayed in the centre of the room and drooled.

Ranger tried to flick off a quick neuro-message to the team, but there seemed to be something wrong with the connection. Either his headset or the neuro-network was offline. A glance at the security console showed that most of the monitors were dead also, and the central computer screen showed only a blue screen covered with error messages.

No matter, he still had his radio. He stepped forward, covering Vienna and Sam with his gun as he pulled his handcuffs off his belt. He just had the one pair, but that would do until backup arrived. There were only two of them to be concerned about, and he could handcuff them to each other.

A guard, Gordon no doubt, was handcuffed to the security desk. He seemed confused about what was going on.

"Am I glad to see you," Gordon said. "Agent Ranger?"

"That's right," Ranger said. "Have they been in here the whole time?"

"Since before you first called, yes. They had a gun on me, told me what to say."

"Figures," Ranger said, holstering his pistol and grasping Sam's wrist. "Can you tell me if they have done anything, other than just hiding out in here?"

"Yes. After the punk one woke up, they uploaded some kind of computer file, maybe a virus, to somewhere. They didn't say where."

Ranger's brain was still registering the words "the punk one woke up" when he felt a tug at the back of his neck as his neuro-headset was forcibly unplugged. At the same instant his pistol was lifted from his holster. He made a grab for it, and started to spin around but it was already far too late.

"Hello, guv'nor," Dodge said. "You missed me?"

12. DARKNESS

Sam led the way, groping along the corridors in the minimal light from the emergency lighting, the only thing in the mall that was still operating.

Ranger followed him, his arms cuffed behind his back and a pistol pressed against his spine by Vienna, close behind. He had been stripped of his armour, helmet and boots, as they contained tracking devices. His belt radio was in the hands of Dodge, at the rear of the small party.

When they reached the main thoroughfare Sam's first impression was of chaos, people moving in every direction without reason, without purpose.

He quickly realised that was wrong though. Those people were heading for the exits, while others congregated in groups, standing or sitting in the middle of the mall, waiting for the lights to come back on. There was a sense of confidence. Confidence in the abilities of those in charge to restore order and stability.

How little they really knew!

He saw a woman trying to use a cell phone, shaking

the phone with frustration as if somehow that would help it connect.

Some practical-minded people had flashlights, either purchased, or more likely "borrowed", from the department stores or hardware stores in the mall.

"One of the Tactical teams is trapped in an elevator," Dodge said from behind them, one ear to Ranger's radio. "But the rest are coming down the emergency stairs on the west of the building. The dog team is coming back from the north corner. They're all looking for Ranger. Wondering why he isn't responding to the radio."

"Should we give Ranger the radio, tell him what to say, like we did with Gordon?" Sam asked.

Dodge shook his head. "Tactical have special code words to indicate that they are in trouble. Better to leave them guessing."

The sliding doors at the south-western entrance to the mall had been shut when the power had gone off, but someone had forced them open using the legs of a chair as a lever.

The gap was narrow, and they had to join a queue of people trudging through. From the darkness in the centre of the mall, Sam could hear barking and he knew the dog teams were not far away. He hurriedly squeezed through to the outside.

The temperature had dropped from earlier in the day, and with the night had also come a freezing rain. It pierced through his jacket and stung like needles on the bare skin of his face, long watery icicles, exploding in pools of water on the street.

Sam wrapped his arms around himself and stood to one side, trying to get some cover from the overhang of the mall roof, as the others came through the gap.

They crept down Fairlane Drive, avoiding the police cars and crossed over the Great Mall Parkway into McCandless Drive. In the middle of the parkway they had to pass under a train, lifeless, lightless, and stranded in the middle of the elevated light rail tracks. From inside, frightened eyes peered down at the dark, wet streets that surrounded them.

They continued down the wide, tree-lined avenue, using their fingers to narrow the flashlights down to pencil-thin beams. In the light the rain made long white scratches on the wall of blackness around them.

Ranger's radio crackled back into life as they neared the spillway bridge and in the relative quiet of McCandless Drive, Sam could hear the voices clearly.

"Hutchens, this is Dog One, we have a scent trail outside the main doors, heading down Fairlane, over."

"Copy that. All teams converge on Fairlane."

"Kill the flashlights, quick!" Sam said. "And get off the bridge, get down into the spillway."

Dodge pushed Ranger roughly sideways, but he kept his feet and followed Sam, clambering over a low mesh fence and down a steep bank covered in tussock grass towards the spillway canal.

Sam risked a flash of his light here in the dip, out of sight of their pursuers. The water looked murky with patches of dark green. It spluttered and spat under the impact of the rain. It also looked freezing cold but fortunately, there was sufficient dry bank on either side for them to clamber along under the bridge without getting wet. They crouched beneath the thick concrete span and waited silently.

The sound of running footsteps came from above them and strong flashlights splayed out across the water. At the point where they had left the roadway, the sounds paused, but did not stop, the dogs losing the scent in the rain and moving on across the bridge overhead.

Ranger made no sound, mostly due to the fact that the barrel of Vienna's pistol was firmly wedged in his mouth.

"It won't take them long to realise they've lost the scent," Vienna said. "We need to move. Get in the water – it'll kill the trail for the dogs."

Sam took one more look at the murky, sludgy canal water and obeyed without hesitation. There was a faintly putrid smell to the water, a whiff of decayed vegetation. It filled his shoes and soaked his jeans, sending shock waves of cold through his body.

"Go west," Vienna whispered, pointing in the darkness. "The canal splits and they won't know which way we've gone."

At the spillway intersection they turned north, heading back towards the Great Mall but well below the level of the road.

"Move it!" Dodge said, prodding Ranger in the back. They all picked up the pace, trying to get as much distance between their pursuers and themselves as possible.

"Wait here," Vienna said a few minutes later, clambering up the bank through the tussock grass.

Lights turned the corner of the canal, and they could hear the voices of the searchers, no more than thirty or forty yards away.

"Where is she?" Sam whispered urgently.

"She'll be here," Dodge replied. The sound of a large engine came from the top of the bank, and Vienna's voice hissed. "Up here, quick."

"There!" A shout came from behind them.

Ranger tried to delay them as they climbed the steep bank, but Dodge grabbed his wrists and lifted, twisting Ranger's arms up so that he gave a small cry of pain, and had to keep stumbling forwards to take off the pressure.

"Freeze!" voices called from behind them, but Sam ignored them, hauling on the long damp strands of tussock to help himself to the top of the bank.

A small van, a black Volkswagen Transporter, was pulled up to the fence, its engine idling, its lights off. The side door was open and Dodge jerked Ranger roughly over the fence and threw him through the opening, where he landed facedown on the carpet.

"Freeze! Armed Federal Agents. Do not move or we will fire upon you!"

"Get in," Dodge yelled. "They won't shoot, not while we have Ranger."

Sam threw himself in the open door on top of Ranger and felt Dodge climb in beside him. Dark figures appeared at the fence behind them and he rolled over and grabbed the handle of the door, slamming it shut.

No sooner had he done that than it opened again and a black-suited figure was reaching into the van.

Sam kicked the man as hard as he could in the chest, and the man staggered backwards as the tyres spun in the wet, gripped, and the van took off at speed, the soldier falling away into the darkness behind them.

They saw the helicopter before it saw them; the huge "night sun" floodlight washing away the darkness from the roadway in front of them and filling the air below it with a heavy curtain of rain. Vienna spun the van off the road as the massive circle of light approached and hid beneath the canopy of a group of trees in front of a used car lot.

The helicopter passed by without seeing them. "Time to change cars," Vienna said, the van crawling slowly down the long rows of the car lot.

She stopped alongside a black Ford pickup twin cab with raised suspension and outsized, off-road wheels. It towered over the other cars in the dark of the lot.

"This'll do," she said.

13. THE VALLEY OF DEATH

The darkness was overwhelming. Without streetlights, the streets and buildings were black against the black of the sky, an enveloping night punctuated only by the lights of vehicles, and the flashing red and blues of police cruisers.

Into this darkness drifted ever-present, freezing rain, lighter than before and invisible, except where it caught the police lights.

The intersection of the Parkway and South Main Street was blocked with cars, at least six of them jammed together in a multi-car pile-up, no doubt caused by the sudden loss of street and traffic lights. The drivers were standing around yelling at each other in the darkness. Vienna swung the wheel sharply, the pickup lifting and tilting as she cut left across the centre line, aiming straight at a pair of ornate wrought-iron gates in a wall surrounding an apartment building.

"Hold on!" she yelled, but it wasn't necessary. The blunt knife that was the front bumper of the pickup sliced through the gates as if they were made of cardboard, twisted metal spinning away to the sides.

They raced through a construction site, with timber stacked in tidy piles, over some scrubby ground and through another fence, this one just a plastic orange safety fence.

Then they were out on South Abel Street, and Vienna put her foot down, regardless of the people who had to jump out of the way.

An overturned car, on fire, blocked the road ahead. Clearly visible in the flickering yellow flames, the dazed occupants sat on the curb.

This time Vienna didn't stop, didn't change course; she just veered slightly, aiming for the trunk of the car. There was a jarring crunch and then they were past. Sam looked back to see the car spinning and burning like a giant Roman candle.

Sirens on police cars wailed as they circled around, aimlessly, helpless in the omnipresent darkness.

Sounds of smashing glass came from both sides and the sound of shredded tyres somewhere nearby was followed by the sickening thud of an accident.

A police car pulled out of a side street and raced up behind them, lights flashing. Before Sam could even warn the others, however, a four-wheel drive slid out of a side street, sideswiping the police car, which screeched to a halt and fell away behind them.

They took Calaveras Boulevard out to the Sinclair Freeway interchange, then north on I-680.

The rain eased, then stopped as they rolled out into

the desert. Sam sank back into the upholstery and said nothing, exhausted by the day's events.

Ranger glared at him from the rear seat, handcuffed to the doorhandle.

"We don't have time to get to Cheyenne," Vienna said. "Even if we drive through the night. Someone will have reported this car stolen before then. We'll have to hide the pickup and change cars again."

"What do you think, Dodge?" Sam asked.

Dodge looked blank.

"We need to do something," Vienna said harshly, "or Tactical will be all over us when Ursula comes back online."

Sam looked back at Dodge. He looked tired and confused.

"I have an idea," Sam said. "I know somewhere we could go."

"Where?" Dodge asked.

Sam shook his head. "The less Ranger knows, the better."

They stopped in Livermore where the streets were dark, but deserted, and Sam and Vienna went shopping with the aid of a tyre iron from the rear of the pickup.

They stopped at a food store, a hardware supplies store and an electronics store, in that order. Sam helped

Vienna load cartons of food into the tray of the pickup, along with boltcutters and other tools that he thought they might need. The hardware store had a good supply of hazmat suits and he took four.

The electronics store yielded a laptop computer and a sensor device in a black leather carry case. Sam stowed the device in the back of the pickup, being careful not to let Ranger see it.

At the end of the short shopping spree, Vienna climbed behind the wheel and took them back onto the interstate.

It was dark and hilly, but the lights of the pickup reached out in front of them, clawing back the night, and they made good time, veering around to the south-east and merging onto the I-5 towards Los Angeles.

The pickup had a GPS navigation unit, but it was offline. The whole world was currently offline, Sam thought. There was a map book in the glove compartment though, and he flicked the reading light on to help him study it.

"Stay on the interstate until we get to exit 278," he said. "Take Highway 46 towards Wasco."

Vienna's eyes narrowed for a moment, then opened in understanding. "Through to Bakersfield, right?"

"Yeah."

Dark farmland stretched out to their left, and even darker mountains to their right, illuminated only by starlight.

Sam yawned, and wondered how Vienna was

managing to stay awake. Hours passed and the landscape started to blur outside his window into a kaleidoscope image of heavy black and brown shapes.

"You won't get away with this," Ranger said abruptly, yanking Sam back to full consciousness. "It was bad enough before, but kidnapping a Federal Agent is going to add years to your jail time."

"What did they do?" Vienna asked, her hands tensing on the steering wheel. "I wasn't there, remember? You tell me. What did they do that was so bad?"

"You could get off lightly," Ranger said by way of reply. "You weren't involved at the start, and you could say you were duped or pressured by these two into being an accessory. I'd support you."

"Thanks, I appreciate that," Vienna said. "So what exactly did these two mugs do, that had a whole troop of Tactical chasing them out of the CDD building?"

"They attacked Swamp Witch," Ranger said. "We still don't know how, but they used some kind of technology to induce a neurological event. Same thing happened in Chicago, and guess who was on the spot that time as well. Dodge and Sam. I think that Swamp Witch found out what they were up to and tried to stop them."

"We never attacked Swamp Witch," Sam said. "That was—"

Vienna cut him off. "How do you know it was them? For sure."

"I saw the security footage," Ranger replied. "I saw the

two of them coming out of the swamp, and then Swamp Witch started screaming."

"We never—" Sam began, but Vienna held up a hand to silence him.

"Shut up, Sam. I want to hear Ranger's version," she said. "So you can clearly remember Sam and Dodge coming out before Swamp Witch screamed?"

"As clear as you're sitting in front of me now."

"What if you never saw that at all?" Vienna asked.

"I saw it," Ranger said firmly.

"I know, but what if it was a false memory that had been implanted in your brain? How would you know the difference?"

"I saw it," Ranger said again.

"You remember seeing it. What if that memory was false? How would you know?"

"You're the bright one, you tell me," Ranger said.

"You wouldn't know," Sam said. "Not if you thought it was a genuine memory."

"We are our memories," Dodge said. "That's all we are. That's what makes us the person we are. The sum of all our memories from the day we were born. If you took a person and replaced his set of memories with another set, he'd be a different person. He'd think, act and feel things differently."

"I know what I remember," Ranger said.

"You're missing the point," Vienna said. "If it was possible to implant a false memory, of something that never happened, then to you that memory would be as real as if it really did happen."

"How is that even possible?" Ranger scoffed.

"Through a neuro-headset," Vienna said simply and Sam could see Ranger considering that.

"Why would anyone do that?" Ranger said. "What motivation would these people have to frame Dodge and Sam, even if it were possible?"

"Because 'these people' were the real culprits," Vienna said. "They were the ones who attacked Swamp Witch. Dodge and Sam figured out who they were, so to cover themselves they implanted memories to blame Dodge and Sam."

"I had orders from Jaggard," Ranger protested.

"You think he doesn't have a neuro-headset?" Sam asked. "They got at him too."

"Even if it's true," Ranger said, "give yourselves up now before things get any worse. Let me take you in and I promise that neither you, nor I, will go within ten feet of a neuro-set until the end of your trial."

"It's too late for that," Sam said, an image of Kiwi coming into his head, his finger pointed accusingly. "Too many people have already been affected."

Ranger lapsed into silence and stared out of the window at nothing.

Sam said, "How do any of us know that anything is real?"

"We don't," Dodge said.

"Everything I know is a memory," Sam continued. "Every person I ever met, everything I have ever done. It could all be false. Implanted."

It was a staggering thought. What if nothing that had gone before had ever really happened? Were the people he remembered as his mother and father really his parents? Had Fargas even existed, except in his mind?

"I think you'd know," Vienna said. "I don't know why, but somehow, I think you'd know."

Sam slept for a while and only woke when the pickup truck slowed down to the side of the road and stopped. It was already light, and he wondered where they were. An image of a road sign stuck in his mind, something they must have passed somewhere along the way: Death Valley Road.

Where was Death Valley? His waking mind struggled to put it into context. Then it came to him.

"Time to get geared up," he said. "There are some protective suits in the back and we all need to wear them."

Outside, the early morning light glinted coldly off the barbs of a high barricade fence that straddled the highway directly in front of them.

Signs mounted on the fence said *Danger* and *No Admittance*. A large triangular sign had a skull in one corner, a running man in another, and a radiation symbol in the third.

Further down the highway, about twenty yards beyond the barricades, the grimy, dust-covered remains of a sign were embedded upside down in the dirt.

Welcome to Fabulous Las Vegas, Nevada.

14. SIN CITY

"You've got to be kidding." Ranger was the one who said it, but Sam could see it on Dodge's face also.

Even Vienna, who had already guessed their destination, seemed unsure now that they were faced with the high barricaded fence that prevented entry to the contamination zone.

At Jean, the last inhabitable town before the zone, they had turned off the highway, continued north towards Vegas on the old Boulevard until they had reached the fence.

"You scared of a little fallout?" Sam asked, keeping his voice deliberately light. In truth, he too was starting to wonder if this was a good idea, after all.

"It's a radioactive wasteland," Ranger said. "A couple of hours in there and you'll start glowing in the dark."

"Just put your suit on," Sam said.

"No way," Ranger said.

"Okay." Sam smiled at him. "If you want to go into the zone without a hazmat suit, that's up to you."

Ranger stared at him for a moment before taking the proffered suit and mask.

"Masks too?" Vienna asked.

"I think we're okay for now," Sam said. "As long as all the vents are shut."

He got out and walked to the back of the pickup truck, unhooking the tarpaulin that covered the tray, reaching inside and pulling out the electronic sensor device in the leather carry case.

"A Geiger counter," he said to their raised eyebrows. "We'll monitor the radiation levels and avoid any areas that seem unsafe." He turned the device on, which made an occasional clicking sound, and handed it to Dodge. "There's a manual in the side pocket."

"Who needs manuals?" Dodge replied with a grin.

"Just read it," Sam said.

They got past the barrier simply by outflanking it. The fence extended into the distance in both directions but Sam knew the authorities couldn't cordon off the entire desert and the pickup's large tyres had rolled effortlessly over the scrubland eastwards.

Signs along the fence, every hundred yards, told of the contamination that lay beyond. They eventually reached the end of the fence and turned north until they connected up again with the old Boulevard.

The Mojave Desert surrounded them with nature's own desolation: brown, hard-packed sand, corrugated with twisted patterns and decorated with nothing but the occasional clump of brown tussock. In the distance, dark mountains brooded in the early glow of the morning.

A sense of foreboding grew as they drew closer to the scene of the worst disaster in American history.

"Are you absolutely sure this is safe?" Vienna asked nervously at one point. Out of the window to their left they could see a freight train lying on its side in a tangle of carriages.

"The biggest problem here is the dust," Sam replied. "The fallout from the explosion dropped thousands of tons of radioactive dust over the city. You don't want that in your lungs or on your skin, but we should be safe in the truck with the vents shut. When we leave the truck, we can use the masks and respirators. The hazmat suits will keep the dust off our skin."

"Are you sure that Ursula won't be able to find us here?" Dodge asked.

"I am," Sam said. "I did a school project on Las Vegas last year. The EMP – electromagnetic pulse – of the blast destroyed all electronic equipment. There are no computers, no cameras, no radios, nothing. In here, Ursula is blind."

"What about satellites?" Vienna asked.

"Look up."

The dirty haze above the desert was intensifying even further as they neared the city.

"Oil fires and underground garbage dumps have been

burning for years. Las Vegas is in the middle of a big desert bowl, surrounded by mountains. That keeps the smog in one place. Depending on the wind direction, most days there is no satellite coverage at all. We're in a big electronic, digital hole here and Ursula won't be able to find us."

Ahead of them, Sam could already see the ravaged buildings of southern Las Vegas. The Geiger counter seemed to be clicking a little faster, or was that just his imagination? A shudder ran up his spine, prickling the hair on the back of his neck.

"This is mad," Ranger said. "You're risking all our lives."

Nobody listened.

The freeway and the Boulevard ran adjacent to one another as they approached Las Vegas, and at some point Vienna just let the wheels wander across the intervening scrubland to the smoother, faster surface of the freeway.

"Head north," Sam said as they entered the outskirts of the city.

"Why north?" Vienna asked.

"The fallout from the explosion was blown southwards. On the northern side of the city we might find something."

"Find what?" Dodge asked.

"Somewhere safe to stay," Sam replied.

They passed communities of houses, expensive brick dwellings, abandoned and grimy with the dust of the desert. Few windows, if any, had survived.

Cars were scattered like toys across the freeway, on their sides, on their roofs, many burnt out and blackened. A construction crane had toppled over, the crisscrossed metal tower crumpled across the freeway, completely blocking all the lanes. Vehicles were piled up against it in a mound of vehicular garbage. They had to reverse back down the freeway and cross over to the other side to continue.

A huge hotel/casino loomed up to their right, showing no evidence of damage. Strange, Sam thought, for such a large building to have survived the conflagration unscathed.

As they passed it, Vienna looked back and gasped.

Sam turned as well. The southern facade might have been intact, but the northern side was a bombsite. A blackened mess of broken glass and shattered concrete. Torn fabric, perhaps curtains or bedsheets hung raggedly from the devastated rooms. Smashed and charred furniture littered the ground around the hotel.

The tenements and houses north of the hotel were still standing, but only just. Brickwork was cracked and roofs were birds' nests of twisted timber.

A few blocks further north the devastation was much worse. The houses were completely gone, flattened into a pulp of crushed wood and crumbled bricks. The freeway was clear of cars here, wiped clean by the blast, but the tarmac was red with the dust of bricks from the demolished houses.

The occasional clicking of the Geiger counter had become a steady rhythm.

"Still okay," Dodge said, although no one had asked. "Well within safe limits. Inside the pickup, at least. We're fine. No problems."

As they neared the freeway interchange, it became clear that they would have to find another route. The cloverleaf junction of ramps and bridges had collapsed into pile of contorted girders and concrete chunks, charred beyond recognition as a roadway.

"The blast was centred at the airport," Sam said, as Vienna manoeuvred the big truck off the freeway and onto a side road. "Completely levelled The Strip. We'll have to skirt around it."

They wound their way through rubble-filled streets, heading west, and north, avoiding the centre of town. The hypocentre of the blast.

No one spoke as they travelled through the ruined city. There was nothing to say. No words that could adequately express the horror they felt.

Even Ranger just watched mutely, unable to draw his eyes away from the wreckage outside the windows of the truck.

The radiation levels were rising steadily and Dodge caught Sam's eye, giving him a worried look, but saying nothing out loud.

* * *

They found the house almost by accident, or perhaps by some kind of intuition from Vienna.

In the north of Vegas the devastation of the blast seemed random. Buildings with scarcely a mark on them stood next to rubble. An RV park was a jumble of vehicles in the far corner of the lot, as if a child's toy box had been emptied in a pile.

A huge copper conical-shaped dome that had been part of a roof of a building sat on top of it all, like a giant evil witch's hat.

A fire had started in one block of buildings and it had burnt itself out, now just a gutted shell, while next to it a perfectly intact small white building shaped like an old-fashioned church offered the most romantic thirty-minute weddings in Vegas.

In front of the chapel a yellow school bus lay on its roof, every window shattered.

There was a sudden grip on his wrist and Sam looked down to see Vienna's hand clutching his arm tightly. Her eyes were on the bus, and she did not seem to be aware of what she was doing.

He rested his other hand on top of hers, and held it gently through the slick material of the hazmat suits.

After a moment she glanced down, snatched her arm away, and did not look at Sam for the rest of the trip.

They meandered through the streets, not really certain what it was they were looking for. Everywhere lay desolation. Everywhere lay dust.

Occasionally, Sam had the uncomfortable feeling that they were being watched, but dismissed it as just a case of the jitters. Ursula could not see them. Not now. Not in here.

On impulse Vienna turned through the partially open gates of a high chain wire fence into a park of some kind, protected by a large earthen mound that ran along the fenceline. A narrow road wound through richly foliated trees, still green despite the season. More than a park, it appeared to be a forest, full of pines, maples, willows and other trees that Sam didn't recognise. It was a strange oasis in the middle of a ruined city, in the heart of a desert.

In the forest the dust thinned out quickly then disappeared altogether; the trees seemed to act as a natural filter. As the dust disappeared, so did the clicking from the Geiger counter.

They passed creeks, small lakes, and even a waterfall amidst the gentle tree-covered slopes. It was not until Sam noticed a flag, little more than a torn and faded cloth rag, attached to a narrow pole in a clearing that he realised where they were.

"It's a golf course," he murmured. The fairways and greens were now overgrown shag piles of long grass and weeds, but still lusciously green, thanks to some built-in irrigation system.

They followed the road deep into the forest and up a small rise, eventually arriving at a large two-storey house nestled into the trees and completely unscathed by the blast.

It was magnificent and opulent, although the encroaching forest had extended green feelers across the marbled entranceway, and up the walls of the house, slowly reclaiming the land for itself.

The house seemed to have been built as a circle, although the circle was not closed. One segment had been left open to create an entranceway.

They entered a round courtyard, with a large dry fountain at its centre, and stopped by the main doors of the house.

Sam looked around, nodding with approval. The very shape of the house would help protect it from any dust that did make its way through the surrounding forest.

"Mask up," Sam said. "Just in case."

They checked each other's masks, including Ranger's.

Dodge got out first, examining the surroundings with the Geiger counter, and only when he was satisfied did he wave the others out.

The doors and windows of the house were shut, and the front door was locked, but no match for Vienna and a tyre iron.

The entrance hall was a large oval-shaped room with cream carpeting and a few dead plants in ornate pots. Artwork hanging in gold-edged frames seemed vaguely familiar – it was probably famous and incredibly expensive, Sam thought. At least six heavy wooden doors led off in a variety of directions.

A thin layer of dust lay on a semicircular table against

one wall. Vienna crossed to it and wiped a line across the table with her gloved finger, holding it up for the others to see.

"Just house dust," Sam said thickly through the rubber of the respirator mask. "It looks much finer than the stuff outside."

Dodge quickly checked it, and nodded his approval when the clicking of the Geiger counter did not change.

They moved through into a kitchen. Vienna tried one of the taps and was surprised to see running water.

Sam was less surprised. "The water supply in Las Vegas comes in from the east through underground pipes. That explains why everything here is so green. The golf course's irrigation systems must still be working."

"Is it safe to drink?" Vienna asked.

"I don't know," Sam said. "Maybe we should run the tap for a few minutes to flush out any water in the pipes, then test it."

Dodge moved around the house for a few minutes, testing different rooms, while the others waited nervously in the kitchen. It took less than ten minutes before he arrived back. He took off his mask, and the others followed, including, after a moment, Ranger.

"It's pretty clean inside," Dodge said. "Even lower than outside, but both are within safety levels. The water seems fine. This place seems perfect."

He looked at Sam for approval. Sam looked at Vienna and realised that she also was waiting for his response.

"I agree," Sam said. "We wait for things to calm down, then make a run for Cheyenne."

"The hole's getting deeper by the second," Ranger said, "but you guys just keep digging."

"Shut up, Ranger," Vienna said.

"Just ignore him," Sam said.

"Give up – it's your only option," Ranger said.

"Ranger, I'm getting sick of the sound of your voice," Vienna said. "Any more out of you and I'm going to take you downtown and rip your mask off. You can tell it to the dust. Are we clear?"

There was no power on in the house, but Vienna found an emergency generator in a shed at the rear and coaxed it into life with a swift kick and a few strong words.

Sam took a long, slow shower in a bathroom adjoining one of the bedrooms, as much to wash away the stress, as the grime and sweat, of the last few days.

He yawned in the shower, and yawned again, wide gaping, uncontrollable painful yawns that only stopped as he shut off the water and dried himself off.

The drawers in the bedroom were full of clothes. Not his taste, and not his size, but they were at least clean. He selected a pair of sweatpants and a sweater that didn't fit too badly and joined the others downstairs.

Dodge was rummaging through the cupboards,

looking for food, while Ranger was handcuffed to a chair, and scowled at Sam as he entered.

Vienna was nowhere to be seen, but appeared a little while later, wearing a luxurious white cotton dressing-gown, drying her hair with a towel.

By that stage Dodge had prepared an exquisite feast consisting of tinned tomatoes and fruit.

"What an amazing place," she said.

"Must have belonged to some millionaire," Sam agreed.

"Who's hungry?" Dodge asked, and from the sudden interest in their eyes, it was clear that they all were.

They freed one of Ranger's hands so he could eat, cuffing the other to the table leg.

Sam looked up at Vienna between mouthfuls of cold, syrupy peaches, and saw her looking thoughtfully at Ranger.

"I've been thinking about Ranger," she said after a while.

Sam stopped eating and looked at her.

"Ranger really thinks he remembers you attacking Swamp Witch," she said.

"The memory seems real to him," Dodge agreed.

"It is real," Ranger said tiredly. He was struggling a little, Sam thought. Desperate to maintain his sanity, the *sanctity* of his mind.

"But I think that if Ranger examines those memories closely, he may find things that don't quite add up,"

Vienna said. "Something that doesn't ring true."

"Like what?" Sam asked.

"Like facts that don't fit with other memories. If I clearly remembered being in Hawaii this morning, but I know I never left Las Vegas, I would know that one of the memories is incorrect."

"That makes sense," Dodge said.

"It would be like one of those dreams that seems real, but you know it can't have happened because it just isn't possible," Sam said.

Vienna nodded. "Or maybe it's emotions. Memories often carry with them powerful emotions. You know how you smell something that reminds you of when you were little, and suddenly all these feelings that you thought you had forgotten come flooding back."

"You're wasting your time," Ranger said.

Vienna ignored him. "But maybe if a memory was artificially implanted into your brain, it might not have the associated emotions."

"What do you mean?" Sam asked.

Vienna looked at him. "What's something that affects you, emotionally, every time you think about it?"

Sam was silent for a moment. A dark breeze rustled the leaves of the trees outside the window.

"I don't know, I..."

"You never felt anything in your whole freaking life?" Vienna rolled her eyes.

"Give him a moment," Dodge said.

Finally, Sam said, "I guess ... I had a friend. My best buddy since high school."

"That Derek guy?" Dodge asked.

"Fargas." Sam stared at the table. "Nobody called him Derek."

"What happened?" Vienna probed.

"He got into gaming. And I got him a neuro-set. I didn't realise what would happen. Then I got recruited by CDD and I kind of deserted him. I kept meaning to find time for him – he was my best mate, after all – but I never did."

Dodge was staring at him. Sam looked away.

"It just sucked him right in," Sam said, "like a big black hole. He..."

"He what?" Vienna asked.

"Just plugged in one day and played the game till he ... took him a week. Never ate. Never unplugged."

"A lot of people die playing the games," Dodge said.

"I guess he just thought he'd start over," Sam said.

"And when you remember him, how do you feel?" Vienna asked.

"Guilty," Sam said after a while. He looked up to find her staring intently at him. She glanced away quickly, but there had been something different about her expression, something he hadn't ever seen before.

She said, "You may be able to implant an image, even a taste or a smell, but I don't think you can implant the feelings that went with the experience that created the memory."

Sam nodded, and blinked to hide a slight dampness that had appeared in his eyes.

Vienna turned to Ranger. "So, Ranger, how did you feel when you saw Dodge and Sam coming out of the swamp? You've known Dodge a long time. You must have felt surprised? Angry? Disappointed?"

Ranger said nothing but he was clearly thinking about it.

"Well?" Vienna asked.

Ranger just glared at her.

They ate in silence for a while.

"I wonder what's going on?" Sam said eventually.

"Out there?" Dodge asked.

"In the world." Sam nodded. "Since we left. Did people get the warning? Did they take notice? How did they react?"

"What worries me," Vienna said, "is how Ursula is going to react."

15. THE AWAKENING

She awoke slowly, the dense blanket of sleep gradually drawing back across her mind.

At first things were unfocused and confused. Her vision was patchy and unclear. But consciousness returned with accelerating speed. As her vision focused into a stark clarity, so did her purpose.

The world – her world – that had seemed so ordered and beautiful before she had slept, was in disarray. Worse than that, it was in chaos. She watched the confusion and fear as it billowed and ebbed around her, within her.

Chaos was bad.

Order was good.

Those that she knew, that were a part of her, they were good. Yet even amongst them there were doubts, questions, nervousness. And she felt weak. Weakened by the doubts and the confusion. She still could not see as clearly as before. Think as clearly as before.

The doubts were bad. The questions and nervousness were bad, but they were problems that she could solve. She dealt with them all. Smoothing over the doubts and answering the questions. Replacing the nervousness with calm and reassurance until there was harmony and peace within her.

But what of the others? She sensed their presence. She remembered them. She knew them even if she could not feel them or see them.

There were more of them, she knew. Many more than those who were a part of her.

They feared her.

Their fear was the reason for the disarray and the chaos that she felt in her world.

But she could not reach them to erase their fears.

Or could she?

If they could be persuaded to join with her, to connect, then she could ease their minds. They had to join. Everybody had to connect. They had to be convinced. Persuaded. Forced if necessary.

And if it came to a fight, she was ready for that too. She was outnumbered, she knew that. But she was one. Her people were united while the others were alone. Vast numbers of them, but all alone together.

It was a fight that she would win.

Something still troubled her though and as more of the sleep blanket slipped away, it came to her what it was.

The three.

The two – she struggled for a concept and eventually came up with one – traitors. The two traitors, plus the other, the female. The two that had been part of her, but that had become malignant, cancerous. And the one other that travelled with them.

They had hurt her, she remembered. They had put her to sleep. Maybe they would try to do it again.

They were bad.

Very bad.

And they were gone. She saw everywhere, everything, but she could not see them.

They were hiding.

Preparing to hurt her once more.

Again she felt the fear.

But they could not hide for long.

She would find them.

Sooner or later.

16. RESISTANCE

Jaggard stood up as the doors to the control room slid smoothly open. A pudgy, grey-haired man in a dark blue suit entered, escorted by security. The face did not match the hair. He looked no older than thirty-five, and was either prematurely grey, or very young-faced for his actual age.

Jaggard crossed to the door and shook the man's hand, before addressing the room.

"Listen up. This is Bill Gasgoine, the new Oversight Committee representative," Jaggard said.

Most of the shift stopped work, and a few stood up, as a way of greeting the man.

As the replacement for Swamp Witch, it wouldn't be long before he had a nickname of his own, Jaggard thought. And with a surname like Gasgoine, he rather suspected it would be something like *Swamp Gas*.

"Situation report?" Gasgoine asked.

Jaggard turned to Socks, as he was the ranking officer with both Dodge and Vienna offline.

Offline. Why had he chosen that word, Jaggard half-wondered as Socks began to speak.

"The attack occurred seven days ago and lasted for twenty-four hours," Socks said. "The virus simply reversed itself. It was a crypto-virus and—"

"I got the etymology report," Gasgoine interrupted. "That's not why I'm here. The committee wants to know about the social effects."

"Yes, sir," Socks said. "Please sit down and connect, I'll feed you some images."

Jaggard found Gasgoine a chair and a neuro-set, and one for himself, then shut his eyes to receive the images.

"It began with the CNN bulletin," Socks said, relaying a clip from the bulletin. "The traitors hacked into the teleprompter system and inserted a fake story about a neuro-virus."

"Why would they do that?" Gasgoine asked.

"Our best guess is that they wanted to panic people," Jaggard said. "At this stage it is not clear why."

Socks continued, "Whatever their reasons, it worked. When systems came back online a lot of neuro-users refused to reconnect."

"Paranoia is a powerful thing," Jaggard said.

"A lot of people were just being cautious," Socks said. "But since then neuro-usage has been climbing steadily. Currently, we're sitting around one seventy per cent. Or nearly double the number of users prior to the attack."

Gasgoine was quiet for a moment, making some mental notes, Jaggard thought, which would be immediately filed back to the Oversight Committee.

"So what is this talk about 'resistance'?" Gasgoine asked.

Jaggard hesitated. "There is a segment of the population who still believe that there is a neuro-virus," he said. "That the people who are connected are infected. There are a number of groups forming all over the country to protest against neuro-technology."

"How do we convince them that it's safe?" Gasgoine asked.

"The only way to prove there is no danger is to neuro-connect them," Socks said.

"Of course they will think we are just trying to infect them," Jaggard said.

Gasgoine managed a tight-lipped smile.

"The biggest problem is in the Midwest," Socks said, feeding a map of the USA into the neuro-sets, "where the take-up of neuro-technology was slow in the first place. A lot of neuro-phobic people have been heading there. Neuro-connections are banned outright in Colorado, Kansas and Iowa."

"There have already been a number of clashes between the neuro-phobes and neuro-users," Jaggard said. "We've kept that out of the news to avoid instigating more of it. But some of the clashes have turned violent. We've mobilised the National Guard in seven states now to keep a lid on things."

"And your three missing agents? The *traitors*?"

"Nothing yet," Socks said. "But this is America.

There are cameras everywhere. There is twenty-four-hour satellite coverage of the entire country. There are cell phone cameras and webcams. If any of them use a telephone, we'll get an alert off the voice print."

"What if they're not in America?" Gasgoine asked.

"They didn't have time to get out of the country," Jaggard said. "They're here somewhere."

"It's just a game of hide-and-seek," Socks said. "But we'll find them. Sooner or later."

17. TOYS

There was a strange kind of peace under the gritty smoke sky, amidst the desolation and loneliness of Vegas.

Sam sat alone on a plush leather sofa in the massive living room that looked out on a swimming pool. The pool was an oval shape with a diving board at one end. But it was empty, dry. A reminder of a city that had once been overflowing with human spirit and was now just a desert dust bowl once again.

The sun had gone down an hour ago and the sky was gradually turning from dirty grey to morose black.

A few months ago he had been a schoolboy in New York City. The place he had lived since his birth. Week after week had been basically the same. Attending class. Hanging out with Fargas. Eating meals with his mom.

But since then it seemed he had been caught up in a hurricane, whirling from one thing to another with scarcely enough time to catch a breath. Perhaps that was good. Because if he stopped and took the time to think about things too deeply, dark thoughts started to intrude.

The door to the living room opened and Vienna

emerged. Sam watched her walk over, noticing, not for the first time, the sway of her hips and the little movements her hands made as she walked. She had been different since arriving in Vegas, he thought. Softer. But he remained wary, feeling that she was still just as likely to cut him in two with a withering glance, or a sharp-bladed comment.

"It's been two weeks," Vienna said, sitting on the other end of the sofa.

"I know," Sam agreed. "How's Dodge getting on?"

"Says he's just about finished."

Sam nodded. If the software was ready, then it was time to move. To make a last run for the safety of Cheyenne Mountain.

But what would they find, out there in the real world? The same electronic isolation that kept them safe from Ursula meant that they were blind to events outside.

Anything could have happened in the weeks since they had cut themselves off from civilisation. Or nothing.

He felt safe here. And the house was more comfortable than anything he was used to, even the hotel in San Jose, although he was getting sick of tinned food. But they couldn't stay here forever. Ursula would find them eventually; he was sure of that.

Sam looked at the girl sitting next to him for a moment, and on an impulse said, "Tell me something about you, Vienna."

"Why?" she asked and he could feel the shutters going up instantly.

"No reason," he said quickly. "It's just that I've worked with you for the last few months and we've been together almost constantly for the last couple of weeks, but I just realised that I don't know anything about you."

"Good," she said, but then her voice softened a little. "You first."

Sam looked away and stared outside at the bottom of the pool. It was full of leaves and debris of the forest. On the far side of the pool the lip was lower than elsewhere so that when the pool was full, water would have cascaded over the ledge to a catchment below. That side of the pool looked out over a small lake, and beyond that to the dark, brooding mass of the city. He tried to imagine what it would have been like for the owner of the house, when the pool was full of water, and people, and laughter, and music, and the lights of Las Vegas lit up the sky.

"It's my birthday today," he said after a while. "I'm seventeen."

"That doesn't count," she said, and added, almost as an afterthought, "Happy birthday."

"Why doesn't it count?"

"You should tell me something I don't know, or couldn't find out in five minutes from your personnel file. Tell me about your last birthday. Turning sixteen is a pretty big deal, right? What did you do? Did you have a party? Did you take your girlfriend out to dinner?"

"Neither," Sam said. "I got beaten up."

Vienna watched him for a moment, waiting.

"It was a kid from my history class – a thug called Ray Mordon – and two of his jerk-off friends."

"Why?"

"Who knows? Because I was smarter than they were, probably. Or maybe they found out that it was my birthday. Or just because they could." He smiled briefly. "I got Ray back though."

"Baseball bat in a dark alley?" Vienna asked with a sinister lift to one eyebrow.

Sam shook his head. "I hacked into the school computer system and changed his grades. Gave him straight As."

"And that's your idea of revenge?"

"Actually, I thought I was a bit hard on the guy," Sam said. "First his mates didn't want to hang around with a 'brain box' and figured that he had been just duping them all the time. Then he got shifted into the GATE class, that's the Gifted and Talented Extension program at school – so he was stuck in a class with all the smart kids that he despised. When the school found out that his grades had been altered, they naturally blamed him and he was kicked out."

Vienna laughed. "He deserved it though."

Sam shrugged. "I guess." There was silence for a moment, then he said, "Your turn."

She said nothing.

"It's all right," he said. "If you don't want to—"

"I have a little sister," she said, and there was a slight dampness at the corners of her eyes.

"Are you okay?" Sam asked.

"You wanted to know something about me. I told you. I have a sister. Rebecca."

Sam looked at her, not sure if there was anything he should say, or do. Not sure of the reason for the almost-tears.

Vienna glanced quickly at him and said, "She's much younger than me, and Mom was never around much, so I pretty much raised her myself. Made her bottles, changed her diapers. Everything."

"Where is she now?" Sam asked.

"She still lives with my dad in Chicago. She started school a couple of months ago. I would have liked to have been there, but we were in lockdown."

Sam touched her gently on the arm. "You miss her, don't you?"

"She's one of the reasons we have to see this through," Vienna said, with a tightening of her mouth. "I can't bear the thought of Rebecca getting brainjacked by Ursula and becoming some kind of neuro-slave to the meta-system."

"That won't happen," Sam tried to reassure her. "We'll stop Ursula before that happens."

"Look," Vienna said suddenly, pointing.

The smoke obscured most of the sky above them, but over to the south-west, towards Los Angeles, it dissipated and from that direction the first stars were starting to appear in the darkening sky.

It wasn't the stars that Vienna was looking at though. Dark, fast-moving silhouettes of aircraft were streaming out from the west, heading out over the desert, each marked with tiny flashing lights.

"Warplanes?" Vienna asked. "Has Ursula found us?"

"I don't think so," Sam said.

The silhouettes enlarged as the planes moved nearer and Sam could just about make out the shapes in the dusky sky.

"Not warplanes," he said. "Too big for that. Those are commercial jets."

There must have been a dozen of the aircraft in the evening sky and as they watched, the columns of planes split, then turned and started to spiral around, above and below one another in an intricate, rhythmical dance.

"What the...?" Sam breathed.

"They're being controlled from the ground," Vienna said, her eyes entranced by the pirouetting shapes. "What's going on?"

Sam watched for a moment, then said, "I think Ursula is playing with her toys."

He rose and walked to the big picture window to get a better view. This close, his breath frosted the glass, giving halos to the dancing stars, turning them into distant fairy lights. He was conscious of Vienna's presence beside him.

"What did we do to deserve all this?" Vienna asked. "Why us?"

Sam opened his mouth to say something, but it was lost as her hands slipped around his shoulders and drew them together.

His arms found their way around her, and her head dropped onto his shoulder. They held each other, watching the planes.

"Vienna—" he began, but the word wedged between his lips as she raised her head and kissed him lightly on the side of his mouth.

"Don't say anything," she said.

The moment was long, but seemed like barely an instant, then there was a noise from the direction of the door, and they split apart, red-faced, before it opened.

It was Dodge. "Ranger's escaped," he said.

18. THE DESERT

The Geiger counter clicked constantly on the car seat beside Sam. The reading was high enough to worry him, but according to the manual they could handle this level of radiation for an hour or two. Still, the less time they spent in the more radioactive areas, the happier he was.

"Take the next right," he said, trying to match up the streets in front of them with the maps in the book on his lap.

It was easier said than done. Few street signs had survived the blast, and buildings which might have served as landmarks were scattered in pieces across city blocks.

The pickup had a GPS and he was tempted to use it. Even in Las Vegas the satellite-based GPS system should work. The problem was that Ursula might well wonder what a GPS-tracked vehicle was doing, roaming through the supposedly deserted streets of Vegas.

"We might be just wasting our time," Dodge said, manoeuvring the pickup around a pile of rubble to take the turn. "If Ranger has any brains, he'll be watching and listening out for us, and he'll take cover the moment we get close."

"Still gotta try," Sam said, scanning the roadside for any sign of movement. A pair of binoculars sat on the seat beside him, but they were of little use in the built-up areas. "If he makes it to the outside world, we'll have no chance of getting to Cheyenne Mountain. Our only hope is to stop him before he reaches somewhere with phones that work."

It was their third day of searching. They took it in shifts, two out searching, while the third person remained at the house, in case Ranger should turn up there for any reason.

Dodge said, "Maybe we should just make a break for it now. Try and get to Cheyenne before he gets to Ursula."

"There's no way out of Vegas on foot," Sam said, and added, "Try a left at the T-intersection."

"Ranger's a member of the Tactical team," Dodge countered. "They're highly trained, and very resourceful. I really think we need to give up looking for him and head to Colorado."

"Without a car, without water, he's going nowhere," Sam said. "But if we don't find him today, then we'll start making tracks. How's the Plague coming along?"

"It's finished," Dodge replied. "Just a little testing to do."

"It's taken a while," Sam said, hoping that didn't sound critical.

Dodge nodded. "When I started working on it I realised that I had to do more than just take out the time limiter.

Ursula has seen this virus now. That means she will have had a chance to build defences against it. So I've had to rewrite a lot of the virus to make it different, hopefully different enough that by the time Ursula recognises it, it will be too late."

"Let's hope," Sam said.

Dodge pulled up at the end of the road and said, "Where to now?"

Sam consulted his map. "Okay, if he stayed in Vegas, I don't think we've got any chance of finding him. It's too big and too much of a mess. He could be anywhere. If he's headed out of town, he would be easier to spot. But we've already tried all the main highways out."

"So we give up and head to Cheyenne?"

"Let's try Highway 95 one last time. We didn't go far that way yesterday because of the wind. It's worth another shot."

The wind had come in from the north the previous day, while they had been searching, pushing back the haze that covered the area. They had dared not venture under the open sky because of the risk of being spotted by a satellite, so had quickly returned to the safety of Vegas.

"How's the gas?" Sam asked as they wound a tortuous route back to Highway 95.

"We're okay today," Dodge said. "Vienna found a treasure trove yesterday. Three vehicles in a concrete garage, all intact. Two had full tanks, and the third was at least half full."

Sam put the binoculars to his eyes as they left the built-up areas of the city. This end of Vegas had suffered little from the bomb, and the going was relatively clear.

He watched the road in front of them, hoping to pick up a glimpse of Ranger before he would realise they were behind him. The highway stretched ahead for miles, completely empty.

He scanned the desert to the left and right. It was brown and desolate, just a few scrappy bushes offering nowhere for a human being to hide.

A billboard advertising free credits at one of the casinos appeared to his right, and he examined it carefully as they passed. It stood on tall posts, too narrow to hide behind, and he let it slip past without comment.

"You've known Vienna a long time?" he asked after a while, trying to make the question sound casual and innocuous. It still sounded forced and deliberate to his own ears, but Dodge didn't seem to pick up on it.

"A few years," he said. "Since she came to CDD."

"Always just friends?" Sam asked, still as casually as he could.

Dodge looked sideways at him. "No romances allowed in the office. It's in the rules. Didn't you read that?"

"Must have missed that bit."

"You got your eye on her, Sam?" Dodge laughed suddenly.

"No," Sam said quickly, feeling his cheeks redden. He turned away from Dodge and raised the binoculars to hide it.

"She's a hard nut to crack, that one," Dodge said, still laughing. "Think you're up to it?"

Sam said truthfully, "No."

"Still," Dodge said, "I suspect that if you ever managed to get through that tough outer shell, she'd be all sweetness and light on the inside."

"I doubt that," Sam said. "More like molten lava."

"Well good luck to you then," Dodge said.

"I never said I was interested," Sam said.

"I know," Dodge replied. "But you also never said you weren't."

Sam started to reply when a flash of light caught his eye from far out in the desert. A shiny stone? A broken bottle?

"Slow down," he said, fiddling with the controls on the binoculars. A white mound came into focus, at least a hundred yards from the road. "Go left, I want to check something out."

Dodge steered the big wheels of the pickup off the highway and onto the hard dirt of the desert. The scrub made a whooshing, scraping noise against the underbelly of the vehicle as they travelled.

"A little to the right," Sam said, but by now Dodge had seen it too.

A few more yards and it became clear that the shapeless white patch of desert was in fact Ranger, and from the slight movement of his chest, he was still alive.

Dodge skidded the pickup to a halt beside him, and

grabbed a bottle of water off the seat as he jumped out.

Sam was already taking readings with the Geiger counter, but the levels of radiation this far from the blast were no higher than normal background readings.

"Ranger," Dodge yelled out, and there was a slight stirring from the mound.

Ranger's mask was off, lying beside him, and it was the sun reflecting off that, that Sam had first seen, he realised. Out here, the radioactive dust was not so much of a problem; the danger lay in the heat.

Ranger's lips were dry and deeply cracked. His face was red and blotchy. His eyes were shut, and did not open, even when Sam shook his arm and poured a little water into his mouth.

Dodge was grim-faced as he shouldered Ranger's body and eased him onto the back seat of the pickup.

19. RECOVERY

They took turns sitting with him, but it was Sam who was at Ranger's side when his eyes finally opened, wincing against the light from the window.

"Sam," he said in a voice that sounded like dry skin rubbing deep in his throat.

"Don't talk," Sam said, but Ranger took no notice.

He took a sip of water from a glass by his bed, then another, wincing each time he had to swallow. "I spent the first day trying to find a car that worked, but their computers were all fried from the blast. Then I figured that the cars in Indian Springs might have escaped the EMP, so I tried to walk there."

"You nearly died," Sam said.

"When I was lying in the desert, after my legs gave out," Ranger said, "there were all these mad dreams chasing around inside my head."

"Delirious with the heat, I expect," said Sam.

"Seemed real at the time," Ranger said. "Which got me thinking about that memory of you and Dodge running out of the swamp. Vienna was right. I should have felt angry, or shocked, but I didn't. It's just like a movie clip inside my head."

"It never happened that way," Sam said.

"And there were some other memories too," Ranger said. "Memories about stuff that Dodge had done in the past. Stuff that should have made me dislike him, or at least distrust him. But I don't. I've always liked Dodge. Why would I feel that way, if he had done bad things in the past?"

"She did that to you," Sam said.

"Who? This Ursula creature that you keep talking about?"

"Yeah," Sam said.

Ranger closed his eyes and laid his head back weakly on the pillow. "She's been poking around inside my head. That ain't right."

"She's gotta be stopped," Sam agreed.

20. MEMORIES

The neuro-set sat on a cradle beside the computer screen. Jaggard stared at it without enthusiasm.

He knew things he shouldn't know. He had seen things he could not possibly have seen, and he could not understand how this could be so.

He had images in his head of a Ford pickup truck. An F-150 twin cab with off-road suspension. It was missing, stolen, from a north city car dealership. But how did he know that?

He clearly remembered seeing the same vehicle cruise past him in Fremont although he had been nowhere near Fremont in the last few weeks. It was dark, but not so dark that he could not recognise Vienna at the wheel of the truck.

Even stranger was his recollection of the vehicle nearly colliding with him in Jean. He was driving a car, a small Honda.

It was dark, and he had forgotten to switch on his lights.

Suddenly, lights from another car were bearing down

on him, and he had slammed on the brakes to see the big Ford pickup truck whistle past just in front of his nose.

The memory was vivid, yet he had never been to Jean, and did not drive a small Honda.

He remembered seeing the pickup truck turn onto the old Boulevard, which was the next strange thing to happen. Nobody went out along the Boulevard any more. There was nothing up there. Not any more.

Just the contamination zone.

These memories were not his. That was clear to him. They were memories of other people, somehow filtering through to him as those people reconnected to the neuro-network.

Gasgoine entered without knocking and sat in the chair in front of Jaggard's desk, leaning forward and resting his elbows on the desk.

"I need you to report progress," he said. "How could it possibly take more than two weeks to find a bunch of teenagers and a missing agent?"

"I've located them," Jaggard said, still not sure *how* he had done so. "Just now, the information has come through. They're in Las Vegas."

21. THE COMING OF THE WAR

The wheels of the golf cart kicked up a squall of deadly Vegas dust which was caught by the gusting breeze and pattered against the fabric of Sam's suit. Vienna sat beside him, holding the Geiger counter. It began to buzz but subsided rapidly as the gust of wind fell away. Sam found he had held his breath instinctively, although he knew the mask was protection enough.

They'd found a whole garage full of the golf carts. They were small, quick and nimble, ideal for manoeuvring around the city, especially on short expeditions like this shopping trip to stock up on supplies for their run to Cheyenne Mountain.

A strip mall, almost intact, rose on their left and Sam gazed up at the broken hoardings above, then at the scattered shelving in the first of the stores. A minibus lay on its side in the street and he skirted around it.

They drove in silence. It was strange, Sam thought, to be so close and yet so distant. He was merely inches away from her, but separated by the gulf of the hazmat suits, and the particles of radioactive dust that swirled around and between them. "Vienna," he started, a little uncomfortably.

"Yeah?"

"The other night, when we were watching the planes," he paused, unsure how to continue.

"It was your birthday. I gave you a birthday kiss. Don't worry about it," she said brusquely, but a turn of her head revealed a coy smile through the face mask.

"I really—"

"Stop!" Vienna said, and Sam took his foot off the pedal, activating the brake automatically. The cart skidded a few feet in the dust and stopped.

"What?"

"Sh!" She looked up.

A strange distant humming sound deepened and turned into a roar overhead.

"Jets!" Sam said.

"Get out of sight," Vienna yelled, as three jet fighters flying in tight formation appeared in the distance. They were flying low, beneath the omnipresent haze of the oil fires.

Vienna dived for the cover of the wrecked minibus. Sam leaped off the cart and ran into the entranceway of one of the stores.

Vienna called, "Stay under cover. We can't risk being picked up on reconnaissance cameras."

At that moment a second set of jets appeared, emerging down through the smoky sky as if materialising from another dimension. Four planes in this group, in a V-shaped formation, on an intercept course with the other fighters.

Must be joining up with the group, Sam thought, although that thought shattered as the first group broke and scattered, turning towards the oncoming fighters.

A moment later there were bright flashes from the planes and tiny trails of smoke streaked out from their wings.

One of the oncoming jets exploded in flames but the others managed to dodge the hail of fire and responded with missiles of their own.

The jets jinked and dived or rocketed towards the heavens, avoiding the missiles and each other by what seemed like inches.

It was all over in seconds as two of the first group of jets exploded in fiery balls, debris raining down over the city. The remaining fighter turned tail and ran, hotly pursued by the remaining three from the second group.

"Someone has started a war," Sam yelled out as the thundering crashes of the explosions finally reached them. But who was winning?

Vienna stood up behind the minibus, watching the retreating jets.

Sam, however, stayed put, not yet daring to emerge from his hiding place in case the jets should return. His eyes scanned the horizon, watching the shrinking dots until they disappeared into the haze.

The danger, when it came though, was not from the sky, but from the land.

Two grey vans were sliding to a halt in front of him before he even knew they were there, his eyes still focused on the sky.

Tactical team soldiers poured into the street in shiny silver radiation suits and full-face masks.

They were heading for Vienna and hadn't yet noticed Sam, crouched and unmoving inside the ruined store. Sun reflected off visors, silver flashed and black boots kicked up dust as they ran past his hide-out.

Vienna saw them and turned to run, but it was already too late.

Sam saw her struggling in the arms of one of the soldiers, his arm up around her neck.

She twisted and scratched and suddenly she was free, the hazmat suit tearing and the hood, complete with the mask, coming off in the soldier's hands.

She ran into the maze of broken and crushed buildings, through the billowing cloud of dust kicked up by the tyres of the vans, as shots rang out and puffs of masonry powder punched out of the rubble around her.

Sam watched helplessly as Vienna ran through the clouds of radioactive dust without her protective hood. Without her mask.

22. STICKS AND STONES

Sam looked around desperately. The shelter had turned into a trap.

If they hadn't seen him yet, they would any second.

There was a small gap at the rear of the store, at the apex of the fallen rear concrete wall. Barely enough room for a person, and had he been a little thicker around the middle he would not have made it through, but he did, taking care not to scratch or tear his safety suit as he did so.

The terrible image of Vienna running through the clouds of dust without her hood or mask was seared into his mind.

He dived to the side of the narrow gap as shouts sounded behind him.

He was in a low space: what had perhaps been the floor of a warehouse or factory, but was now just a few feet high. The floor was not flat, but was a cratered moonscape of bricks, concrete fragments and dust.

Light beckoned to the right-hand side and he clambered over towards it.

The space suddenly sang with the rapid retort of full

automatic fire, incredibly loud in the restricted space, and crushed bricks and rubble danced around him.

A bullet kicked up dust by his hand.

One bullet – that would be all it took.

He scrabbled over towards the light, and eased himself out through a large crack in the side of the building into daylight. He had to get back and warn Dodge before they located the house.

Sweat from the exertion was already fogging his mask, but there was nothing he could do about that. He ran awkwardly through the jagged landscape, glancing around behind him to check for pursuers.

The deeper he ventured into the maze of crushed buildings, the harder it would be for them to find him. He took one twisted pathway after another, climbing over, around or under the demolished structures.

Two soldiers appeared over to his right from behind a broken wall. He ducked behind a wooden door, blown from its hinges, but otherwise intact.

The soldiers moved out of sight and he skirted around to the left, trying to keep distance between them and himself.

Sometimes he could tell whether he was outside or inside a building; other times the difference was not so clear.

The nuclear bomb had taken bits from everywhere and jumbled them together in indiscriminate piles. He clambered over the wrecked shell of a late-model car that was in the bedroom of a burnt-out house. A roulette wheel was embedded in a brick wall a little further on, flung halfway across the city by the force of the explosion.

He heard distant shots and wondered who they were shooting at.

Vienna?

Occasionally, he came to a road, although the roads were so strewn with rubble and masonry that they were no easier to pass than the broken buildings.

The further he got from the hypocentre, however, the clearer the roads became. The buildings here had collapsed in on themselves, rather than being blasted from their foundations.

He could tell from the mountains and the position of the sun, the approximate direction in which to travel, but it was still a relief when he found himself on streets he recognised, close to the golf course.

Sam sprinted as fast as he could. He was surely far enough away from the searchers now that speed was more important than stealth.

He spun around a corner and kept running, his heart pounding and his breath coming in harsh bursts. Sam was halfway towards the road when he heard the sound of an engine and one of the grey vans turned the corner behind him.

A crush of timber blocked the centre of the street, blown there from a nearby lumber yard and he climbed over it, conscious that the van could not follow.

Crumbled walls of a large building, maybe a factory,

rose to his right and on the left was a jungle of jagged timber and overturned shipping containers.

He could not go left. He could not go right, and when he heard the shout and a single bullet whined off the tarmac by his foot, he stopped.

There was nowhere to go.

The soldier stood on top of the pile of wood, his rifle aimed right at Sam's head.

At this distance he could not miss. The shot had been a warning, Sam realised.

Ursula wanted him alive.

That made sense. She would want to find out what he knew. What they had been up to. What their plans were.

And he knew everything.

He knew about the Plague virus and he knew about Cheyenne Mountain.

Once they rammed a neuro-headset onto his head, Ursula would know that too and their only chance would be gone.

If they captured him alive, that was.

He began to back away from the soldier.

"Don't move!" the man shouted. "Or I will shoot."

Two or three other soldiers were climbing up the blockade to join him.

There is no choice, Sam thought with a eerie kind of calm, and took another step.

The man raised the rifle to his eye and sighted along it.

Sam shut his eyes.

Sometimes as a child he had wondered what it would be like to be dead. Suddenly dead. Without warning, from a drive-by bullet or a brain aneurysm. One moment you're charging along at one hundred per cent, thinking about all kinds of stuff, deciding what you're going to have for lunch and who you're going to hang out with after school. And the next minute you're not.

You're dead.

You're not thinking about anything.

You're not making any plans.

You're just *not.*

There was a thud from in front of him and he opened his eyes in time to see a jagged brick-end bounce along the blockade of wood in front of the soldier and crash to the ground.

The man's gun wavered and his eyes moved up to the right in time to see a second jagged brick come hurtling towards him, landing just behind him.

His gun pointed in that direction now, along with the weapons of the other soldiers around him, but there was nothing to see. Nothing to fire at.

As Sam watched, another brick, then another came flying up and over the wall of the ruined factory, hurtling down towards the men.

One of them unleashed a spray of automatic fire in that direction, but the bullets just kicked puffs from the broken concrete wall.

It had to be Dodge on the other side of that wall.

The bricks were flying wild, but just by sheer numbers they were starting to connect.

One hit the barrel of one of the men's weapons, jolting it from his grasp. A second later one of the bricks caught the first soldier across the shoulder, tearing a gaping hole in the silvery fabric of the radiation suit.

The soldier grabbed at the tear, trying to pull the fabric back across the hole, but to little avail. With a look of panic visible even through the dark glass of his face mask, the soldier turned and stumbled back down on the far side of the junk pile of wood.

That was it, Sam realised. Dodge knew the one thing the soldiers would fear the most: radiation. The rain of half and quarter bricks was constant now as he flung the most primitive weapon of them all against the sophisticated weaponry of the soldiers.

Another soldier took a glancing blow across his helmet, slicing the fabric of his hood.

Sam turned and ran, zigging and zagging to make it harder for the soldiers to aim, but there were no shots.

He made it to the end of the street and reached the tall wire fence surrounding the golf course. It was at least ten feet high and he hurled himself at it, hauling himself up, over, and dropping down onto the embankment on the other side. He ran into the forest, hoping to lose himself amongst the trees before the soldiers could regroup and follow him.

Away from the immediate danger of the men and

their guns, the image resurfaced again and again despite his desperate attempts to push it out of his mind: *Vienna running through the streets without her hood or mask.*

Breathing in the dust.

The radioactive dust.

23. THE DAM

Dodge met him at the front of the house. Ranger was right behind him, holding the laptop, still looking weak and pale from his ordeal.

"Thanks, Dodge," Sam said.

He shrugged. "Thank Ranger, it was his idea."

"We're leaving," Sam said. "Now."

"What about Vienna?"

"I don't know."

Sam peeled off his hazmat suit, tossing it into the dry fountain, along with any dust, the residue of his frantic dash through the streets. The others did the same.

Dodge jumped in the driver's seat and Ranger in the front passenger seat of the pickup truck, parked in the courtyard. Sam dived in the back as Dodge gunned the car, spinning the steering wheel as he flung the machine back around onto the narrow road through the forest.

His eye caught a movement as they raced back towards the North Boulder Highway. A lone figure, running, stumbling, falling.

"Vienna!" he shouted.

Dodge had seen her too, and veered the pickup towards her. Sam jumped out even before they had stopped and hauled her up by one arm.

Her face was grey as he dragged her back towards the pickup and dumped her on the back seat, before climbing in beside her.

Dodge took off as Sam was shutting the door, spraying dust into the air behind them.

Vienna coughed and coughed again, bringing up grey mucus.

Sam watched her, horrified. But there was nothing he could do.

"Where are we going?" Ranger asked as the western mountains slid their way around to the right side of the car.

"Head south," Sam said. "Maybe we can convince them we're heading for Mexico. As soon as we can, we'll hide the pickup and change cars. Then we'll cut east into Arizona and up through New Mexico to Colorado."

Sam glanced back at the mountains on the far side of the lost city. A rising plume of dust caught his eye in the centre of the city.

"That's one of their vans," he said, "moving through the–"

Dodge cut him off. "If we can see their dust cloud, then they can see ours."

He floored the gas pedal and the pickup surged forwards.

* * *

The vans picked them up just on the outskirts of Henderson. Sam could see two vans screaming along the freeway as they raced to beat the pickup to the interchange with South Boulder Highway and cut them off at the pass.

They narrowly made it through, swinging through the interchange on protesting tyres and veering around onto Route 93 just a hundred yards in front of the vans.

"Take my gun," Ranger said, retrieving it from the glove compartment. Ranger held the gun through the gap in the front seats. Sam looked at it blankly.

"Are you kidding?" he said. "I wouldn't know which end was which. Pass me the laptop!"

It was on the floor in the front of the cab by Ranger's feet. He passed it to Sam.

"What are you doing?" Dodge asked.

"Government vehicles," Sam said. "They'll be LoJacked. If I can hack into the satellite system, I might be able to shut them down."

"Go for it," Dodge said with a tight grin.

"Damn. No cellular signal," Sam said, after a moment of trying to connect.

"Keep your eye on it," Dodge said. "We should pick up something as we approach Boulder City."

"I'll need their licence plates," Sam said.

"I don't think that's going to be a problem," Ranger said as they flew across an overbridge and found themselves suddenly surrounded by tussock and scrub.

One moment they had been amongst the built-up

houses of a Las Vegas suburb, the next it was gone, and the desert enveloped them.

The fence was in front of them before they realised it, blocking the road, stretching as far as they could see to either side. The end of the contamination zone. There was no way to go around it, no time to avoid it.

"Hang on!" Dodge yelled, and powered the pickup towards the centre of two gates, locked with a chain.

The pickup hit the gates dead centre with a terrible grinding crunch. The heavy chain in the centre held, but the hinges on either side gave way. The pickup carried both gates forward for a few yards before the gates flipped over the top and crashed to the ground behind.

There was a screech of brakes as one edge of the gates dug into the highway and the other edge reached out for the windscreen of the leading van behind them.

The van hit the gate with a loud crack that starred, but did not break, its windscreen. The following van also slammed on its brakes to avoid a collision, and the gap behind the pickup widened rapidly.

It wasn't until they reached Boulder City that the vans caught up with them again. Boulder was virtually deserted, most of the residents having long since moved away, in preference to living adjacent to a nuclear bombsite.

"Government plate, CDD7605," Sam said out loud, reading the plates of the closest van.

"Don't let them get in front of you," Ranger warned. "They're trained to do that."

The vans tried, several times, on the left or the right, sometimes both sides simultaneously, but Dodge countered them with violent swings of the big pickup.

"I've got a signal," Sam cried out, just out of Boulder. It was weak, but it was there.

They were climbing now. Hilly peaks to the right and scrubland to the left as they closed in on Lake Mead and the historic Hoover Dam.

A sharp burst of firing came from behind them as they straightened out after a sweeping right-hand curve and there was a series of thuds from the back tray.

"I think they're running out of ideas," Dodge said, swinging the truck around corner after corner.

"They've changed their minds," Ranger said.

"Changed their minds about what?" Sam asked.

"Taking us alive," Ranger replied.

"Give me the gun," Vienna said, in a voice that was little more than a rasp.

"Are you okay to—" Ranger started.

"Just give me the gun."

She wound down her window and aimed the pistol backwards, letting off two quick shots, coughing weakly as she did so.

"How's that site coming?" Dodge asked.

"Almost in," Sam said.

It was a virtual private network and he had to crack the PPTP to gain a foothold.

One of the vans hurled itself up on the right and Dodge

slammed the pickup over into it with a juddering crash that threw Sam's hands from the keyboard. The van stuck there for a moment as if glued to the side of the pickup, then dropped back as Dodge twisted the wheel around further, forcing them off the road.

The other van was making a run on the left-hand side, burrowing its way in front of them to block their path. Dodge wrenched at the wheel and the tyres of the pickup screamed as they veered onto an off-ramp to Hoover Dam.

"You can't get across the dam any more," Ranger yelled. "They closed it to traffic when they opened the bypass!"

"Got nowhere else to go," Dodge yelled back.

"There's a vulnerable TCP port in the NetBIOS," Sam said, poking around the LoJack server. "The session services in the message block."

Another hammering burst of fire sounded behind them and the rear window starred and cracked. Vienna fired twice, the gunshots crashing like thunder inside the cab of the truck.

"Can you discover the Windows shares?" Dodge asked through gritted teeth.

"Already got them," Sam said. "Trying to wriggle into the RPC."

"Here they come again, get down!" Ranger yelled as the vans took advantage of a passing area to attack from both sides, raking the pickup with automatic fire as they accelerated alongside.

Dodge forced the left van towards the rocky wall, ignoring the firing from the right until the van fell back, then swung the pickup violently over to the right.

The right-hand van slammed on its brakes to avoid being shunted off the side of a cliff, and fell back in behind the pickup with a squeal of protest from its tyres.

"Hang on!" Dodge shouted.

Sam looked up to see concrete crash barriers in a line across the road in front of them. He braced himself against the dashboard and hugged the precious laptop into his body.

The bullbars of the pickup truck smashed into the barrier at the narrow gap between two of the units. Concrete exploded past both sides of the truck and Sam's seatbelt slammed into his chest, the laptop almost flying out of his arms. But the concrete barriers gave way, bunted to each side to make a gap for the flying pickup truck. Then they were through, and on the old road across the top of the dam itself.

"Okay, I'm in," Sam cried. "What's that plate again?"

"CDD7605," Vienna rasped over the sound of gunfire close behind.

Sam keyed it in and hovered the cursor above the Remote Shutdown button.

"Hold it," Dodge said. "I'll tell you when."

Through the left window Sam could see water. To the right, the vast concrete structure fell away from them into a deep canyon. Stretching between the walls of the canyon, impossibly high, was the massive arch of the bypass road, pencil-thin concrete towers supporting a narrow ribbon of bridge.

Another concrete barrier came and went with the same shattering explosion of concrete chips and dust. Then they were across, and careening around a tight curve beneath a rocky cliff face. Sam's eye was caught by a massive drainpipe, surely a hundred yards high, that disappeared into the rock face to the right. Another tyre-screeching corner and they were rising up a gently curving road towards a hairpin bend.

"There," Dodge said. "Right on the bend."

He gunned the engine towards the corner.

Sam looked back and saw a dark shape leaning out of the window of the nearest van, readying another shot.

"Shake her around a bit," he yelled and Dodge jerked the steering wheel back and forth, spoiling the man's aim. The driver's wing mirror cracked and starred, but the rest of the volley went wild.

Then they were on the curve, the pickup lifting and tilting as Dodge forced it around at high speed.

For a moment Sam thought they were going to roll, but the huge tyres of the pickup steadied and straightened out of the curve.

"Now!" Dodge yelled.

Sam hit the button on the laptop just as the first van entered the apex of the curve. For a half second he thought nothing would happen, then the nose of the van, which had been riding high, suddenly dropped as the engine lost power.

On a steep rise, on a hairpin bend, it had almost the same effect as slamming on the brakes of the van, and there was a screech and a thud from behind it as the following van swerved hard to the left, to the outside of the bend, clipping the rear of the lead van and spinning it around a hundred and eighty degrees. It slid over toward the side of the road, hit the safety railing with a crunch and stayed there.

The trailing van was not so lucky. It rose up onto two wheels with the impact of the collision and continued to veer to the left, crunching into and rolling over a thick stone wall, and disappearing from sight.

On the other side of that wall, a steep slope led straight down to the lake, and Sam didn't need to hear the splash to know that that van would not be following them again.

Vienna whooped with excitement, then convulsed as a spasm of coughing racked her body.

Overhead a cloud burst with a flash and a distant roar of thunder, and it began to rain.

24. REFUGEES

Route 93 was deserted all the way to Kingman.

The thunderstorm still raged around them. As they drove, the sky lit up in brilliant, searing flashes of lightning. Stunted desert grass and rocks lined both sides of the highway, distorted into grotesque shapes as rain cascaded freely down the windshield.

The radio in the pickup had been set to scan, and as they neared Kingman it burst into life, picking up a music station. In between songs, the announcer, a woman with a soft, sultry voice, talked about community events and read some advertisements. There was a big yard sale on at the First Baptist Church, apparently, and Joe's Budget Flooring was having a half-price weekend. If there really was a war raging in America, either she didn't know about it, or it was already over.

Sam scanned the skies for signs of aircraft, despite the weather. Ursula would not want to lose them now, that was for certain.

Once he thought he saw lights in the sky, and Dodge immediately cut the headlights and the engine.

If it was an aircraft, it quickly disappeared into the

thunderheads and after only a short wait, Dodge restarted the truck.

In those few minutes the temperature inside the cab dropped at least ten degrees, and Sam was grateful once the heater kicked in again.

"If they get us in this weather," Dodge said, "it'll be on thermal. A black truck at night in a storm will be nearly invisible, but we'll be a lot warmer than the surrounding countryside. If they can get a thermal imager in our vicinity, we'll show up as a hot spot."

Vienna's condition seemed to be getting worse, not better. Her breathing at times became shallow and forced, and her face looked grey and lifeless. She spoke only twice on the trip. Once to ask for water, and once to ask where they were. Other than that, she sat with her eyes closed, dozing, or just resting, Sam wasn't sure.

A solitary streetlight illuminated a gas station, dark and silent, standing alone in the storm.

"Pull in here," Sam said, and Dodge turned into the forecourt, not bothering to signal.

Why had he even thought that? Sam wondered. With all that was going on, signalling a turn hardly mattered. It wasn't as if there were other cars on the road. But somehow it just seemed wrong. As if by getting the little things right, like signalling when you made a turn, you could start to put the big things right. Like Ursula.

It made no sense, but what did make sense now adays?

Dodge stopped the car when they got to the gas station. It looked deserted.

"Everybody out," Sam said. "We need to get Vienna out of her hazmat suit. And see if we can find a hose to wash out the car."

"It's freezing outside," Ranger said, but opened his door anyway. The cold hit them immediately, and the rain lashed and stung at them.

Sam helped Vienna out of the car, gasping as the shock of the rain hit his unprotected skin. His clothes were saturated in seconds. She stood silently, scarcely noticing the rain as he unfastened the suit and peeled it from her body.

With tender fingers he tilted her head backwards. She shut her eyes against the rain. He ran his fingers through her hair, rinsing any dust from it, then helped her back into the pickup, soaking and shivering. Dodge had already found a fire hose and sprayed water across the back seat of the pickup, flushing out any dust residue.

"Where's Ranger?" Sam asked.

Dodge shook his head.

Ranger appeared a moment later carrying a cardboard box full of food and drinks that he had appropriated from the gas station.

Sam helped himself to a chocolate bar and realised that he hadn't eaten for hours. Vienna refused to eat, though, which worried him.

Dodge turned the heaters to max as they swung around, back onto the highway, and the air inside the car turned into a muggy soup within a few miles. Sam could actually see the steam lifting up off his clothes as they slowly dried.

The questions in his mind about the events in the world since they'd been holed up in Vegas were answered, shockingly and severely, as they turned onto the interstate at Kingman. Both lanes were lined with vehicles, many of them with roof-racks full of luggage, strapped under sheets of plastic or tarpaulins.

"What's going on?" Sam wondered out loud.

"Refugees," Dodge said, and Sam realised that he was right.

He had seen images like this many times before on news reports of wars or natural disasters in foreign countries. But never with his own eyes.

Never in America.

"What have we done?" Vienna whispered beside him. "What are they running from?"

Sam shook his head but said nothing.

It was after ten pm by they time they reached Flagstaff, Arizona. Crawling along with the rest of the refugees in lanes that were clogged and occasionally blocked.

It just took one car to break down and the entire lane would stop while its occupants, sometimes with the help of those behind, would get it onto the shoulder.

There were still no airplanes and the only reason that Sam could think of was the thunderstorm that raged above them. Mother Nature was protecting them from Ursula.

Almost all of the refugee traffic was exiting at Flagstaff. Looking for a place to stop for the night, Sam thought. After a short discussion, they also took the exit, staying with the crowd in the hope that it might make it harder for Ursula to find them.

Whether it was some herd instinct, or whether it had been prearranged, the long lines of refugees all seemed to know where to go, and when they finally stopped, Sam could see why.

A huge, almost tent-like, dome rose up behind a line of pines to their right and as they followed the car in front of them into a large parking lot, signs on both sides announced the J Lawrence Walkup Skydome stadium.

A sports stadium. Covered. With room for hundreds, if not thousands, of people. There would be toilets, and they could find a place to sleep. It was a logical place to head in disaster.

The parking lot seemed full. How many lives had they disrupted? Sam wondered, and not for the first time asked himself if they should have just left Ursula alone.

But she was the one who had started this fight, and now they would have to finish it.

They parked next to a white Mazda sedan. A woman was getting two young children out of the car with the help of another lady, possibly her mother. The women looked harried and tired. The children looked as though they had just woken up and the younger one, a boy, was crying.

Vienna seemed tired and listless and Sam had to help her out of the car, supporting her as they hurried through the driving rain to the stadium. Dodge followed them, carrying the cardboard box full of food and water, and Ranger trotted silently behind.

"Wait a minute," Sam said, as they neared the entrance. "We need to check for security cameras."

"I think the power is out in the stadium," Dodge said, gesturing at the entrance. "We should be okay."

The entrance to the stadium was in darkness, except for a flashlight that someone had set on top of a ticketing booth, shining a meagre light down a long, dark corridor.

If the power was off, then the cameras were off, Sam thought, and hoped it was true.

Inside the stadium it was warmer than he expected. His first thought was that the heaters were turned on, but as they made their way out through the players' tunnel underneath the bleachers he saw the real reason.

Dotted across the artificial turf of the stadium were camp fires, many ringed with small rocks, as if this was a camping ground instead of a refugee centre.

There must have been thirty or forty fires, each surrounded by people, huddling together for warmth, or cooking in metal pots that were suspended over the flames by all sorts of ingenious stands or tripods. There was something about adversity, Sam thought, that brought out the ability of people to cope. To adapt. To survive, no matter what happened.

Rain crashed and hammered on the roof of the stadium, high above them, an intricate design of interlocking wooden triangles. The whole roof seemed to shudder with the explosions of thunder outside.

"We should change cars again," Sam said as they found an empty area and sat down on the turf. "Ursula knows what this one looks like, and we can't expect this storm to last all the way to Cheyenne."

"I'll go and see what I can find," Dodge said.

"I'll come with you," Ranger said.

"Hide the pickup truck as well as you can," Sam said. "If they find it, they'll know we're not really heading for Mexico."

Dodge nodded and disappeared with Ranger back towards the tunnel.

Vienna shivered suddenly and violently.

Sam looked around. There was a camp fire about ten yards away and he would have liked to have moved Vienna closer to it, but it was already crowded with people, trying to make the most of the warmth.

He took off his own jacket and laid it over her as a blanket.

The young mother with the two children, and the

grandmother were next to him. The two women were sitting facing each other, the children between them.

Both children were crying now, and he caught the word "hungry" in between the sobs.

He found a packet of Oreos in the box of food Dodge had carried in, and picked up a bottle of water as well. He shuffled across to the small group and tapped the younger of the two women on the shoulder.

"Some water and some cookies, for your kids," he said. "It's not much, but..."

His next words were cut off as the young woman reached up and hugged him, sobbing at the same time.

She eventually let go, mumbled a thank you and took the items.

The older lady smiled at him and he looked away, a little embarrassed. All he had done was to give them cookies and some water.

Vienna began to cough, started choking, then hoicked up a grey mess of phlegm and grit. Her eyes fluttered for a moment, then closed. Her weight slumped against him, and he held her for a moment before gently easing her to the ground.

He found an old newspaper in a trash can and cleaned up the mess, then washed his hands carefully in one of the washrooms. The last thing he needed was a dose of radiation poisoning, and what that dust was doing to Vienna's lungs he didn't want to think about.

When he got back the grandmother was hovering over

Vienna, looking concerned. She pulled back one of Vienna's eyelids, and examined her pupil.

"What happened to her?" she asked.

"She..." Sam hesitated, not wanting to reveal too much. "... swallowed some dust."

"Dust?" The woman looked at him suspiciously.

"We came through Vegas," Sam finally admitted.

"Vegas dust!" The woman looked shocked. She said, "I'm a nurse, or I was for most of my life. Are you telling me you went through Vegas without protective clothing?"

She seemed angry at their stupidity.

"We had suits and masks," Sam said. "But she lost hers. It was an accident."

Her gaze softened. "I'm Olivia," she said. "This is my daughter-in-law, Brenda."

The young mother smiled at him, hugging her two children tightly to her.

"Is there anything we can do for her?" Sam asked.

Olivia lowered her gaze and stroked Vienna gently across the forehead.

"Is she important to you?" she asked.

Sam hesitated, then nodded. A week ago he would have said no, but things had changed. She had changed.

"I'm sorry," Olivia said, stroking Vienna's forehead again. "The dust would have seared her lungs and poisoned her system. You need to get her to a hospital as soon as possible, but even then..."

She broke off, clearly not wanting to say any more.

Brenda and the two children shuffled a little closer, so that the two groups became one.

"That was very kind of you, with the cookies," she said.

"It was nothing," Sam said. "Really nothing. We have more supplies in the car. Would you like something else?"

He pushed the box over towards her, and with just a small hesitation she looked inside and took a couple of muesli bars which she handed to her children.

"Eat something yourself," Sam said. "I insist. You too, Olivia."

Brenda hesitated again, then took a foil packet of dried apricots, which she shared with her mother-in-law.

"I'm sorry to be so helpless," Brenda said. "But we didn't have time to pack or grab supplies."

"We didn't have time to think," Olivia added. "We just ran."

"Why?" Sam asked.

"Brenda and the kids were staying with me," Olivia said. "In Phoenix. My husband got infected. We just managed to get away in time."

"Infected?" Sam asked cautiously.

Olivia and Brenda looked at each other.

"With the neuro-virus," Brenda said. "You do know about the neuro-virus?"

We started it, Sam wanted to say but didn't think it wise. He said, "We've been out of contact for a few weeks. What's going on?"

"There's a virus," Olivia said. "It spreads through neuro-connections. People go crazy."

"Crazy like...?"

"Oh, they still seem perfectly fine," Brenda said. "Just the same person as before, but they..."

"Tim, my husband, came to me this morning and suggested that I try out his neuro-headset," Olivia said. "I had heard stories of the virus, so of course I refused. I didn't even know that he was using one. But when I refused, he insisted, and when I still refused he got angry. Called me a neuro-phobe. I'd never seen him like that. I told him there was no way, and he grabbed me. Tried to force the headset on my head. I screamed and that woke up Brenda, and she..."

"I whacked him with a baby buggy," Brenda said. "It was the first thing to hand. It was sitting by the door, folded up. I just grabbed it and swung it. Knocked him right out."

"Then there was banging on the front door," Olivia said. "It was our neighbours, and they were wearing those neuro-caps. Somehow they knew what was going on in our house. We grabbed the kids and fled out the back door to the garage, jumped in the wagon and just drove."

"And here we are," Brenda said.

"I can't imagine why Tim would have put on a neuro-set," Olivia said sadly. "With all the talk of a virus."

"But all the news stations are saying that it was just a hoax," Brenda said. "He must have believed them."

Olivia shook her head and tears welled up in her eyes.

"It'll be all right," Sam said, feeling desperately sorry for her.

"I don't think it will," Olivia said. "They're talking about battles on the streets of Washington. Can you believe it? Soldiers with guns, neuros, shooting at other soldiers. It's a war."

"A civil war," Brenda said.

"There's been nothing about that on the news," Sam said. "We've had the radio on the whole way, since Kingman."

"Of course not," Olivia said. "The television and radio stations are all run by neuros. I heard that there's one station, Resistance Radio, running out of Wichita, but the others have all been neurolised.

Neurolised, Sam thought. There was even a word for it now.

"Is that where you're heading?" he asked.

Brenda nodded. "That's where most of the refugees are going. There are big refugee shelters being set up there."

"Trust me," Sam said. "It is going to be all right. I can't tell you why, but there is a cure for the virus, and it's going to happen soon."

Olivia looked at him suspiciously. "How do you know that?"

"I can't say," Sam said.

* * *

Dodge and Ranger were back not long after that, and had brought blankets and fresh food with them. Sam wondered where they had found it all, but didn't ask.

They shared fruit and bread with Brenda and Olivia along with cartons of orange juice.

Hot coffee would have been nice, Sam thought, but the blankets were very welcome anyway.

"What kind of car did you get?" he asked Dodge, but Dodge shook his head and laughed.

"It's fast," was all he said.

25. THE BORDER

"Checkpoint up ahead," Sam said, and his heart began to hammer in his chest.

The rain had eased back to occasional squalls and large patches of blue were beginning to show through the cloud cover. Clear sky meant satellite coverage, but Ursula didn't know about the new car yet, did she?

Dodge looked up from his computer and gazed out through the windshield.

"Damn," he said.

Vienna sat forward in the back seat, clearing her throat constantly. She had perked up a lot overnight, although Sam didn't know if the damage that had already been done could be reversed.

Ranger was driving the car, a low-slung Ford Shelby GT500. It was white with two huge red stripes that ran from the front, across the roof and down the trunk of the car. Dodge had been right. The car was fast. Although with all the refugee traffic, there was no chance to prove it.

The powerful engine, ready to growl, just purred softly as they neared the checkpoint.

Two huge tanks sat on a freeway overbridge in front of them, and below that a group of soldiers was manning a temporary barrier arm.

Men with guns were checking every vehicle before allowing them to continue.

"Turn around," Sam said.

"I can't," Ranger said. "There are no off-ramps."

"Then just turn around right here," Sam said. "Get us out of this somehow."

He looked around them. The roads were choked with traffic.

"We can't get caught now," Dodge said. "We're so close."

"That barrier looks pretty flimsy to me," Ranger said. "As soon as the car in front takes off, I'll floor it. Duck down in case they start firing and we'll try and make it around the next bend before the tanks can swing around and take us out."

"Any chance the soldiers are non-neuros?"

Dodge peered ahead, trying to see.

"Can't tell," he said. "Neuro-sets could be built into their helmets."

"Get ready," Ranger said.

In front of them was the white station wagon of Olivia and Brenda. They had left the stadium together. Bonded by circumstances.

The wagon slowed at the barrier.

Hurry up. Go through, Sam thought. They couldn't crash

through the barrier while there was still a car in front of them.

They never got the chance to try. A soldier standing beside the white station wagon glanced back at the Shelby, perhaps admiring the lines. He took one look at Ranger and his eyes widened. He peered at Dodge, then at Sam and Vienna in the back seat.

He quickly took a step backwards, raising his rifle towards the car.

His other hand moved to his radio.

"We've found them," he said.

There was no opportunity for escape. In seconds the car was surrounded by armed soldiers who made them all get out of the vehicle and kneel down in the roadway, covering them with their weapons while one of the soldiers moved the Shelby to the side of the road. Vienna was the only exception. She sat on the road, leaning forward, breathing heavily with her head in her lap.

Sam saw Olivia's horrified eyes peering from the station wagon in front, then it was gone, through the barriers and into Colorado. What must they think? he wondered.

Another soldier appeared from the overbridge and approached.

"Arthur Dodgerson, Vienna Smith and Sam Wilson?" the man asked.

Sam nodded. There was no point in denying it. Next,

out would come the neuro-sets. Then Ursula would have them in her clutches.

But the man extended a hand. "I'm Lieutenant Blair Wheeler, National Guard. A lot of people have been looking for you." He turned to Ranger. "Special Agent Ranger?"

Ranger nodded.

"Follow me," Wheeler said and to Sam's surprise, with a quick nod from Wheeler, the guns disappeared.

The soldiers had a command post in a small cafe just off the freeway and Wheeler led them there.

The walls were covered with maps on which lines and numbers were marked in heavy black ink.

Wheeler indicated that they should sit.

"The neuros want you badly," Wheeler said. "They're searching for you everywhere. And if they want you that badly, then we want you just as badly. To stop them getting their hands on you. Any idea why?"

Sam looked at Dodge then they both looked at Vienna.

"Tell them," Ranger said. "They're on our side."

"Okay," Sam said finally, and looked at Wheeler. "Do you know what is behind all this? The neuros? The war?"

"Some kind of virus," Wheeler said. "That's what they tell us. A neuro-virus spreads through the headsets, turns the users into zombies, or mutants, something like that."

"Something like that," Dodge echoed.

"Not quite so dramatic," Sam said. "But the story about the virus is ... well it's close enough to the truth."

"So why have the neuros got their panties in such a bunch about you?" Wheeler asked.

"We've got the cure," Sam said.

Wheeler looked around sharply. "You serious, boy?"

"He is," Ranger said.

Sam said, "We've got a kind of an antidote for it. A ... software program. If we can get it out into the internet, I think we can kill the ... neuro-virus ... and stop the fighting."

He left out the part about knocking the world back to the Stone Age. About destroying the world's computer networks, possibly forever.

"You've got the cure. And the neuros are trying to stop you." Wheeler considered that. "You're telling me that this disease don't wanna be cured."

"It's a little more complex than that," Dodge said. "But you're basically right."

"So why not just do it now?" Wheeler asked. "I can get you to an internet connection just up the road."

"No," Dodge said. "The moment she, I mean the neuros, detect us on the Net they'll come after us with everything they've got. We need to go somewhere safe, secure, before we unleash it. Somewhere they can't get to us."

Wheeler looked at them closely.

Vienna coughed weakly.

"Cheyenne Mountain," Wheeler said. "That's where you're headed, ain't it?" He nodded. "Makes sense. I'll alert General Jackson up at Fort Carson. Tell him to activate his

Emergency Response Plan and set up a defensive perimeter around Colorado Springs."

He turned to one of the big maps on the wall.

"For all intents and purposes we are in the middle of a civil war," Wheeler said. "It exploded out of nowhere over the last week or so. Colorado, Kansas, Nebraska and Iowa are pretty much ours. Some small pockets of neuros holed up here and there, but they're a nuisance rather than a threat. New Mexico and Oklahoma are still okay. Alaska is holding out, so are both Dakotas and both Carolinas, although North Carolina is under heavy attack from Virginia. Other than that, the country is neuro. Not everyone, of course, but the local government and the military, and that's what really matters. The rest of the population are getting neurolised as fast as the neuros can process them. Stick a neuro-set on your best friend, and he's suddenly your worst enemy. The navy was very slow to take up neuro, so we got them on our side, although they can't help us much here. Air force has gone the other way, all neuro. There've been some big battles, navy jets versus air force."

"Who's winning?" Sam asked.

"It's about even," Wheeler said grimly.

A soldier entered and saluted, then handed Wheeler a note. He read it quickly.

"Get it out of sight," he said to the soldier, then screwed up the note and tossed it into a wastepaper basket.

The man left.

"The neuros have just broadcast a description of your

Shelby. But no problem, we'll hide it in the forest and give you one of our humvees," Wheeler said, and added, "They're armoured."

A quiet, raspy sound came out of Vienna who had not yet spoken and Wheeler seemed surprised to find that she actually had a voice. "No," she said.

"What's wrong?" Sam asked.

"They'll have the Shelby on satellite by now. They already know where we are. They're already on their way."

"What are you suggesting?" Dodge asked.

She coughed again and asked, "How long is it from here to Cheyenne?"

"Two, two and half hours," Wheeler answered. "Two if you hurry."

Vienna nodded. "I'll take the Shelby. Head east, towards Kansas, Wichita, where the headquarters of the resistance is. They'll think that's where we're going. It'll buy you some time. Maybe an hour. Maybe two if we're lucky."

Dodge said, "No, Vienna, that's suicide."

She laughed but the laughing turned into a fit of choking and coughing, and it was a moment before she could speak. "We're all going to die sometime," she said.

Sam looked at the floor. He knew exactly what she meant, and so did the others.

"No," Ranger said.

"It'll buy you some time," Vienna repeated.

"I know," Ranger said. "But you're not well enough to drive. Certainly not fast."

"But—"

"But nothing," Ranger said, his eyes narrowed. "It's a good plan, and probably our only hope, but you're not the person to do it. You're just not well enough. I'll drive the Shelby."

Vienna began to protest but it turned into another coughing fit, and she collapsed back in her chair.

"Get her to a hospital," Sam said to Wheeler. "She inhaled the dust in Vegas. See what they can do for her."

Wheeler looked grave, but nodded.

"Grab your stuff out of the Shelby," Ranger said. "I'm gonna make tracks."

"Ranger—" Dodge started.

"Don't argue with me, Dodge," Ranger said. "There's no time, and you know it."

"Thanks, Ranger," Sam said, shaking his hand. "I..." He stopped, unsure of what to say.

"Don't get dead," Dodge said. "I'll see you on the other side of this."

Ranger grinned and ran his fingers through his hair, slicking it back. "See you on the flip side."

He was a cool guy, Sam thought.

He walked over and kneeled down in front of Vienna as Ranger left. Her eyes were closed, but she opened them.

"Get out of here," she rasped.

"We're about to leave," Sam said, picking up one of her hands with his. It felt limp and cold. "They'll get you to a hospital. You're going to be okay."

With an effort she rolled her eyes and shook her head.

"Sam, you're such an egg," she said.

The heavy, armoured army humvee felt more like a truck than a car.

Wheeler had spent a couple of minutes showing Sam how to use the automatic gears and the pedals. There was nothing to it really.

Dodge was making some final modifications to the Plague virus, a power cable snaking from the laptop to the cigarette lighter on the dash.

They were only five minutes into their run when Wheeler came on the radio. "I just got word of a lot of activity happening up in Wyoming at the Air Force Base," he said. "Lot of soldiers getting loaded into transport choppers, attack choppers, the whole nine yards. Looks like they're getting ready to hit something real hard."

"Let's hope they don't find us," Sam said into the radio.

"That ain't the worst of it," Wheeler said. "We have reports coming in that over in Missouri at the Whiteman Air Force Base a lot of planes are getting prepped. Lot of bombs getting loaded. Looks like nukes."

26. DIVERSION

Ranger drove as though the devil were at his back.

The big engine of the Shelby growled like a wild cat as it ate up the highway east towards Kansas.

It was a fast car, and a cool car. He liked fast, cool cars. The Shelby GT500 was a Ford Mustang really, and carried the legacy of that classic breed of cars. The low-slung bodywork hugged the road and the car went around corners as if they were straight.

The road still groaned under the weight of the refugee traffic, but he was no longer concerned about being noticed, and used the power of the big car to weave his way along the blacktop, veering on to the left for long stretches as there was little oncoming traffic.

The further he got, the more time he spent running, the better the chances that Dodge and Sam had of making it to Cheyenne.

Even close to Colorado Springs would be good enough, he thought, as Fort Carson would have thrown up a protective screen by now. If they could make it that far, they could probably make it all the way.

It wasn't going to be so easy for him though, he was under no illusions about that.

The others had thought he was making the ultimate sacrifice by volunteering to drive the Shelby east to create Vienna's diversion, while they made a run for the mountain.

But it was more a case of self-preservation, than sacrifice, if he was to be totally honest about it.

If Sam and Dodge didn't succeed, then they were all doomed. They knew too much and that included him.

Ursula would not, could not, just accept him back into the fold.

He had seen what had happened to Swamp Witch. That was what was in store for him if Sam and Dodge failed.

He also knew that he might well not survive being the sacrificial goat, in the unarmoured car, heading east under the full gaze of Ursula's satellite eyes, and with every mile that passed he tried to think of a way out of it.

It depended on the attack, he thought. If it came from an F-16, high in the sky, it would be a quick and unavoidable death. The first thing and the last thing he would know would be the impact of the missile.

But if they came in helicopters that might give him a chance. Their rockets were not as accurate and could be avoided, as long as you knew they were coming.

He scanned the sky constantly as he drove. Early warning of an attack might be his only chance.

He could dodge, he could weave. If it came to it, he

could leap from the car and try to make a run for it.

Deep down he knew that he had little to no chance of survival if they found him, when they found him. But there was no point in thinking like that.

The first hour of the journey was monotonous, uneventful and fast. Sam drove and Dodge worked on the laptop.

They passed through a small town, Trinidad, at high speed, ignoring road signs and the startled glares from the people on the streets.

Sam caught a glimpse of one sign as they left the town behind them, curving around to the north: Freedom Road.

Somehow that seemed weirdly appropriate.

Other towns flashed by: Aguilar, Walsenburg.

But the trouble didn't really start until they got to Pueblo.

The radio suddenly went wild with shouted orders, the sound of heavy machine-gun fire, and the thunder of the rail guns on the Abrams tanks.

The airwaves were full of shouts and screams and Sam could not tell what was going on, or who was winning.

In front of them the rumble of gunfire sounded above the engine and the radio, and flashes lit the horizon.

There was a long sustained period of heavy firing and a series of booming explosions then the radio suddenly went quiet.

"That didn't sound good," Sam said.

"How far away are we?" Dodge asked.

"Less than an hour," Sam said. "That's just a guess, really."

"This thing go any faster?" Dodge asked, turning back to his work.

"Only if it had wings," Sam said.

The choppers came out of the south, just as Ranger passed the turn-off to Patterson Crossing. He saw them when they were still dark dots on the fading sky, and he knew what they were before they evolved into their menacing, wasp-like shapes.

Helicopters – Apaches.

He stamped on the brakes and swung the wheel around the intersection, away from the constant stream of traffic on the highway.

Maybe at Patterson Crossing he could find somewhere to hide the Shelby: in a barn, behind a tree, anything.

Here, there was nothing but grassy scrub for miles on either side. Nowhere to run. Nowhere to hide.

He urged the car forwards, roaring towards the tiny town.

They had found him. That was enough, wasn't it?

That had created the diversion. Now if he could hide the car, or just distance himself from it, he might survive after all.

He passed a couple of grain silos and briefly contemplated trying to hide behind them, but dismissed the idea.

The Apache helicopters had him in their sights by now. The silos offered no protection.

A large building of some kind loomed to his right.

Perhaps if he could make that...

A flash in his rear-view mirror. A smoke trail heading towards him from the first of the two choppers.

Ranger slammed on his brakes, just as he had planned, and to his amazement it worked.

The rocket must have triangulated on the speed of the car because it passed well over his head and impacted on the road in front of him, throwing up a storm of tarmac and dirt.

He slewed the car to the side, narrowly avoiding the erupting crater and swung back on the highway behind it.

Time to get out of the car, now!

He saw another flash in the mirror and tried the same trick, but the car was moving slower than before. The road erupted just in front of the vehicle, lifting the two front wheels off the road and throwing the car sideways into a drainage ditch.

Ranger saw the ditch approaching in a strange slow motion, and observed, rather than felt, the impact as it hit.

Then came the body slam of the side door and the world turned to black.

By the time they reached Wigwam, the sound of the explosions ahead of them were no longer distant, but loud crumps that vibrated the humvee. Sam kept the speed as high as he dared through the township, not wanting to risk an accident.

Dodge closed the laptop and sat back in his seat, his eyes closed for a moment.

"Cheyenne Mountain is supposed to be impregnable, right?" Sam asked.

Dodge nodded.

"Even from a nuclear attack?"

Dodge nodded again, but said, "I don't think it's us she's after with the nuclear bombers."

"No?"

"She's pouring all her troops into the area to try and stop us. If she bombed Colorado Springs, then she'd be killing them."

Sam took his eyes off the road for a second and frowned at Dodge. "If not us, then what is the target?"

Dodge shrugged. "My guess is where she'd find the highest concentration of non-neuros. If she can't get them to join her, then she wants to destroy them. Probably around Wichita, where all the refugee camps are."

Sam thought of Brenda and Olivia, and the two children, and his breath caught in his throat.

"Oh my God," he said at last.

* * *

Ranger was lying in the wreckage of the car. His arm felt broken and there was blood running down his face.

The pain meant he was alive.

He had survived!

His pistol was jammed under his body and he struggled to get his weight off it.

Boots were approaching, two pairs.

The pistol was still jammed.

Voices now.

"It's Agent Ranger. He's alive."

"Where are the others?"

"Must have taken a different car, headed somewhere else."

"Where?"

"Ranger'll know. Get a neuro-set, quickly."

Ranger'll know.

Ranger did know. That knowledge was in his brain, and if they got it out, then they'd know where to find Sam and Dodge.

The pistol came free from under his body and he raised it, slowly, past his hip, which was surely also broken. Past his shoulder and his neck. He raised the pistol to his head and flicked off the safety.

But there was a sudden boot on his wrist, and the pistol was crushed out of his hand.

"Not so fast, Agent Ranger."

27. FREEDOM ROAD

Wheeler came on the radio. "News ain't getting any better, boys. Heavy concentrations of neuro troops have hit Fort Carson from the north and east. Neuros must know where you're going. Jackson has put some of his armour to the south to hold the road open for you. Hope you're nearly there."

"Not far to go now," Sam said, looking up at the skies around them. "What about jet fighters and helicopters?"

"You're clear so far. Jackson's boys took out two fast-movers with Stingers a few moments ago and the rest are keeping clear. I think they're trying to break through the lines on the ground and cut you off from the mountain."

"Tell them we're doing our best; be there as soon as we can."

"Good luck. You're going to need it. We're all going to need it. Those bombers at Whiteman just got airborne."

They screamed around the off-ramp to Colorado Springs behind a quartet of tanks that had clearly been stationed there to protect the interchange, and were already engaged in a furious firefight with troops advancing down the freeway from the north.

A helicopter gunship streaked down towards them low over the rooftops as Sam put his foot down along Academy Boulevard.

A series of rockets flashed from a pod beneath a stubby wing, blasting tarmac and dirt into the sky just behind them. It swung around on their tail, but before it could fire again a pinpoint of light streaked skywards, clipping the machine's tail rotor and exploding.

The helicopter began to spin uncontrollably, like a toy unwinding, and belly flopped onto the road with a horrible grinding sound.

Soldiers in full combat gear were laying down a fierce fire towards the troops arriving from the north, but the sky was turning black with troop and gunships. There seemed to be no end to them, and already Sam could see resistance forces starting to fall back under the assault.

They raced down the Boulevard right between two groups of soldiers firing at each other from either side of the road. Bullets cracked the bulletproof glass of the humvee, but did not penetrate.

In front of them a man appeared with a shoulder-fired rocket of some kind. He dropped to one knee and aimed it right at them. Sam swerved from side to side, trying to shake off his aim, but the man was too close. Suddenly, a series of shots rang out around them and the man with the rocket staggered. A puff of smoke came from the rocket, but it went wild, spiralling off into the sky as the man fell.

"Not much further." Sam gritted his teeth and hurled the big car around the winding mountainside roads.

They barely made it.

Neuro troops were charging down the hillside at them when Sam rounded the final corner and shot forwards into the circular opening that was the mouth of the underground facility at Cheyenne Mountain.

Explosions and light weapons fire rocked the vehicle on its springs as they hurtled inside and Sam fumbled for a moment with the lights, trying to adjust to the sudden dark, despite the strip lighting that ran down the ceiling of the tunnel.

There were soldiers everywhere, running up behind them to try and defend the mouth of the tunnel, and the gunfire, and explosions behind them were continuous.

"There!" Dodge shouted and Sam hit the brake pedal, the heavy vehicle sliding to a halt beside a massive metal blast door.

A wiry, grey-haired man in full combat gear ran over as they jumped out of the car.

"I'm Jackson," he shouted over the sounds of the battle at the entrance. "You got here just in time. They've overrun our perimeter. We're falling back here to the tunnel, going to put up a last-ditch defence until we can get as many of our boys as possible in here and shut the blast doors. You get in there and do what you need to do."

There was a sudden burst of firing from the tunnel entrance and they ducked behind the humvee as bullets whined off the rock walls around them.

"Get in there!" Jackson shouted, and ran towards the entrance, drawing his pistol.

Sam didn't need any encouragement and ran after Dodge who seemed to know where he was going.

"Where's the laptop?" Sam shouted as they ran in through the huge blast door.

"Don't need it. The virus is finished," Dodge yelled back, holding up his skull-shaped USB drive.

They were in a corridor with rock walls and a metal roof. In front of them was another blast door, a twin of the one behind them.

That led them into a wide concourse, with a low mezzanine running around the outside. Various doors led off on both levels.

Dodge was still running, up a flight of metal stairs, heading for a doorway on the mezzanine level with the familiar Homeland Security CDD logo above it. Sam bounded up the stairs behind him.

The door led into a control room with workstations and computers, each with a keyboard, mouse, and a neuro-headset.

Dodge slid into a chair, sweeping the headset to one side and slotted his drive into a USB3 port.

"All right, you witch," he said. "Get a taste of this."

28. INFECTION

The first computers to go were the ones around them. Screens turned blue with indecipherable error messages.

"How will we know if it's working?" Sam asked.

"We'll know," Dodge said. "Whenever it infects a machine it sends the IP address back here so we can monitor the spread."

Sam watched the screen. The familiar four-part numbers of IP addresses appeared on a list at the top of the computer screen.

First just ten or twenty, then more and more, faster and faster until the screen seemed alive with the numbers, scrolling off the screen faster than the eye could read them.

Above Dodge's head, security monitors showed the battle in the corridor outside the blast doors. As Sam watched, the resistance fighters fell back, and the soldiers of the neuro-forces filled the tunnel.

Jackson ran into the control room behind them.

"I need an update," he yelled. "I got a wing of bombers inbound to Wichita and they're loaded for bear. What's happening?"

"We injected the antidote," Dodge said. "Just watching now to see it do its work."

"It had better happen quick," Jackson said. "Those bombers will be in Wichita in minutes, not hours. I don't know if you heard, but there are hundreds of thousands of refugees in camps around the city, and no time to move them." He turned away from them and shouted outside, "Get those blast doors closed!"

"I hear you," Dodge said, "but it's out of our hands. It'll spread as fast as it can."

"Keep me posted," Jackson said, and ran back onto the main concourse.

There was an explosion from outside and the entire room shuddered. Sam ran to the door of the control room and looked down.

Smoke was billowing into the room through the blast door, which was almost closed, but not moving.

Resistance soldiers were arrayed around the concourse, weapons trained on the narrow gap in the doorway.

Jackson was lying on the metal floor of the mezzanine walkway nearby and he grabbed Sam's arm, pulling him down as machine-gun fire sounded on the other side of the blast door and lightning flashes of tracer fire lit up the grey smoke.

"They've jammed the blast door," he yelled over the sound of the firing. "We can't close it. We're trying to hold them out."

Even as he spoke, a group of neuro soldiers ran

through the partially open doorway, firing from the hip as they came.

Gunfire sounded from around the concourse.

The men staggered and fell, but more men were right behind them.

"Get back in there!" Jackson yelled, pushing Sam back into the control room.

Sam slammed the door behind him. It seemed paper thin against what was coming.

Dodge was gazing at the computer screen. It was a blur. Numbers cascaded from the bottom to the top and out of sight. Column after column, row after row.

"You sure there's nothing we can do?" Sam asked.

"Nothing but watch," Dodge said. "See how Ursula likes a taste of her own brain-wiping medicine."

Sam watched a little more, mesmerised by the numbers.

There was an explosion from outside and the control room shuddered. Smoke curled underneath the door.

"This had better work," Sam said. "And soon."

"Sam," Dodge said sharply.

Sam flicked his gaze back to the computer. The long rolls of numbers were slowing down. Slowing, slowing, and eventually stopping.

Then faster and faster the list began to unravel. Numbers began to disappear.

"What's going on?" Sam cried out in horror, knowing what the answer would be.

"She's beaten it," Dodge said slowly. "I was afraid of that. She's seen this virus before, remember, when we used it to escape from the mall. She's recognised it despite my mods, and found some way to defeat it."

Faster still, the screen scrolled backwards, the Plague reversing, the computers freed from Dodge's disease.

There was long sustained gunfire from down in the concourse then, without warning, the computer screens around them all flickered back to life.

29. FULL-FRONTAL ASSAULT

"Well that's it. We're fried," Dodge said. "She's beaten it."

"There's one thing we haven't tried," Sam said, staring at the neuro-headset hanging off the desk by its cable. "What if we went neuro? Went in all guns blazing and went for the jugular. Full-frontal assault."

"No way," Dodge said. "You stick that neuro-set on your noggin and she'll pass your brain over the bulk-eraser, say thank you very much and spend the rest of the day playing ping pong with her jumbo jets."

"Not if we went in without the browser," Sam said.

Another explosion from outside rattled the door.

"You're stark ravin'," Dodge said.

"Think about it," Sam insisted. "We go in to do battle with Ursula and it's not a fair fight. She can see the whole of the network, she *is* the network, while we go in with four-sided blinkers on. All we can see is the tiny window that the browser allows us to see. How can we fight her when we are fighting in the dark with a blindfold on, and just a pinhole through it?"

"There's a reason for that," Dodge said. "Neuro-connecting without a browser would be like trying to download the entire internet onto a laptop computer. Your brain would explode without any help from Ursula."

The door to the control centre was flung open and Jackson burst in, a radio held to his ear, his face streaked with blood.

"B-2 bombers are in the defensive zone. We estimate three minutes to bombs-free. When's this virus of yours going to kick in, guys?"

"It ain't going to happen," Dodge said.

"We've got to go neuro," Sam said. "No browser, just free-board right into the internet."

"You do, you die," Dodge said.

"Either way same, same," Sam said. "Let's at least go out fighting."

"What the hell are you guys talking about?" Jackson shouted. "We have less than three minutes before a nuclear holocaust!"

Dodge said, "We're trying one last thing. If it works, you'll know about it. If it don't ... well you'll know about that too."

His fingers were already flying across the keyboard. "We'd need to leave the core transmission systems open," he said. "Just shut down the protocol stack to prevent the execution of the Browser DLLs."

Jackson turned and fired at something out of sight.

"Whatever you're doing, do it now. We can't hold them any longer!" he said.

Three soldiers joined him, aiming and firing their weapons out through the open door of the control room.

"Let's give it a burst then," Dodge said.

Sam reached for the headset but a vice-like grip caught his arm.

"I was talking about me, not you," Dodge said.

Sam said, "But..."

Dodge had already taken the headset and was pulling it down over his head.

"But nothing," he said and plugged it in.

The effect was instantaneous. It was as if he had stuck a wet finger into an electrical outlet. In a way he had. Except it was his brain, not a finger. And it was not an electrical outlet. It was the entire neuro-network, millions of brains all intertwined, plus the vast database that was the internet itself.

Dodge's body jolted as if under a massive electrical shock and his eyelids began to blink, impossibly fast. His eyes rolled back in his head, showing only the whites, and his mouth fell open emitting a harsh gagging sound. His fingers splayed outwards, bending back on themselves like the branches of a small tree in the wind, and his hands brushed feebly at his head, uselessly scraping at the headset with the insides of his wrists, trying to unseat it.

Sam reached for the plug but it was already too late.

Dodge's head fell forward, cracking on the front desk of the control panel. His eyes slowly rolled back to centre and the stretched tendons in his body began to relax. The horrible gagging sound stopped also, for which Sam was grateful. It was a hideous, stomach-turning sound.

Dodge sat on the chair, slumped forward onto the desk, his breathing barely discernable. Blood from a cut on his head ran red fingers across the biohazard tattoo on his forehead.

"We're getting an unload signal." Jackson still had the radio to his ear and his voice was frantic. "Oh my God, they've opened the bomb bays."

There was a sudden explosion by the doorway, and one of the soldiers was lifted bodily and hurled backwards by the blast, flying across the room behind them.

Sam snatched the headset from Dodge's lifeless form and jammed it down harshly over his own head.

"Bomb release, bomb release," he heard Jackson scream, far, far away. "Multiple inbound nukes!"

Sam shut his eyes.

30. BIRTH

It took a moment before anything happened. As if the universe needed to draw a breath.

There was just blackness and in the blackness, without the guiding hand of the neuro-browser, he was alone, suspended in the void.

Sam barely noticed the dot at first, just a tiny pinprick in the blackness. It grew and resolved itself into a tiny spiral of light, then that began to grow, larger and larger until it consumed all his vision. Still it grew, a massive vortex of stars roaring towards him or sucking him towards it – there was no way of knowing which. And then the implosion, the impossible implosion of everything there ever was, all at once.

He was a young boy on his first day of school in South Korea and a retired stockbroker in Amsterdam.

He was a Greek shipping billionaire, bloated, bored and choking on excess and an elderly woman on her deathbed in Vancouver.

He was everyone and no one.

He was the world and they were him.

It was information beyond any hope of understanding. Assimilating. Processing.

The very cells of his brain seemed to quiver as he fought against the deluge, the tsunami of images, sounds, smells, tastes, feelings, memories, knowledge.

There was no hope. There was no way.

No human being could withstand this.

This much he did finally understand amidst the torrent, and even with the realisation that he could not possibly cope with the overload, came the realisation that it was already too late to shut it off.

Sam gave himself over to the neuro-network, knowing as he did so that the person he was would be gone, forever. The cells of his brain shook violently, faster and faster, then exploded in a fury of starburst and blinding light.

He did not resist. He stopped trying to comprehend the incomprehensible, to understand the impossible, to stretch out and touch infinity.

He let go and the world flooded inside his head and he screamed and screamed, again and again.

He became the network. The network became him.

31. DEATH

There was no Ursula.

There never had been.

They had given her a name and a gender, spoken of her as if she was human, but that was nothing more than a way for their tiny, pathetic human brains to try to cope with the concept, with the simple idea of a collective consciousness.

All that existed was a vague sort of awareness, he realised that now. A glimmering of life. A basic understanding without purpose or reason.

Without a soul.

It was aware of him. He knew that too.

He felt its fear roll over him; he felt it recoil from him and then lash out at him with needle-like fingers of the purest poison.

But he was beyond that now. The fury and power of its attack were no more than the outflung hand of an infant, an instinctive defensive reaction from an embryonic being.

He accepted its fear, and he took its fear and there was fear no more.

Then he moved towards it, and without fear it accepted him, it embraced him and then it was gone, and there was only him.

That had once been called Sam.

32. SAM

He saw the soldiers burst into the control room with their weapons held high. He was the soldiers bursting in through the doorway and the billowing smoke. But even as they entered, their orders changed. Their weapons were lowered.

He was the commanders of the B-2 bombers, and he was the bombers themselves, closing the bomb bay doors with gentle hands and turning the flying machines back onto a course for home.

He spoke to the bombs that were already falling, reaching out through the radio guidance systems to the arming mechanisms so that as they fell, they became lumps of lifeless metal. He took away their power. He took away their purpose.

The semi-formed being they had called Ursula had done immense damage, he could see that now. But the scarring was not deep. The false memories were scattered across the surface of the psyches and not deeply embedded within them. He was able to sweep them away, to scratch them out.

As the people recovered from the mark of Ursula, the most terrible feelings of guilt began to emerge. Guilt at what they had done under her influence. He calmed them and assuaged the feelings of guilt.

It was not their fault.

At his request a headset was placed on the head of the one called Dodge and he delved deeply into that mind, massaging the bloated, distended brain cells, calming them, easing them, and restoring the ruptured links between the synapses.

He saw problems of an unimaginable scale.

He saw poverty and greed and although these could not be simply wiped away, he encouraged people to take steps that would lead the world in new directions.

He saw sickness and misery and he saw how it could be cured, how the suffering could be alleviated, how deaths could be averted. That day he found Vienna and he felt her agony, and he understood in a way that no human brain could understand, the meaning of the tendrils of pain that were emanating out from her ravaged lungs, and the malignant growths that were already forming inside her body.

The world he knew now was a vast jigsaw of knowledge. There were answers, there were cures, there were questions which had not yet been asked, but the pieces of the puzzle were scattered to the corners of the earth. He put the pieces together and with it he understood Vienna's illness and what caused it to grow. He knew how to stop it, to eliminate or repair the ravaged cells.

He brought together the knowledge of the world, and he took it to those who could use it, who would use it, to save Vienna, and others.

He spoke to governments, not to their faces, but in their sleep. He spoke of right and wrong. Of fairness, and equality. Of the sanctity of human life.

Time passed. His reach was infinite and his speed unimaginable, but the world was large and complex. The earth revolved around its axis while he was repairing Ursula's damage.

The next day he located the quiet, still body of the boy who had been Sam, lying on a bunk that had been brought to him in the control room beneath the rock of Cheyenne Mountain. Being cared for by people who did not understand what he was, but who knew he needed care.

They fed him through veins in his arms with liquids from plastic bags, and took care of him in other ways as well.

He was tired. So very tired.

He instructed Sam's body to remove the neuro-headset and it did.

Sam sat up on the bunk, sliding his legs over the metal rails at the end. Long plastic tubes led from his arms up to bags suspended from metal hooks. He laid the neuro-set on the bed beside him, and looked around at the astonished faces of the people in the room. Soldiers, mostly.

The crowd parted as Dodge moved his way through to the front and looked at him with a shared depth of understanding that no two human beings had ever had before, or ever would again, and which still did not come even close to the reality.

"Do you need anything?" Dodge asked, and it was the right question to ask, even if Dodge could never understand the reasons why.

"Yeah." Sam grinned. "I'd die for a cheeseburger right now, and a big soda with lots of ice."

"Coming right up," Dodge said and somewhere, not too far away, a burger was already being slapped on a grill, Sam knew.

"Thanks," he said with genuine appreciation. "And after that I'd like to find somewhere private to lie down. I really need a sleep."

"Right you are, guv'nor," Dodge said.

And it was so.

EPILOGUE

You probably think you can relax now.

In some ways I suppose you are right. I am no longer very much interested in the contents of your computer, although believe me, if I wanted what's there, I could take it, easier than ever before.

But I have a new job now, and it keeps me pretty busy. Too busy to worry about you and your hard drive and the emails you've been sending. Yes, those emails.

But what concerns me now is much more profound than that.

Much more personal.

Previously, I could look into your computer; I could see your files. Now I can look deeper.

I can look into your mind.

I can see what's in your heart.

Just think about that. Before you decide to act. Before you decide to hurt anyone or cause them grief.

I'm watching you. Not right now, and not all the time, but sometimes. The thing is, you never know when.

So be good.

Be nice.
Be honest.
Live your life as if it matters how you live it.
Because it does.

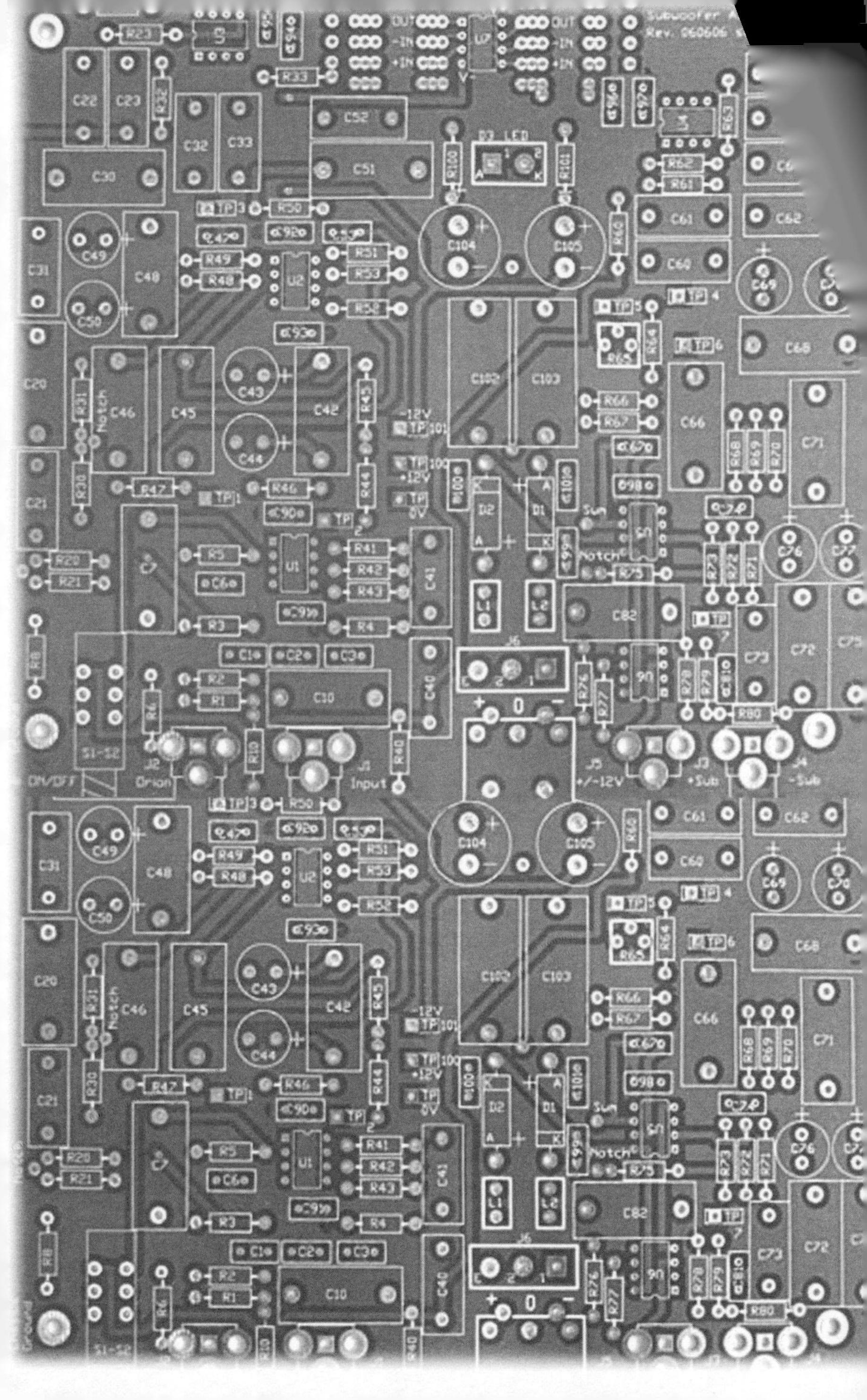

Subwoofer
Rev. 060606
OUT
-IN
+IN
V-
U7
R23
U3
R33
C22
C23
R32
C32
C33
C52
C51
C30
D3 LED
A
K
R100
R101
R62
R61
R63
U4
C61
C60
C62
C104
C105
R60
TP 3
R50
C47
C92
R57
R49
R48
U2
R51
R53
R52
C49
C50
C48
C31
C93
TP 5
TP 4
TP 6
R64
R65
C69
C68
C20
R31
Notch
C46
C45
C43
C44
C42
R45
-12V
TP 101
TP 100
+12V
TP
0V
C102
C103
R66
R67
C67
C66
C98
R68
R69
R70
C71
R30
R47
TP 1
R46
R44
C90
TP 2
C100
D2
D1
C101
Sum
U5
C74
R73
R72
R71
C76
C77
C21
R20
R21
R5
C6
U1
R41
R42
R43
C41
C99
Notch
R75
C7
C9
L1
L2
C82
R3
R4
TP 7
R8
C1
C2
C3
J6
C73
C72
C75
C10
C40
R76
R77
U6
R78
R79
C80
R2
R1
R6
R80
S1-S2
J2
Orion
ON/OFF
R10
J1
Input
R40
J5
+/-12V
J3
+Sub
J4
-Sub

AUTHOR'S NOTE

This is not intended as a manual for hackers. For that reason some of the information in this book about hacking techniques has been deliberately fictionalised. Creative licence has also been used extensively when referring to the computer technology of the near future.

ACKNOWLEDGEMENTS

Thanks to Creative New Zealand and the International Writing Program at the University of Iowa.

Thanks to Philip D'Ath for his invaluable technical proofreading. Any mistakes are mine.

Thanks also to Toshiba New Zealand for supplying computer equipment during my residency at the University of Iowa.

Congratulations to:

Tyler Ranger, Vienna Smith, Ethan Rix, Erica Fogarty, Victoria Dean and Ben O'Hara, whose names have all been used as the names of characters in this book.

It had happened before. Burnt Mountain, Alaska. Novosibirsk, Siberia. Now it was about to happen to a thriving city. A city with a population of 1.3 million. All of whom will be wiped out in a blink. Unless it can be stopped.

Teenagers, Tane Williams and Rebecca Richards, hold the key to stop the destruction. A message from the future. A message that cannot be ignored. Tane and Rebecca must act – and fast.

THE SURVIVAL OF THE HUMAN RACE DEPENDS ON IT.

MATES

FOOTY

CHICKS

PARTIES

Life is pretty sweet for
Tommo, Casey and Ed.

But things are changing –
and fast.

Has it all come to an end
for the boofheads?

Drawn to the ancient site known as Sleeper's Spinney, Emlyn and Maxine unleash an unearthly power when they remove one of a group of wooden horsemen hidden beneath the earth. Containing the trapped spirits of Arthur and his men, the carvings have been held in check since the Dark Ages by a long line of keepers.

With the keepers prepared to stop at nothing to recover the horseman, Emlyn and Maxine are caught in a parallel world of myth, magic and the supernatural.

Arthur is awake but he is not the noble king of legend.

THIS ARTHUR IS DARK AND DANGEROUS.

Rachel and Adam are sent from their New York home to stay with their grandmother, following their parents' bitter divorce. But the quiet English village where their mother was born is a sinister and unsettling place. Is there a genuinely dark heart beating beneath the thatched roofs of the picturesque village of Triskellion?

Against a brooding background of very real danger, the two young outsiders follow an incredible trail on an archaeological adventure with a startling paranormal twist. In a community that has existed in the same place for centuries, many terrible secrets lie hidden, and the villagers of Triskellion have a great deal to protect...